Also by Isabel Cooper

DARK POWERS
No Proper Lady
Lessons After Dark

HIGHLAND DRAGONS
Legend of the Highland Dragon
The Highland Dragon's Lady
Night of the Highland Dragon

DAWN OF THE HIGHLAND DRAGON
Highland Dragon Warrior
Highland Dragon Rebel
Highland Dragon Master

STORMBRINGER
The Stormbringer

THE STORM BRINGER

BRINGER

ISABEL COOPER

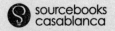

sourcebooks
casablanca

Published by Sourcebooks Casablanca, an imprint of Sourcebooks
P.O. Box 4410, Naperville, Illinois 60567-4410
(630) 961-3900
sourcebooks.com

Printed and bound in the United States of America.
OPM 10 9 8 7 6 5 4 3 2 1

To my parents, Dan and Kathy Kunkle,
for support while I wrote large parts of
this during a lockdown with them.

Part I

Call: What is the number of the gods?
Response: *The gods are five in number. Four are friends to the world. One betrayed it.*

Call: What is their nature?
Response: *Poram rules the wild, the sea, the world in the raw. Sitha is the weaver, the Golden Lady, mistress of crafts and civilization. Tinival, their son, the Silver Wind, governs justice and wisdom. Letar is the Dark Lady, the Threadcutter, the patron of death and healing, love and vengeance.*

Call: What is the nature of the fifth?
Response: *Treachery. Subjugation. Greed. The dagger in the back, the poison in the cup, the fetters locked unjustly. All of these are Gizath's domain.*

—The Catechism of the Temple
of Sitha, Part I

Know, Your Grace, that the downfall of the world as it was once known began in the shining city of Heliodar. There Lord Thyran, fancying himself betrayed by his common-born wife, came to see the world and all within it as corrupt. There, in the course of a single night of horror, he spilled the blood of his bride, her paramour, and his servants, a dedication to Gizath unlike any the Traitor God had ever known, and from there he fled into the north. His power summoned some of his minions from the places outside the world. Others swarmed to his banner. Many were changed. The lands of the south paid little heed until the day he and his armies came forth...

—From the Letters of Farathen, scribe
to the young Duchess of Bethal

Chapter 1

BLOOD SOAKED THE STONES OF KLAISHIL.

Some—too much—was as red as Amris's own. It didn't quite blend with the darker, viscous ooze that spilled more in blobs than in rivulets and ate into whatever was beneath it. Both pooled around crumbled stones, abandoned possessions, and bodies of all sorts.

Those still moving, living and otherwise, fought above the corpses of their comrades without looking down. Amris knew his soldiers couldn't chance the distraction. He suspected—or knew, in the cases of the undead and the beasts—that Thyran's troops simply didn't care.

Trapped with his back to the burnt shell of a house, he ducked a massive blow from a scaled fist. Jazmin, his last living lieutenant as far as Amris knew, seized the moment, sprang onto an abandoned cart, and fired a crossbow bolt into the single eye of the creature menacing him. Her aim was keen, despite days without rest: the monster grunted and fell backwards.

Amris followed it forward a few steps, spun, and cut through the dead arms reaching for Jazmin.

She smiled her thanks from a soot-smeared face and leapt down to his side.

"Have we any others?" he asked.

"Blaise, Vada, and the Pine are coming up from the

southwest. Or were. Edan and ten of us are getting the last of the priests out of the temples. Nadusha and her squadron are dead. Building collapse."

Amris made the sign of the Four Gods with his free hand, wearily, wishing them peace. Compared to the last few years, they'd have it anyhow. "Damos's squadron? Lady Winthair?"

"I've seen nothing of them today."

The previous sign of the Four would have to cover them too. Amris needed both hands on his sword and all his focus at the other end, for coming down the street was a squad of twistedmen: Thyran's shock troops, redly and wetly skinless, with curving black talons on their huge hands and faces that were mostly sharp-toothed mouths.

Amris had killed a score or so of them since the sun rose, and it was near noon now, but there were always more.

Creatures with wings of tattered flesh circled overhead, riding icy winds below black clouds. One raised its eyeless head and screamed, and a building near it shivered. Another dove, exhaling a purple cloud, and vanished behind a row of still-standing buildings. Amris couldn't see its prey, which was just as well: he and Jazmin were too far away to aid in time.

A month ago, he'd been in front of a fire with Gerant in his arms.

They'd had no illusions of peace then. Thyran had been burning a path across the world for years. They'd both heard what had happened to Vylik, the first city he'd attacked, whose baron had tried to surrender. Some said that baron and a few score of his citizens still lived, after a fashion. Amris had already beaten Thyran to a standstill twice, forced him to retreat once, and knew it was only a matter of time until the next attack. Their last, desperate plans, based on months of magic on the part of Gerant and the High Priestess of Sitha, had even then been going forward.

But for a few weeks, they'd been safe, warm, together, as they'd been before either of them had heard the name Thyran of Heliodar.

Now as Amris felt claws scrape against his armor, he stabbed, cut, and thrust mechanically, and didn't even feel the creature's ribs breaking beneath his blade. He registered them, which was a different, much more abstract matter. The world was action and response, mission and path, and much else to be ignored, like screams beneath the sky and how much colder it was than it should have been in June.

Another storm was on its way. The last had been a nine-day blizzard. If patterns held, this would double it in strength and duration. After that? Even Amris, not half the scholar Gerant was, could see the arc rising and cringed, fearing it as he'd feared few things in battle. If Thyran couldn't "purify" the world with his armies—or if he simply felt the process was taking too long—he'd evidently try other ways.

The final twistedman fell, twitching. Amris and Jazmin moved forward into the clear alley beyond them, and on toward where it opened onto what had once been the Plaza of Winds. The crumbling walls blocked much of Amris's view of the plaza, but he could still see the huge, pillar-flanked staircases that led to the duke's palace.

His Grace, well into his old age, had gotten out, along with his bride and his eldest son's family. Amris had made sure of that, perhaps the only triumph he'd had in the last three days. Lord Bauspar himself had stayed behind to defend the city he would have one day inherited, and had been devoured the evening before by one of the winged creatures. His sister, as far as Amris knew, lived and fought yet.

There, running toward the steps of the palace, Amris saw the remnants of the army he led, the soldiers that hadn't already retreated to guard Klaishil's fleeing citizens or stayed to hold Thyran off a little longer and given their lives in the process. The spiked helmet of the Pine towered above the shorter forms of stocky Vada with their spear and shield and Blaise, his dark braids loose since his helm had broken the previous dawn. Amris noted their presence, but his heart didn't lift the way it would have done at such a sight when the war had begun.

Too much weighed it down now.

Sword in his hands, Gerant's rose—an enchanted weapon no one would think to suspect—secure in his belt, he dashed toward the meeting place. To one side, he saw Jazmin, crossbow up: she could fire while running, at need, and with wicked aim.

Each step leading to Klaishil's palace was huge, ceremonially so. Amris saw the bodies lying strewn across them, but used as he was to passing corpses in the streets, he didn't focus on any until one raised a dark, mustached face and he saw what had once been Damos.

Blaise's profanity filled the air, even above the sounds of battle. Amris couldn't have gotten sound from his throat even if he'd taken the time to curse. He simply bolted for the step where the other man lay, more of a puddle than a body and yet somehow still living.

"The man himself," Damos rasped, as Amris came within earshot. What was left of his mouth strained over the next words. Amris would have given his life to not need to hear what came next, to be able to tell his sergeant to rest easy and lie quiet. He held still, listening. "Came. Blasted us. Five minutes gone, or so. Went up," Damos went on, gesturing to the palace with the boneless remnant of a hand. "Lady's there. Was firing on them. A couple guards with her. We slew his. I tried for him. I thought I'd struck, but…I'm sorry, General."

"No," said Amris, his voice sounding no better than Damos's, even though he had lungs. "You did well. Go with the gods."

He brought his sword down on the man's neck. The light in Damos's eyes faded, and he slumped back against the bloody marble, to Amris's relief. Sometimes even beheading didn't end the suffering of Thyran's most immediate victims.

"General?"

It was Jazmin, red-eyed, broken-voiced, but tearless—tears took water, and they'd all lacked that for a long time. The others were beside her, waiting.

If Damos was right, Thyran was alone, or nearly so.

Amris alone could use the rose he carried: the others who'd received them were on other battlefields, or with Letar. None of the half dozen who watched him with weary, grimy faces could end the five years of hell, and he wished with all his heart he could have simply considered that and bid them go.

Yet Thyran was not invincible. The fighting might have worn down even his shields and contingencies. A succession of attacks, when the sorcerer had no guards, might do likewise, could buy Amris time to act or even mean he didn't need to. He couldn't let himself hope so far, but he couldn't discount the possibility either.

"We go in," he said, and began to climb the stairs.

Inside, Thyran had left a trail of warped doors, twisted walls, and bloody boot prints. The palace hadn't stood long before his onslaught, any more than most people did, and he'd taken no care to hide his course. Amris would likely have been able to guess regardless.

The first of Lady Winthair's guards lay dead at the foot of the inner stairs—truly dead, in a mercy that had likely been mere convenience for Thyran. His ribs had grown outward from his chest, sprouting white and red through his armor. Amris didn't look longer, but ran on.

He heard the scream midway up the stairs. It almost masked an assortment of wet sounds. Afterward, metal clanged against stone. Amris gripped his sword tightly in one hand, Gerant's rose in the other.

"If you can, get the lady out," he told Jazmin. "I'll chance the rest."

There was no time to argue, nor reason for it. Noble blood wasn't sufficient protection from Thyran, not even when tied to the land, but he got power from making that nobility bow before him, and everybody broke in the end. Lady Winthair's ties to Klaishil had helped them for a while. Now they'd be a liability, should Thyran get his hands on her.

Jazmin nodded. Neither she nor Amris wasted breath speaking while they climbed the stairs, but their eyes met as they'd done a score of times in battle, conveying messages in the shorthand of those who'd fought together for years.

This time, the message was *goodbye*.

It wasn't completely certain—if all went well with the plan Gerant and Her Holiness had concocted, they'd meet again, with Thyran defeated and a world to rebuild. All very rarely went well. Every one of the people ascending the staircase with Amris knew that.

At the top of the staircase, he caught sight of Thyran's robe, gray silk billowing in the cold wind as the sorcerer strode down the hallway. The armor of another guard lay on the landing behind him. What was within could no longer properly be called a body.

Thyran was muttering to himself as he walked, lashing out with dark power at every door he found, and that gave Amris and his troops a few moments of cover before he heard them. They used the time to scatter, as much as they could in a hallway, and the Dukes of Klaishil had built their halls wide. Jazmin and Blaise ducked through the nearest door. They'd make their way to the lady by inner door or secret passage, Amris knew, or climb along the windowsills as a last resort. He and the Pine spread out, each taking a different wall.

Magic was already bursting from Thyran's fingers when he turned. The Pine whipped his shield up in front of his body. Amris, charging, saw the metal melt without heat, fusing with the arm behind it, and heard his soldier's shout of agony.

He couldn't stop. They'd both known as much.

There was Thyran in front of him, the ordinary middle-aged face topped by a crown of jewels and bone, the milky blue eyes aware, yet empty of all feeling Amris could have recognized. As Amris slashed for the sorcerer's throat, that changed: he did recognize alarm in the other man's expression, and was glad of it, for a fleeting moment before one of the jewels flickered and his muscles locked in place.

That had happened before—not with Thyran, and not defensively, but Amris knew the sensation. He could still breathe, and he did. Thyran glared at him, recognition dawning first, then a more specific hatred than the sort he seemed to have for the world. His hands started to glow again.

Amris remembered Gerant: rolling over to face him with a sweet smile, sunlight pouring over them both, pacing the study gesturing with enthusiasm over a new theory, and sleeping peacefully beside him. *Dark Lady, be with my love,* he prayed, feeling his muscles begin to relax, *until we meet again.*

He raised the rose as Thyran lifted his hands. "Be still," Amris said—and time itself froze around them.

Chapter 2

105 years after Thyran's War

A SKULL WAS GNAWING ON HER HEEL.

Darya kicked backward into the nearest wall and heard bone shatter, but the jawbone held on. She couldn't kick very hard, lest she bring down the tunnel of ruined masonry she was crawling through, and she didn't have enough room to stand or turn around.

Undeath isn't contagious once they're down to the bones, Gerant said in her mind. The emerald in the hilt of Darya's sword flickered to the rhythm of his speech.

"That's a relief," she said, "but I'd rather not hunt a cockatrice with half my foot gone. Get *off*, you stupid thing—it's not like eating does you any good!"

Flailing her leg didn't manage to shake the skull loose. Her boot was holding up, though, and the teeth were only mild pressure and irritating movement. She'd ignored worse. Darya sighed and started squirming forward on her belly again, focusing on the light ahead of her and gripping her long knife in one hand, in case she met an enemy that leather couldn't hold off.

So far, there'd been two of the walking dead—one with flesh, both in the rotted remains of armor—and a puddle of black ooze that moved on its own, not to mention the cockatrice she was chasing. Its trail had ended at the collapsed hallway, but then, the cockatrice had wings. Not being so gifted, Darya had to search for another route up.

"Some days," she grumbled, pulling herself along and trying to ignore the skull, "I think I should have sworn out at thirteen and gone off to be a pig farmer."

You'd be no good at it. Besides, just think of all we're discovering.

Gerant wasn't wrong. The city, what was left of it, was beautiful. The years and the wilderness had done a lot of damage, but some buildings still spiraled to the sky, and even those that had fallen had come down in chunks of vividly colored marble, some inlaid with gold and silver; Darya's prey had made its nest in what had clearly once been the wealthy part.

One more wiggle of her shoulders and her head was past the wreckage. Darya drew herself out into a larger room, where moth-eaten tapestries still adorned the walls and a staircase of pale-blue stone led up—graceful, spiraling, and likely about as stable as a house of cards.

As soon as she was free, she reached down, wrenched the skull—now mostly a jaw and a shattered braincase—off her heel, and flung it across the room. It did shatter then, and the sound was extremely satisfying.

The staircase didn't seem sturdier up close. She could actually see cobwebbed cracks in the marble, and three of the steps in the middle were sunken in, as though a giant had stepped on them. It was the best way up Darya had yet seen, though, and *up* was necessary if she wanted to catch her prey; the Traitor God and his minions hadn't consulted her opinion in the matter of winged monsters.

She put her weight lightly on the first step, held her breath, and waited for a crucial part of the stairs to come crashing down. When it didn't, she continued to the next—cautious, wary, and yet full of the excitement that always gripped her at such times, when she pitted herself against the world with her life on the table.

If you die here, said Gerant, *I'll spend centuries being extremely bored.*

"Should have thought of that..." The stair shivered below Darya's feet, and she shifted her weight hastily to the side, her free hand on the wall. "Before you agreed to be in a soulsword."

The service of the gods is very demanding.

"Don't I know it." Two more steps up, she leapt from edge to edge like a gazelle, catching herself on the wall when the unstable footing got the better of her.

The hallway ahead stretched out clear for a while, barring a few armored skeletons that didn't seem to be animate, then ended in a pile of rubble and daylight streaming through a gaping hole in the roof—ideal for Darya's purposes. Vines covered the walls, blooming here and there with roses in a rainbow of colors: bloodred as Gizath's wings, sunset orange, blue like the summer sky, darkest black. They were lovely. They also grew thickest over and around the rubble, keeping Darya from seeing past it.

"I wonder if they'd eat me if I tried to take cuttings," she said. "Seems a shame that none of the scenery in this place has been portable so far. The only ones to appreciate it are you, me, and the ooze monsters."

Gerant didn't reply. The emerald glowed as usual, so Darya wondered if she'd stepped on some metaphysical toe. "Sorry," she said, and took a step forward. They could talk about it at length later, when they were out of hostile territory, but the apology was important.

Behind her, the world shifted.

Darya had felt it change half a dozen times since she'd followed her quarry past the mist-cloaked walls of the city. She doubted a normal mortal would have, just as nobody normal would've been able to find the city itself. Even she couldn't quite define the feeling: the closest she could come was a solid *thock* in the back of her mind, as though a phantom finger had flicked her there.

So far, none of the changes had been directly dangerous. They'd all been damned inconvenient, though, so Darya didn't even look behind her at first. "The stairs are gone, aren't they?"

In a sense.

They were still, strictly speaking, present, she discovered. But they'd folded in half lengthwise, then curled up. Darya stood facing a marble snail's shell, suspended in air in a way that hurt to look at.

She raised her hands and let them fall back against her thighs. Even swearing was beyond her for a moment. Wheeling around, she started down the empty hall.

After a few minutes of walking off her frustration, it occurred to her that Gerant was still silent, and that he'd sounded distant when he'd answered her before.

Normally the instantly folding stairs alone would have sent him into a frenzy of theory: being dead hadn't gotten rid of his wizardliness. "Are you all right?" she asked. "Do you know this place?"

No, said Gerant slowly. *Unless my memory or my logic has gone very badly wrong, it's Klaishil, but I never visited.* As he spoke, Darya felt his attention turning to the roses, as he looked not quite with her eyes and not quite with his own. *I know the spell that grew those, though. It was one of mine.*

The real distress in Gerant's "voice" silenced all the smart replies that rose to Darya's lips, from comments about his taste to asking whether he'd also made ornamental mazes. "I've never seen one like it before. Didn't let this one get around?"

I'd only just worked it out when the storms broke. And I had the help of Sitha's High Priestess, who died in those storms. Nobody since has been able to bear so much of the Golden Lady's power, and the spell wouldn't work without it.

The rubble was higher than Darya's head, but the rose stems would work for handholds: she'd had worse pain than a couple of thorn scratches, and she'd yet to find the poison that could cause her more than a moment of discomfort. As she reached for the first, she saw that it was bent already, and by someone with at least as much strength as she had.

She froze and listened. The hall remained silent, even

to her enhanced hearing. Whoever had come that way was likely long gone.

"You want to tell me about it?" Darya asked, when she felt safe speaking again. "If you don't, I won't ask about anything that won't kill me."

It's an enchantment of stasis, Gerant said. He didn't hesitate—Gerant would never be hesitant, talking about magic—but he spoke slowly, as though he stripped all feeling from each word before he let it leave his mind. *Beyond this, likely not far beyond, time has stopped. Those there when the spell was cast can't be hurt, and they don't age, but they... Sleep is the best word for it.*

"That doesn't sound too bad."

I came up with it during the war. I was needed elsewhere, but I discovered how to put the spell on a physical object. A rose. I thought it made a poetic symbol. I was young. I gave it to my lover.

"General Amris var Faina?"

The very same. I thought he'd died before he could use it, when Thyran was destroyed.

They'd talked about Amris a very little during their years together. Gerant had broached the subject rarely. Darya hadn't pushed. She'd lost comrades and friends, but grief like Gerant's was foreign to her, as it was to most of the Order, and she'd always known herself out of her depth in those conversations. She felt the same way now. "Should I—"

All we can do is go and see.

She climbed quickly until she could just see over the top of the rubble, then paused.

Beyond, a man stood with a red rose in one out-stretched hand. He was tall, lean, but muscled like a warrior, and both the sword in his other hand and the plate mail he wore bore out that impression. An ornately old-fashioned helm, rich with gold and set with sapphires, hid his face, but Gerant didn't need to see it.

Amris, he said, and his voice held more love and anguish than Darya had ever heard before.

Chapter 3

"What can I do?" The question felt foolish, and Darya didn't know why. The spell was Gerant's, so of course he'd know how to break it.

Indeed, his answer was quick and sure. *You have to be unarmed. Then you must approach him, very closely, and speak his whole and true name.* Gerant hesitated, though not from any mistrust of her, Darya knew. *Amris ap Brannon var Faina.*

It was only a description of the man's lineage, but Gerant said it slowly, bringing it out from where he'd kept it close down all the years and putting it in front of her, who'd barely known him for ten—which usually seemed a long stretch.

She went over the wall and down the other side, feeling helpless in a new, foreign way. There was no monster whose death would stop Gerant's pain, or avenge it. She might be able to bring Amris back, but the years that had passed wouldn't come with him. And she couldn't simply wish Gerant the best, take her payment, and ride off.

There was nothing for it but to fix what she could. Darya unbuckled her sword belt and laid it carefully on the floor. On top of it, she put the knives from each of her boots, the smaller venom-coated ones from each of her wrist sheaths, her short bow and her quiver.

"Let's hope he doesn't kill me before I can explain

myself," she said, but didn't get an answer. It was harder
to talk to Gerant when she didn't have the sword on. "Or
that something else doesn't before I can get armed again."

Glancing over her shoulder with every other step,
she approached Amris. The burn marks grew fiercer in
a circle around him: the wall behind was scorched black,
and three broken arrows lay at his feet.

Up close, closer than Darya generally got to anyone she
wasn't trying to swive or kill, she started to notice details:
the dents in Amris's breastplate and gauntlet, for instance,
accompanied by smears of blood from a battle four generations past, and the copper-colored leather wrapping the
hilt of his sword. His face, under the helm, was strong, with
dark bronze skin, a sharp, square jawline and chin, thin
lips, and a nose like a hawk's beak; his eyes were the dark,
misty gray-green of pine and spruce, with surprisingly long
dark lashes. They were narrow, made more so by the fact
that he was glaring—had been glaring for a hundred years.

Darya inhaled, sounded out the words in her mind to
make sure she had the name right, and then slowly spoke
it: "Amris ap Brannon var Faina."

———

The world was silent, and that itself told Amris the spell
had worked—not that he'd ever doubted Gerant's skill,
whether at magic or anything else. It was a different
matter, though, to be transported, in the space of two
breaths and two words, from the screams and crashes of
a pitched battle to utter quiet, save for a single voice.

Because the voice wasn't Gerant's, nor any that he recognized, Amris's reflexes carried him backward several steps and brought his sword up in front of him. He realized that the person who'd woken him was human and not Thyran, and hastily readied himself to defend rather than striking out, but it was a close thing.

The woman hissed and darted backward herself, moving with more than human speed or grace.

She *was* more than human. That became apparent as soon as Amris saw her eyes, unnaturally bright green and glowing in the dim light. Her skin was paper-white, her braided hair dark around it, and those could be human enough, but the eyes were a different matter.

"Easy, there," she said. Her accent stretched the vowels out more than Amris was used to, and the words came more quickly, but he could understand her rightly enough, particularly when she held up her hands, palms out. "I'm on your side."

Anyone could say so. "What side is that, pray?" Speaking felt odd. Gerant's magic had kept his muscles from degeneration through however much time had passed, so he felt no worse than a little stiff, but just as sound had taken a moment to become words, Amris had to think at first: move the tongue this way for w, the lips and throat so for i.

The woman shrugged. "The side that doesn't love the Traitor. The Order of the Dawn, the Sentinels… I think we were starting when you—" She waved a hand.

When he trapped himself in time in a desperate bid to stop the murderous warlord. "Yes. Only just."

Still Amris didn't lower his sword: the woman aside, there was no virtue in dropping his guard before he knew the situation. He did let the rose fall from his gauntleted fingers, and used that hand to pull off his helmet, a necessary compromise between defense and intelligible conversation.

The state of the hall became clearer to him as he did so—the years' worth of dust and cobwebs, as well as the silence. The woman's clothing—plain dark leather pants, jerkin, and gloves over a shirt of brown cloth—was plainer than he was used to, without even the embroidery that most peasants wore. Practicality, given where she was, or asceticism?

"I should tell you two things right off," said the woman. "You might want to sit down first."

Amris shook his head. "Best to face it on my feet."

"All right," she said. "First, you've been…" Another vague wave of her hand. "Stuck. For a hundred years or so."

She'd spoken wisely when she'd advised him to sit. The knowledge traveled up through his feet as well as in through his ears, making the room spin around Amris, and yet it seemed not to reach his head or his heart. The sweat of battle was still wet in his hair, he still felt his cuts and bruises, and the rose on the floor was as fresh as it had been when he'd plucked it for Gerant.

That reached head and heart both. Gerant was as human as he. Had been as human, rather—in a hundred years, a babe in arms would grow, sire or bear their own children, see grandchildren, and die, and Gerant had been a man in his prime when they'd parted. He'd be long dead by now.

They'd both known that parting might be forever. Toward the end, any farewell might have been the last. Amris had never pictured it taking this form.

"Here." The woman took a small metal flask out of her boot and brandished it in his direction.

The contents tasted roughly as they smelled. Amris had been a soldier long enough to swallow, nod his thanks, and trust that his throat wasn't truly on fire. "Strong."

"I keep it to clean out wounds." One eyebrow quirked, and her mouth twisted in a wry smile. "I'd say this counts."

"Truth." A hundred years. A hundred years, and only now had somebody come to awaken him, but the hall was empty otherwise. "Before you tell me the second truth, lady," he asked, "was there another man nearby? There, roughly speaking?" He gestured to the place where Thyran had been standing at the last.

"No," said Darya, peering at it, and then frowned. "But…wait."

A small, uneven mound of gray powder lay heaped on the stone. Darya knelt and touched it with the tip of a gloved finger, feeling the texture as much as she dared. "Ash," she said, "and—yes, bone. Bits of it. Wait." There was a larger shape within the ash, but that wasn't entirely why she'd stopped. As many shocks as it had gone through, her mind was still capable of calculation. "You're looking for Thyran, aren't you?"

The question sounded completely absurd. Thyran

had shaped, bred, or summoned an army of *things*, led them against humanity, and cursed the world to years of barren cold when he'd begun to lose. Thyran was the Father of Storms and Abominations. He wasn't somebody people looked for.

"Then you know of him," Amris said, utterly serious.

"Bad children and old wives everywhere know of him. The Order taught us a little more of the real histories." Beneath the ash lay a long finger, five-jointed, with a black talon at the end rather than a nail. Burial in the ash had kept most of the insects away and held off some rot, but the finger was still fairly disgusting. She grimaced. "Was he human at the end?"

"Mostly, in appearance," Amris said slowly. He knelt beside her, squinting in the dim light. "Far harder to kill than mortals, or even any of his creatures." Slowly he breathed out, sending ashes scattering. "And one of his defenses was dark fire."

Darya glanced up and knew they were both remembering Amris's own reaction to being awoken, and seeing the same scene—a man, or a once-man, not inclined to be nearly so merciful with any unknown force.

"The messenger creature that came to wake him died, then," Amris said, "but not with its task undone. Its master walks again, and I doubt that a hundred years have lessened his hatred for the world that would not order itself to his liking. I fear I bear much fouler news for you than you brought me, lady—for you and all who live now."

Chapter 4

THE WOMAN SWORE, COPIOUSLY, VENOMOUSLY, AND with a command of profanity that would've impressed any sailor or soldier of Amris's acquaintance.

He knelt silently meanwhile, hands clenched against his thighs, as he tried to see a road forward, tried to see anything past sick, cold anger and the thought *then it was all for nothing.*

Find out more, Gerant would have advised him. To the wizard's mind, more information was never an ill, and either the facts themselves or the quest to discover them might show a way to proceed.

A swarm of questions came to mind. Amris picked one: straightforward, polite, unlikely to further shatter his composure. "Forgive me. What is your name?"

"Darya."

"I cannot say it's a pleasure to meet you, but you have my thanks."

She nodded, a quick jerk of her head. "Couldn't leave anyone stuck like you were, even if... Oh, hell. That was the second thing." Darya was rearming herself as she spoke, with knives, a short bow, and a long sword that had a large square-cut emerald in the hilt. She looked down at the stone, gave a brittle laugh, and said, "I wouldn't *normally* forget. It's not a minor matter. I'm sorry."

"Your...soulsword, they were calling them in my time. It holds a spirit, yes?"

"Yes." Darya laughed again, with no more amusement in it than the time before. Her face itself was no paler than it had been when Amris had first seen her, but color had drained from her lips.

Amris could do nothing about Thyran's return, not just then, but he offered what reassurance he could think of. "Have no fear—I know that they go willingly. I don't think you a necromancer."

"That's good," she said. "That's very good. Because the soul in mine is Gerant."

"I—"

He didn't know what else to say. He didn't even say that much, in truth: the sound emerging from his open mouth meant nothing to him. Meaning itself was a slippery concept right then.

"Gerant." Amris clung to the name and all the images it brought up, memories that were more solid in that instant than the hall of dust and roses surrounding him or the strange woman standing there. "Gerant?" It was a question that time, as he looked at the emerald in Darya's sword and tried to reach out with his mind.

Sympathy softened Darya's expression. "He says... Well, he says hello," she told Amris softly, "and he loves you, and he's very glad you're alive. Only the Sentinel bonded to a sword can hear them, mostly. I'm sorry."

"No," said Amris, with no thought behind the words. He wasn't entirely certain he could think; his mind felt numb, frozen. "No, of course. I presumed...foolish of me. I'm glad he..."

What was he glad about? Was he glad at all? Should he

be? Part of him rejoiced at Gerant's presence, while the rest said that such joy was selfish, when his lover could have been in Letar's Halls long ago rather than trapped in a gem. "I hope he's well," Amris finished, flat, uncertain, and embarrassed.

The slight pause before Darya responded was nothing Amris would even have noticed normally. Now it stretched out into the edge of a razor. When she said, "Generally, yes," he heard it in Gerant's voice, at those moments when he'd combined thought with dry humor, and fought not to flinch.

"Though he admits the situation isn't ideal," she added, with a gesture around them. "And I agree. To say the least."

That brought back some perspective. For the first time since Darya had mentioned Gerant, Amris really looked at her, seeing the lingering animal panic she'd first quashed and then pushed aside for his sake. "Forgive me," he said. "There are larger stakes, I know, and I'd give much if I had any knowledge that would help."

"We know he's back now. That's a hell of a lot more than we did ten minutes ago, and might help the whole world." Darya glanced past him, down a long hall lit only by spots where the crumbled walls let the sunlight in. "If we can find a way out."

———

It was never supposed to last this long, Gerant mourned as they started walking. *We thought if we separated Thyran*

*from his forces, it would be enough of a blow that our armies
could drive them off. Then we could go in, bring Amris back,
take down Thyran's defenses at our leisure, and kill him.*

"Decent plan," said Darya, before she'd thought.
Other Sentinels were used to conversations that sounded
one-sided, outsiders found them odd regardless, and
until Amris gave her a questioning look, it didn't occur
to her to explain. "The plan you two had originally. And
Mater Whoever-She-Was, Gerant said."

"Kasyila," Amris replied absently. "Among others. I
admit I can't regret it, nor find fault, given what we knew
then."

"It kept Thyran off our backs for a hundred years.
That's not nothing." She thought she was being sincere.
It was hard to know. Darya had used up all her day's abil-
ity to feel, she was sure, between sympathy for Amris and
Gerant and...*terror* didn't entirely cover her reaction to
Amris's news. *The creature under the bed is back, and he's
got friends.*

They passed an open door, and Darya poked her head
in hopefully, but inside was only a small bedroom, likely
for a servant: no stairs, just one tiny window. Not even a
child would fit through it.

Action was settling her mind, letting her think past
the fear. "Going by the finger, assuming it rotted like
most things," she said, "then he's only been back for a few
months. Three, I'd say, at most."

"Do you know where he might have gone from here?"

"Probably north. He'd find plenty to work with there."

"The Twisted?"

"Many things, but them too. We've never been able to get farther than this. I'm the first to go as far as Klaishil, for that matter, though there are stories about a city that appears in the summer. Even I wouldn't have come except I was hunting, and I wouldn't have been able to find the place if not for the goat."

"Goat?"

Darya remembered the reason she'd come to the city in the first place. If she'd been distracted by anything less than the potential end of the world, she would've been embarrassed. "Right. We have a stop to make on the way out. I need to kill something."

You can't be serious.

"Of course I'm serious. I have a job to do. This thing's eating people. And an hour more isn't going to make a difference, not when Thyran's been free for the better part of three months."

If both of you die, and nobody's left to take word back to civilization, it very well will make a difference.

"He doesn't have to come, and a fucking cockatrice isn't going to kill me," Darya snapped back.

Well, overconfidence will certainly be an asset in the battle.

"Look—"

Amris cleared his throat. "Cockatrices are as I remember them, yes? Large, winged, not so smart as a man but smarter than an animal? Poison breath?"

"Right. Smart enough to be mean, mostly. And I don't need to worry about the poison."

Only the claws, and the fangs, and the size.

She was about to say that she'd bound herself to a sword, not a mother, when Amris sighed. "It gives me no joy to contradict you, love," he said, which sounded damn odd when he was looking at the hilt of her blade where it rested a little above her waist, "as I believe myself to be doing, but I think we should slay the creature ere we leave. I wouldn't leave anything more intelligent than a beast here where it might bear tales, nor would I want a creature so malicious waiting at our backs."

Gerant said nothing at first, then: *You're... He's... better with tactics than I am. Very well.*

Given the circumstances, Darya wasn't inclined to gloat. "I'll be careful," she said. "Honestly, this time."

"How do you come to be unbothered by poison?" Amris asked, in an obvious attempt to break the tension, but one that Darya silently thanked him for.

"The Forging—wait." As they left the room, she glanced back at him over her shoulder. "You said the Order was just starting when you...in your day. No magical enhancements yet?"

"A few of us had enchanted weapons or armor. Did such things become more commonplace over the years?"

"Not much," said Darya, "maybe less, from everything I've found. There are soulswords, of course, but most wizards don't remember how to make magic stick to objects without some part of a person being in there too. Or so I hear." The only wizard she really talked to was Gerant, but she'd brought back enough tiny novelties, still powered by wisps of enchantment, to draw some conclusions. "We stick them in ourselves instead. As you might have noticed," she added, gesturing to herself with her free hand.

The other hand she kept on her sword as they walked down the hallway toward the older pile and the hole above it. Lots of things could come in through a hole.

"I had noticed, and wondered, but combining magic with flesh was not an art any had mastered in my time. We had Letar's healing, and Thyran and his patron had their...arts...but that was all. Even lesser living things, animals and plants, resisted change. Gerant was one of the first to manage it," he added with a fond, sad smile. "None had seen anything to match those guardian roses."

He was the one to give me the notion, said Gerant. *He'll not tell you that, but he was quite the gardener. Good with all sorts of growing things, really. People never expected it from a warrior.* Without lungs, he still sighed. *Go on.*

"I'm sorry," said Amris at the same time. "I ask and then interrupt. Please go on."

"It's all right," she said. "I expected worse." He hadn't said any of the normal things, now that Darya thought about it—hadn't even asked *what are you* when he'd first seen her. "Anyhow, when we're old enough to choose and we want to stay in the Order, there's a trial. The Forging, because we're the gods' weapons. If we survive, the gods give us gifts, or the magic shapes us—there's a lot of talk either way, when the wizards are drunk."

At her side, she caught Amris's smile. "Often that happens."

Some of my best discoveries came out of drunken wagers, Gerant added.

Darya grinned too. "It's different for each of us," she went on. "Almost always changes the way we look, improves our sight and hearing, makes us faster and stronger and quicker to heal. Usually we get a major blessing from one god, and a minor from another. Some get two minor gifts. I think it comes down to how much reshaping you can endure."

"It sounds a fearsome thing."

"What isn't?"

"Well," said Amris quietly, "there is that view of the matter, yes." He was silent for a while, as they passed fallen rose petals and crumbling walls. "And one of your gifts was to take no harm from poison."

"Poram's blessing, most likely, unless I got two from Sitha—you find poison among the wild as much as among men, and the other way around." She paused before the other end of the hall, where the midafternoon light streamed through onto tumbled masses of stone. Slowly, patterns resolved themselves, and connections became apparent. "And my second gift means you should follow me."

"Sitha's as well, you said?"

"Aye. I can see the safest way to use anything made by man, even if it's ruined." Carefully, she climbed onto the first bit of broken masonry. "That's *safest*, mark you, not a promise of safety. I can't make any promises here."

———

Even if Darya hadn't warned him, Amris would've been loath to feel fully confident in the route: her gift showed as the safest path for *her*. He was taller, likely half again her weight by himself alone, and wearing another stone of beaten steel. Thus, he followed faithfully but slowly, waiting always for the signs the pile would collapse under him, trying never to rest his weight in one place fully or for too long.

Ahead, Darya never paused very long either, but from her, it appeared less a matter of caution and more the innate nimble leaping of a doe. Neither her weapons nor the haversack on her shoulder seemed to impede her. Against the faded, dusty stones, she was a slim patch of darkness, and the sunlight drew bright-green flashes from the emerald set in her sword's hilt.

Gerant.

He'd talked sometimes of the potential for gems to hold human souls, just as he'd spoken of other forms of magic—spells to shape plants, the nature of divination. With his colleagues, the discussions had been long and theoretical, often verging on argument and sometimes passing that border. To Amris, Gerant had spoken more simply, translating his enthusiasms for a lover who lacked most of the context for them. Just as Amris had talked of new recruits and well-made swords, of the conformation of horses and the weather for planting. When it came to other subjects, they'd met on equal ground.

Tears stung his eyes. He let them fall, blinking them away only when they impeded his climbing. Darya kept her silence, and indeed Amris had no idea whether or not she noticed. She looked back rarely, and his face was wet before long regardless; both the weather and the work were hot.

It was a strange, piebald sort of mourning. Gerant had lived long enough to see theory become practice, and was not wholly gone—but never again would Amris drop a kiss on the back of his neck as he sat bent over his notes, or stretch out in front of a fire at night with his head in Gerant's lap. That was ended, as done as was the world Amris had known. And if humanity had survived, enough for hunters of the Order to be searching ruined cities, still some of Darya's speech suggested more danger and less grace in the world that remained.

Gerant, as he existed now, was a creature of that world as much as Darya was: her partner, perhaps her mentor, and certainly, from the way she spoke of him, her friend. Even in mourning, Amris was glad of it. The light in Darya's verdant eyes reminded him of Gerant's enthusiasm over a new sculptor's work, or a well-done landscape, and after their quarrel, she'd spoken with kindness and understanding. Amris didn't doubt they worked well together.

"There," said Darya, rousing him from his thoughts. She'd pulled herself out of the hole and up onto the domed roof of the building. As Amris emerged too, she gestured to a nearby rooftop. The bulk of the dome blocked a direct view, which was fortunate. Even so, Amris could see a circle of filth and carrion atop that roof, and the massive scaled bulk upon it, its comb dull red against the gray-black of its coils.

His first battle in a hundred years waited. The danger would almost be a relief.

Chapter 5

THERE WAS A RHYTHM TO HER KILLS. THERE ALWAYS had been; they were like the dances she'd learned as a girl. If the creature and the situation differed, those were just changes in the tune and the order. The figures stayed the same. Darya had never seen that so clearly until she reached the top of the rubble, saw the cockatrice waiting for her across several hundred yards of stone and air, and felt the comfort of an old pair of boots even as her blood started racing with the nearness of combat.

"I will be careful," she promised Gerant, as she took her bow and arrows from her back. It was an admission and an apology too; she didn't know how much of her confidence earlier had actually been the urge to escape from the world-shattering to the familiar, but her thoughts had not been as clear as she'd assumed.

You'll be effective, he said, doing his part in the language they'd developed over the years. *You always are.*

Darya smiled and turned to look at Amris, the new element, neither a fellow Sentinel nor a hostage to be rescued. Once in a while, she'd worked with packs of soldiers or guards. He felt different. "You'll want to duck down once I start shooting. Weapons ready, but generally just try not to be a target."

"My strength has returned quickly," he said. "I can yet fight."

"Your lungs won't stand up to poison, I bet, and after it breathes, I usually finish too quickly to need help," said Darya. The string went easily onto her bow and twanged with a rich, supple sound when she tested it. "But if you see a chance and take it, gods know I won't complain."

"Can you spare more of…" He gestured to the boot where she'd put her flask. "That substance?"

"Lignath. Or rotgut, as you choose." Darya passed it over, a little surprised. It wasn't uncommon to need false courage before a fight, but Amris hadn't seemed the type. Then again, it was his first battle in a hundred years.

Next, he surprised her more, drawing a faded scrap of cloth out of his belt pouch and pouring the lignath onto it. "It smells somewhat of fish," said Amris, surprised and not thrilled by his discovery.

"Probably is. Or maybe pelican. Good idea," Darya added. "I keep forgetting you've done this before."

"Fought cockatrices, yes, and other poison beasts. I wouldn't call this"—he waved a hand at the ruin, and her—"a familiar experience."

"Variety broadens the mind. Ready?"

Yes, said Gerant.

Amris saluted with the hand not holding the cloth, then drew his sword and sank behind the dome.

The cockatrice bent its head, plucking a final shred or two from the remains of its prey. The curve of the thick neck was like a column of dirty smoke on a windy day: burning far less cleanly than a wood fire and less honorably than a cremation ground. Darya drew back the arrow and then loosed.

Join hands.

As the string snapped against her glove, she was grabbing another arrow, not bothering to look where the first had gone. She knew it would hit. She also knew it wouldn't kill the thing. The scales on a cockatrice were as good as armor or better, and she was no longbowman of Myrias, whose arrows could punch through shields. Her bow was small and portable, made for hunting of all sorts.

Her arrows would hurt, and they would annoy, and cockatrices, like everything the Traitor God had made, gave in easily to their anger. That was what Darya counted on.

Corners cross.

Another arrow, and the monster rose shrieking into the air, spotted the source of its pain, and dove at the speck that stood by the dome, clear and dark against the pale stone. Its wings beat the air, shedding gray-black feathers onto the rock below, and its leprous beak opened wide, showing yellowing teeth that no real bird had ever grown.

Lead down.

The cloud that poured out was a sickly pink with green undertones, like rotting flesh. It flowed over Darya, and while it didn't hurt her to breathe, still the burning-hair scent of it turned her stomach. She swallowed and tensed, ready, and the cockatrice dove closer, thinking to finish off its prey. More feathers fell around her. She saw the edges of the monster's scales and the malice in its tiny pink eyes.

Balance and swing, circle and close.

Darya leapt, up and forward in a neat arc. With one gloved hand, she grabbed the cockatrice by its comb. That gave her a grip and something to push against. She pulled her sword back, twisted her hips for more power behind the blow, and then thrust straight for the thing's chief artery.

Her sword went an inch into the cockatrice's neck, then met solid steel.

The impact screamed all the way up Darya's arm, rattling her bones and numbing her hand. She clutched her sword harder, compensating for her body's wish to do the opposite, but that was all she could make the arm do, and the cockatrice whipped its head sideways, trying to throw her off into the abyss of ruined buildings below.

"*No*," she snarled, and sunk her fingers harder into its flesh. Up close now, she could see patches of scales and skin peeling away from its neck, revealing metal beneath, and she would have asked several questions had she not been preoccupied with survival.

The cockatrice was hard to grip, though. The comb slid between her fingers, half-rotten. It was not what Gerant would have called a *tenable situation*. Darya could feel his magic working desperately, increasing her shields as much as he could—which might still not be nearly enough to let her survive the kind of fall that waited to her left.

When the neck whipped to the right, Darya held her breath and jumped again.

She landed hard against one of the broken walls and managed to jerk her sword up in front of her. It seemed to weigh twice as much as normal, but she slashed out as the cockatrice tried to grab her with one of its foul yellow claws, and the steel bit deep. Yellow blood came oozing out. The cockatrice shrieked again and retracted the claw—then grabbed Darya from behind with its tail, pinning her arms to her sides.

It started to lift her into the air, and squeezed her in the process. Darya's ribs creaked under the pressure, but that was far from her main concern. She could just swing herself far enough forward to kick its body, and did so desperately, putting all her weight behind the blow and aiming at the place where its wings joined to its back.

The hit was a solid one, but the cockatrice's reaction seemed all out of proportion. It reared its head back and howled, releasing its hold on Darya. She fell to the stone, able to control her impact more this time, and puzzled until she saw Amris, raising his sword for another blow at the monster's wing.

As he made contact, Darya darted around him, moving as fast as the cockatrice could swivel its neck. Face-to-face, she snarled an oath as she stabbed again, aiming for a spot under which she was pretty sure there was no metal.

Her blade thrust smoothly, almost neatly, into the cockatrice's right eye. Darya stepped forward, driving the sword in and easily dodging the snapping beak now that the creature was half-blind. Another cloud of poison, that one a last desperate measure, surrounded her; she ignored it, hoped Amris had gotten his cloth up in time, and kept going, breaking through eye and brain until the tip of her sword lodged against the cockatrice's skull and yellow ichor was oozing out onto her shoes.

Then, with a quick backward roll, she withdrew her blade. The cockatrice pulled back as well, but feebly: the last twitching responses it could muster before death. The wings beat a few times, and then it fell with a *thump* that rattled the whole building.

———

After the shaking had passed, when Amris was certain the dome was in no danger of collapsing on his head or Darya's, he rose from his crouch and cleaned cockatrice blood from his sword. He had missed no part of that; the stuff was glutinous and as putrid as the creature from which it had flowed.

"Have they grown thicker scales, all of a sudden?" he asked.

Walking toward the fallen cockatrice, Darya shook her head. "No. It was metal. Watch."

There were few things Amris would have liked less, but for the sake of information, he paid attention as Darya slit open the flesh of the cockatrice's throat, then, with puckered lips and held breath, peeled back the meat and the skin to show iron. It hadn't even rusted.

"By the gods," he breathed.

After the moment of faraway-looking silence, which he'd learned meant she was listening to Gerant, Darya said, "Growing flesh around metal is beyond anything the wizards have ever heard of."

"See how far it goes. If you wouldn't mind," he added, pulling himself back before he could slip into old habits. The woman wasn't one of his soldiers. "I would, but the blood is poisonous as well, or was in my day."

"Oh, good things never change."

She began to strip meat from the monster's neck with the swift, economical movements of a skilled butcher. Halfway through, she added, "Thank you for stepping in back there."

"It was the least I could do." He watched her work. "Have you been all your life with the Order?"

"As much of it as I remember." Darya didn't look up, but it didn't seem as though she was hiding from his questions, only giving her mind utterly to the business at hand. "I was two years old when they took me in."

Amris realized he was still polishing his sword, mostly so he'd have a means of occupying his hands. He resheathed it and asked, "Is that the usual custom?"

"More or less. You get a few younger. People get careless about herbs, a woman dies in birth and nobody's around to take the babe on, that sort of thing. Once in a while, older orphans come to the Order, or kids whose parents can't feed them anymore, but they say it's impossible to survive the Forging if you don't start training before you're past ten or so. Your body's too fixed."

"Dearest gods," said Amris. He responded not to what Darya said, but to what she revealed: a band of metal about twice the width of his hand, looped all the way around the cockatrice's neck and etched with many strange figures. "It has a collar," he said.

"Not common in your time, huh? Not in this time either. I could almost feel sorry for the damned thing"—she paused—"especially as Gerant knows how it'd be done. *Has a theory*, he wants me to say, so you don't think he's been going around doing it himself. Ugh."

"My sentiments precisely. When did this creature settle here?"

"Couldn't say that for sure, but animals started going missing about a month ago. A shepherd boy vanished ten days back. It probably ate him, but the locals thought it was wolves and set a watch. They sent for me when someone saw the cockatrice grab a watchman. These things usually expand their hunting grounds gradually, so I'd say two months."

"And you say Thyran would have been brought back no more than three months ago."

By the way Darya's lips thinned, Amris suspected she was thinking as he was—or that Gerant was, and speaking with her. "Either his flunky did this and rode the thing in," she said, cleaning her own blade and backing away from the cockatrice, "or Thyran woke up, summoned it, and slapped on the collar."

"Both, perhaps. He was ever ready to make use of the tools at hand," Amris replied grimly.

"Must have had another ride out, then."

"Awake, he could transport himself easily enough to one of his places of power. But he chose neither to take it with him, nor to leave it loose to pillage more freely in the countryside." Beyond confirmation, Darya's nod of agreement was a relief. The world was still alive enough to offer better prey than being tethered to an abandoned city would allow. "Why?"

Realization flashed in Darya's eyes, bright as Gerant's emerald for a heartbeat. "Watchdog," she said. "They had to leave you behind, alive. He set a watch in case you woke, escaped." Slowly she looked around them, turning her head from shoulder to shoulder, and although she'd never appeared truly relaxed in the short time Amris had known her, her frame strung itself like a bow again, as it had before the fight.

He was in accord with her, body and mind alike. The sun was slipping down the sky above them, gilding the ruined city with, suddenly, too much light. There on the dome, Amris could see the vast expanse of shattered buildings that lay between them and the forest. The sky was too wide, the air too open. Anything could see them.

"Can he speak to it across distances?" Darya asked. "Or would he have felt its death?"

"I don't know," said Amris, and the words echoed across the rooftops.

Chapter 6

"YOU KNOW," SAID DARYA, "PEOPLE OF YOUR DAY didn't put nearly enough stone ornaments on their buildings."

A distinct fault of ours, and our eternal shame.

"My home had plenty, for it was proud of its stone-work," was Amris's reply. "I admit that's of little help to us just now."

Darya peered down over the rooftop. Below, all was smooth stone by design, unstable masonry where time, war, and weather had done their work. "You should've sent some builders up this way. Damned lack of foresight, I call it."

Joking only helped so much. The back of her neck itched, the target of imagined scrutiny. Had the building been half its height, Darya would have jumped and damned the consequences, trusting her reflexes and Gerant's shields. She unfurled her hands and tried to breathe in patience. Another quarter hour would likely make no difference in whether or not Thyran knew Amris was alive or not, killed them or not, brought an army swarming across human lands or not—

Patience was not working.

Tie the rope to a leg, said Gerant.

"Huh," said Darya, and took a coil of rope out of a small bag on her belt. When she walked over to one of the cockatrice's protruding claws, her intention was likely obvious. Amris didn't ask, at any rate, though his silence made her unsettled enough to explain. "This thing's heavier than both of us combined. And it's maybe less likely to change shape when we're midway through climbing. Did this place do that in your day?"

"Change shape?"

"Mm-hmm." She told him about the stairs as an example while she tied the knots.

"No," said Amris when Darya had finished, blinking but not looking completely nonplussed. He, like Darya, was probably running out of surprise. "I would have remembered."

I think, Gerant said cautiously, *that the spatial distortions are over. They were likely a product of the spell, one I didn't intend, or of having it half-broken for a while. Now that you've lifted it fully, I expect that stairs and walls will remain in place.*

"Well." She filled Amris in, adding, "So all I need to worry about is a bunch of undead and oozes. And not getting my rope back. I've got more, but I paid a silver coin for this."

"Perhaps you could add it to your account, next to the goat," he suggested with a smile.

It was a nice smile: not a flashing grin, but genuine, crinkling the edges of his eyes. Nice eyes, too, when he wasn't glaring. The contrast with his dark eyelashes was striking, and Darya knew she shouldn't have been noticing any of that. The man's lover had been her companion for the last ten years, he was in her sword, and while he couldn't read her mind, he got echoes of her senses.

Darya would have apologized, but that would have only drawn attention to her gaze—particularly as she'd have had to speak aloud and then explain herself.

"It was a goat, yes?" Amris asked. Clearly she'd gone too long without responding. Oh, she was doing *wonderfully* today.

"It was," she said. "With a bag of colored powder tied to one leg, so it'd leave a track when the cockatrice grabbed it. Got me here, and after that, there were only so many places to go. So."

"Tying things to legs seems a winning tactic of yours."

"This one's Gerant's," she said quickly. "Let's hope it works as well the second time."

———

The descent went slowly. Amris passed darkened, broken windows and walls with cracks spidering through them, briefly resting his feet or his grip on the remains of a windowsill. Always he was aware of the weight of his own body, and of his armor beyond that.

About half again his height from the ground, the rope ran out. Amris tucked his head downward and let go; the fall was hard, particularly in his armor, but he picked himself up with no more than a few bruises and pulled twice on the rope, their signal in case Darya couldn't spot him on the ground. He couldn't see her any longer, certainly.

The place he'd landed was an alley, once likely a route for servants to enter the great houses and tradesmen to drop off goods. Shadows were thick on the ground, as was wreckage. Plants had grown up through some of the fallen stones, and all of them were a feeble, sickly green from lack of light.

He waited with sword drawn, listening to his breathing slow back to normal and watching the shadows for motion.

———————

He's safe. Gerant said it like a prayer, and then, more like himself as Darya knew him, *Well, he's down.*

"If he was fighting Thyran," Darya replied, "he'll put paid to any walking corpse or bit of ooze easily enough."

Starting downward, she stared into the windows as she passed them. In the midst of dust and darkness, the graceful lines of statues and vases revealed themselves. Half-rotted tapestries disclosed the shape of a unicorn here, a pair of intact woven eyes there. Darya had no chance to salvage anything she saw, but she could remember beauty—and there might be other journeys, if the world survived.

That coda chilled her, and she suspected it was going to become common.

"How quickly did things start going wrong, back then?" she asked. The outline of the war she'd gotten from her tutors had been sketchy. Thyran had come with an army and storms, people had stopped the army, and the blizzards had hit regardless, though maybe not as badly as they might have otherwise. Sentinels-to-be had needed to know the sort of monsters the army had left behind. History was history. "Did Thyran just fly in on the back of a storm with his creatures below him?"

Gods, no. There'd been five years of fighting before the blizzards started. Some said only four—there was a harsh winter before, but still winter and less dramatic. And, to be fair, the monsters may have been attacking before then as well, but put down to stories of drunken soldiers and old wives. It was only in the second full year that I became at all involved.

"That's a comfort." Beyond the latest window, a shadow moved, small and close to the ground. Darya hurried past the windowsill and then paused, watching, until the source revealed itself as a legless torso, mindlessly dragging itself up and down the hallways where it had died.

"Never thought those things would be a relief," she muttered, continuing downward.

Comparatively, they're harmless. Only flesh.

"So am I."

They descended a few more feet in silence. Then Gerant asked, *Why a comfort?*

"Huh? Oh, because it means we have plenty of time." Gerant's silence did not bode well. "Don't we?"

I can't say for certain. Divination was never my specialty, and it's tricky even for those who master it. But…it's likely that delay was because Thyran had to discover the methods of causing the storms and creating his armies, as well as gather the resources to do so. Now he knows what he's about. And some of the creatures that followed him still remain, despite your—our—efforts.

"Well, shit," said Darya.

Just so.

The rope ended before it hit the ground: a distance, but not a fatal one. Darya glanced down, preparing to jump, and blinked as she saw Amris reaching toward her. "Ah. Um."

Do it. He can take your weight, and that's six feet and a bit less to fall. There's little point in you breaking a bone out of pride, especially now—and I'd rather not use power to shield you when I don't need to.

She couldn't very well voice her other objections. If she did, Gerant would have doubtlessly said that sparing his feelings wasn't worth a broken bone, either, and Darya abstractly agreed. Still, she cringed before she let go of the rope and tried not to feel the warmth of Amris's arms—one at her shoulders, one at her knees, large hands and nimble fingers curving around her body. Silently Darya thanked the gods for both of their armor, which made a considerable leather-and-plate barrier between their chests.

"Thank you," she said. She looked into his face for that, and so she noticed his eyes again, and the sheen of sweat on his dark skin.

"Glad to be of service," said Amris, sounding only calm. That should have been an unmixed relief. That it wasn't entirely, made Darya want to slap herself.

While he set her down, carefully, she delivered a short but firm silent lecture to her body, to the effect that there were plenty of attractive men two or three days' ride away, and none of them had been the great dead love of her sword-spirit's life. Then she stretched, trying to shake off lust along with cramped muscles.

Chapter 7

KLAISHIL HAD BEEN SMALLER IN AMRIS'S DAY.

That wasn't strictly true, or factually true at all. If any person had stayed in the city after the last battle, it hadn't been for long. Certainly nobody had lingered or returned to build. All the same, a smallish city had become an unending maze.

In part, that was due to Amris's state of mind. The more practical side was that he and Darya *couldn't* walk across the city as he had done in the past. Dodging around crowds and carts didn't compare to picking their way across small, unstable heaps of stone, nor to backtracking and trying another road when fallen stone blocked the path they'd been taking.

After one such retreat, Darya frowned upward at the purpling sky. "I don't think we'll make the forest by dark," she said, "and I want to pass the night under wards—gods know what comes out in this place once the light fades. Watch for a place that'll do."

"Have you any particular requirements?"

"No. A roof would be nice, if you can spot a place that's not big enough to have hidden undead and won't collapse on our heads."

Amris tried to picture their road in what he knew of the city. "Which direction are we going, generally speaking?"

"West. Southwest. My horse is there, and he can carry two back to Oakford, though he'll not be happy about it. That's our nearest outpost."

"That way, then." Amris pointed along a street that doglegged toward the setting sun. "We'll find the temples. If any building still stands here, it'll be Sitha's, and if any is free of walking dead, it'll be Letar's. That is, if these are the sort I remember, though I'd think the Threadcutter would drive all of them away."

"Gerant says he doesn't know how much power the temples would still have. They're not *likely* to be defiled, unless Thyran and his crew stopped on the way out, but disuse isn't great either when it comes to keeping a place sacred. On the other hand"—she shrugged—"the undead I've seen so far have just been lurching corpses. Mindless, drawn to warmth, eating things even though they can't actually eat, and so on."

"Masterless forces," said Amris, grimacing at the memory. "A few of Thyran's lieutenants were skilled with the dead. One in particular."

"Lovely talent. Anyhow, without a leader, they're not much of a threat. Nasty if they take you by surprise or you stumble into a nest, but I don't mind clearing out a few to make camp. I just don't want to run into one in the middle of the night."

She fell silent. The fading light picked out her pale face in sharp, severe profile; she could have been on a coin. Light and leisure let Amris notice that her skin wasn't entirely white, but slightly iridescent. Faint rainbows flickered across it while they walked.

"Is Oakford your home?" he asked.

"Only the closest fortress. We've two Sentinels there permanently, plus a few more who come and go. Maybe a hundred regular army, one or two of Tinival's paladins if they're traveling through."

"You're one of those who come and go, I take it."

"So long as I have legs. I'm based in Kvanla, by the sea, but—" Darya smiled sheepishly. "Truth to tell, I like it out on the edges."

The street opened up into a circle, and Darya gave a quiet whistle. While storms, war, and time had touched the temples, the contact had been a feather stroke compared to the fate of the other buildings. Three stood with smoothly curved domes and colored stone walls intact: the red and black of Letar, the Threadcutter; the blue and silver of Tinival, the Lord of Justice; and the many-hued gold of Sitha, the Weaver. In the middle of the plaza, a tall jade fountain in the shape of a pine tree gave tribute to Poram, ruler of the wild. Water yet ran up the trunk and fell steadily from the branches; below, a patch of grass and weeds spread outward through the cracked stone of the plaza, and the green was actually verdant, not the pale, whiteish color Amris had seen earlier.

"Good idea," Darya said, replying to whatever Gerant had suggested. Her voice had fallen to a hush, almost reverent. "*Very* good idea."

Chapter 8

OLD TEMPLES WERE FAMILIAR GROUND FOR DARYA in one sense. The world had plenty of abandoned towns and cities. Naturally, most of them had a few places to worship. Most of the places where she'd been had been smaller, though, and the temples likewise. Most, too, had been more damaged; the gods' power might have kept away the undead and let the temples weather the worst of the storms, but when mortal hands set fires or catapults launched boulders, the divine didn't help very much.

She gawked like a peasant girl at a fair, but she also went to the fountain, made a quick holy sign, and refilled one of her waterskins, then drank and splashed her face as well. The water tingled with more than cold as it hit her skin.

"Honor to Poram, lord of the waters and wild," said Amris, before he bent his head to take his own drink.

He spoke sincerely, but the prayer had a practiced note to it. "Poetic," said Darya, inviting more information but not asking. The man might not want to talk about the past more than he had to—and he would likely have to again before too long.

"A common blessing in Silane," said Amris, and then chuckled, "and I do mean 'common.' Like as not, I kept the habit as much out of defiance as any true reverence when I came among men of rank."

Plowboy, said Gerant affectionately. *Despite all my best influence.*

"I'm not exactly a duchess myself." Darya looked from the fountain to the temples, considering the line of three. "Sitha has my vote. I can fight undead, but I can't do much if a roof falls on me."

"When you put it that way, I can muster no counterarguments."

And since I'd be the one trying to shield you from the roof, I'll make third and all.

They first entered a long anteroom, big enough for twenty or thirty people to stand at need, without furnishings or much ornament. On the walls, golden sconces shaped like spiders held burnt-out torches in their forelegs, and the maple double doors were carved with raised images of webs and looms.

In the shadows of the far corners, shapes began to drag themselves forward. Bone and rusted armor scraped against the marble floor. Darya saw long yellow fingers, a burnt-black skull dragging itself along with its spine, and—"Three walkers."

"Two at the other end."

Without thinking about it, she'd turned away from Amris and stepped backward. Either he'd responded or had the same thought, for they stood back to back, each with a sword drawn. "We could go for the doors," she said. "Get into the main room and shut them out."

"They'd only be here when we need to leave." He was echoing thoughts she'd had herself, confirming but mostly making conversation, while the bones made their slow, grisly advance down the corridor. A helm on one of them still had red feathers. "The temple may yet stand, but the back paths could be blocked."

"Damn. Here we go, then."

———————

Amris recognized none of the armor. There were no faces left to identify: his right-hand opponent had only patches of dried flesh and skin clinging to its skull, and the one on the left lacked even such adornments. He was glad of it. Thyran's monsters had been monsters, but the undead had often been friends and comrades up until their death.

His first overhand strike beat aside a skeletal arm and smashed through several ribs on its way down. His opponent wobbled but kept coming, clutching at air with fleshless hands. Feeble sparks of grayish-pink light burned in the deep sockets where its eyes had been, and its jaw worked steadily on the air, teeth clashing and parting and clashing again.

All of them did that, each slightly out of rhythm with the others. *ClackCLACKclackCLACKclclclCLACK*.

The sound of Amris's sword hitting bone, and of Darya's doing the same behind him, was the only source of relief. Darya wasn't silent, as she had been with the cockatrice, but kept up a constant stream of muttered profanity, lyrics to the macabre concert the seven of them were putting on.

Another stroke from him took the head off one of the skeletons. The body lurched blindly onward, still clutching.

Its companion grabbed at Amris, but he hacked its arm off at the shoulder, spun, and split the headless one's spine lengthwise at the same time as he kicked in one of its knees.

"They're brittle," he said, stomping down on a severed foot. "I'll say that in their favor."

"Like fine, disgusting porcelain."

A chop to the hip took care of the corpse that yet stood. The remaining arms and legs still twitched, though Amris noted with relief that the persistence didn't extend to individual bones. "Or chopping firewood," he said, and suited actions to words.

"Gerant says that Optyras... I'm guessing he was the... Oh, piss off, you"—a smash did, indeed, sound like a milk jug falling onto a stone floor—"the proud father of these things. Gerant says he never did consider the future."

"Among his many other failings."

Amris heard a series of tiny crunches and very deliberate stomps. "Be fair, both of you," Darya said. "I don't think I've ever thought *Will this body hold up against people with swords in a hundred years?*" She stopped talking long enough for another crash, then added, "Yes. Yes, it is."

When the skulls were split in half and the hands had stopped clawing at the air, Amris said, "Hmm?"

"Huh? Oh. Why I'm not a world-conquering necromancer. I lack foresight. And necromancy."

"Alas."

He cleaned off his sword and turned to meet Darya, who was doing the same. The exertion had left her flushed, and her pink face brought to mind the rose

Gerant had given him. He'd left his old life with one lovely weapon from the mage, and it seemed he'd been brought into his new existence by another.

═══════

The doors weren't locked. Darya almost fell when she went to try one and it opened easily, which Gerant found very amusing. She wished, not for the first time, that she could glare at a sword without feeling silly. She also wished Amris hadn't been present to witness, or to put out a steadying arm.

"Strange," she said. "I'd have thought they'd barricade themselves in here, at the end."

The room beyond was a great hall, with an arched roof and carved pillars, a huge altar at the front, and pews carved of the same red-gold maple as the doors. There were many corners where bodies could lie, and maybe they did, but Darya couldn't see any, nor did she hear the scratching sound of bones moving.

"Not here," Amris replied. "Here, there was some warning. Any who would leave the city, did. All who remained turned out to fight, and... I know not what happened to all of them."

The storms broke hard—likely, I now know, it was as soon as Thryan was no longer there to control them—and the city was at the center. Those who fled headed south. A quarter survived the journey. They said it was better to die of exposure—or attack—in the storms than starvation in Klaishil.

"They left ahead of the storms," said Darya. "Some of

them made it." She watched Amris take the news, face still. "One day," she said, "I'll get to tell you some good news."

With that, she left, not wanting to make him hide his pain in front of an audience, and went through the doors into the main room of the temple.

Even Sitha's power couldn't protect a disused temple completely from every misfortune in a hundred years. Dust lay thick on every surface, the burgundy carpets were thin—moths and mice apparently did survive in Klaishil, resilient creatures that they were—and half the tall arched windows were broken.

The last light shone in rainbows through the ones that were still intact, though. The stained glass picked out golden spiders and female faces in the corners. In the centers, larger pictures showed fields of wheat, smiling families at dinner, scholars bent over their books, a woman at a spinning wheel, and other scenes of craft and civilization. As Darya reached the altar, she saw the cloth covering it was still fine and richly embroidered beneath the dust, and the candlesticks atop it were delicate creations of branching gold, studded with topazes in the shape of spiders.

"I'm bringing these back to the temple in Oakford," she said as she reached for the first of them. "As a gift, not for sale."

"It would've been no place of mine to ask," said Amris. "Well."

He was right, and he wasn't, and it was awkward as hell to suddenly have a witness other than Gerant, who'd gotten used to her long ago. Darya looked down at the candlestick. It was important to pack such things with care.

"And it would be a shame," he added, "to let beauty be lost, when so much of worth has vanished already."

That, said Gerant, *is why I loved him. One of the reasons; nothing has only one cause, as I've told you on an occasion or seven.*

"Without you," Darya replied, only half-joking, "I'd be an uneducated clod."

Amris's chuckle drew her gaze up to his face again. His eyes were soft, but he didn't seem quite as sad. "He's not changed very much with the years, then."

Piled up more knowledge, I would say, and only had one person at a time with whom to share it, but I fear neither time nor death has changed the essentials.

"Neither of us is really complaining," said Darya, which drew another affectionate laugh from Amris. This time, she felt as though she was part of the connection between him and Gerant, not in a limbo between translator and intruder.

The inclusion was pleasant—too pleasant to linger in, or she'd come to expect it and start imposing herself. Darya fastened the flap of her pack and stepped back from the altar. "Moving on," she said. "Unless either of you think we'll be smote for it, I say here's the best place to make camp."

───────────

A hundred years before, Amris had knelt in front of the same altar and prayed for victory. Even then, most of the priests had left: fleeing the city, fighting with the army,

reinforcing the walls, or helping with the wounded in
Letar's temple, where holy power had to be reinforced
by human effort. Always tired, always hungry from half
rations of biscuits and dried meat, a bandaged cut down
one leg still aching, he'd looked up at Sitha's gentle, con-
templative face and wondered how much use she could
be, even as he asked for her aid.

The face was still there, carved in relief into the wall
behind the altar. Now, her smile seemed more knowing.
Amris didn't think the gods would have been vengeful
enough to punish him for his doubts, but perhaps she
was saying *And now you see* or something similar. He knelt
and prayed again. It could only help, and he had time.

Darya was walking in a wide circle around the altar and
the room beyond, one that covered as much free space as
possible before bumping into the pews. She went slowly,
with her sword naked in her hand and pointed toward
the floor, and a line of green light appeared on the stone
below it. As the circle grew, the light rose, slowly forming
a dome half the height of the ceiling, until Darya came
back to the point where she'd started and the structure
closed.

A faint green hue tinted everything, but the air felt no
warmer or cooler, and a breeze still stirred it; it wouldn't
go stale on them. Amris rose from his prayers. "May I
touch the circle?"

"You can try, but you'll go through," said Darya. She
sat, sword sheathed now, and Amris thought she was
paler than usual. "It's not really there to block passage for
either of us. Gerant says it knows our souls."

"Is the casting often so hard on you?"

"Not always."

"That is to say, not without a second person to include. Once again, I'm in your debt."

"It's good practice."

Amris joined her on the floor. It was stone, but as it was also smooth and not freezing, he'd had worse, and it was good simply to take weight off his feet. He pulled off his helm and gauntlets, which was a greater relief, and began to undo the catches on his breastplate, while Darya divested herself of her simpler armor far more quickly. With supple grace and long practice, she toed off one boot, then the other, and leaned back with a contented sigh.

"At times I thought," said Amris, "that I could be dead three days and still enjoy this moment." The last catch finally fell away. He lifted his armor off and took a truly deep breath for the first time in…in more than a hundred years. So it always felt, but the literal truth was disconcerting.

"Here," said Darya, holding out a small parchment-wrapped bundle. "It's not much of a first meal, but you probably need it."

As Amris expected, the package contained a square of hardtack and two strips of dried meat. "Thank you," he said, and was about to protest when he saw Darya take another such bundle out of her pack and open it herself.

"I can hunt when we're outside the city. Here, all we're going to get is rats, and I don't want to risk their meat in a place like this." She held out a leather bottle. "Water?"

He accepted and washed down his first few bites of hardtack. It tasted just as good as it had a hundred years before; for all he knew, it could have been made in his own time. Outside, the purple sky turned black, and the shadows inside the temple became darkness, lit only by the faint silver light of the stars.

In that light, Amris looked at his rescuer—Gerant's companion, the woman who fought monsters and talked of eating rat meat as though it was commonplace outside of sieges. She met his gaze evenly, and her eyes glowed in the dark.

"I'd not bring this up at mealtime, nor just before bed," he said, "but I fear I can't choose my time. What has happened to the world since I left it?"

Chapter 9

"Good question," Darya said. "Big question. Um." It was also a question a more forward-thinking person would have been ready for. She took a bite of hardtack, which was good for stalling while she chewed. "All right. I'm going to start at the beginning, and this is going to be pretty general, and there's a lot I don't know. Probably a lot even Gerant doesn't know."

"A first in both of our experiences," said Amris. "Still, I'll value what you can speak of."

Darya took a breath. "When you took Thyran out of the picture, it made the storms hit their hardest, right then."

That was not *Thyran's plan,* Gerant put in, all the more emphatic for the dismayed expression on Amris's face, and Darya repeated his words as quickly and as strongly as she could. *We may not have been able to stop the storms at all by that point. What we did—what* you *did, was interrupt the building of energy.* Darya felt him struggle to put it into words that nonmages understood. *Those that came before fed into one another, and the whole effect was like drawing back an arrow. Removing Thyran, we forced the storms to loose when they were only half-drawn. Because of what they were, that was still enough force to damage, but it could have been much, much worse.*

Some of the shadow lifted from Amris, but not by any means all. "How bad was it?"

"Bad." Gerant didn't add details. Darya felt him withdrawing from contact slightly, as he did when she took lovers or attended to other bodily needs. He didn't go as far off, though, so she felt an echo of his memories as she spoke, filling in details they'd never talked about and she'd never wanted. "For a full year, blizzards worse than there'd ever been. Plants died. Animals died. People couldn't grow anything, or hunt, and that wouldn't have mattered because the cold would mostly kill you in minutes if you went outside."

It was summer, and they'd had no meat to cook, so she hadn't bothered with a fire—there was nothing to burn in the temple, in any case. As she relayed the story, Darya wished for one. The warmth would have helped with the memories, and she could've stared into the flames. She rubbed her hands against her thighs instead, watching her fingers, pale against the dark cloth of her pants. They made her think of the plants in the city, and of dead things.

"The priests and the wizards did what they could, multiplying food and giving people protection from the cold, but there were limits to their power." Without thinking about it, she fell back on the wording of the official histories, as her tutors had told them to her when she'd been barely a woman. "And while Thyran's armies had scattered, the monsters endured the storms better than most humans. Death made others. So did desperate actions, or vicious ones. There were many threats in those days."

Amris was silent.

"Some fared better than others. It wasn't as bad in the south, or in places that could get food from the sea. Hills blocked the wind, and that helped too. But my teacher told me, when I was training, that there were half as many people living then as there were in your day. That was fifteen years ago, after a couple generations of breeding."

She didn't say: *They ate the food, they ate dogs and rats and horses, they ate the candles for tallow, they ate the bark off the trees and the leather of their boots.* She didn't say: *By the end, many of them ate one another, and it didn't help.*

All of that had been history before: sad, and horrifying to think about, but distant, and so well known that neither she nor Gerant had needed to speak of it. Now, Darya saw blood on the snow, faces that were half skulls, bodies burning in the streets, and those who wanted to live unable to move away from the stench.

A hand—large, warm, and callused—settled on top of hers. Darya looked up into Amris's face and managed a quick, guilty smile. "I think I'm supposed to be comforting you, considering."

"You have, and will again, but—" He shrugged. "Shock and memory are each their own sort of pain, and they strike at different times. Just now, I have reserves."

He was speaking to her and Gerant both, Darya knew, and she spoke for them both when she replied, "Thank you," and laced her fingers through his.

"A year, you said," he prompted her.

"Yes." This part was easier. "After that, the storms started getting milder, and further apart. Winter's still worse than it was, they say, and longer, but we have the other three seasons again. The wizards and priests developed some magical techniques, too, or improved on what existed—stored light, different crops, city defenses, that kind of thing. Travel is still very risky, though, especially when it's not summer, and there are plenty of places like this." With her free hand, she gestured around to mean the city, then rethought. "Not exactly like Klaishil, that is, but...lost."

I'd already died, Gerant added, *before we knew that Heliodar or Nerapis had survived, and it wasn't until halfway through my first Sentinel that a person could trust a map for more than five miles.*

Darya repeated that. "Most live and die no more than a day's journey from the place of their birth, even now. The Sentinels are different, but we were made to be."

"I recall your founding," said Amris, "though not the swords. You were always intended as a"—he stopped himself from saying *breed,* obviously—"a force apart."

"Good work, then," she said.

———

In truth, Amris wasn't sure how strange the Order was, at least not as represented by Darya. Her appearance aside, the quickness of her speech was alien, and the casual hardness she displayed had been rare in his time—though that had been his time, before half the world had perished—but in action, she felt like one of his own comrades, and he'd not hesitated before taking her hand.

Some of that was Gerant's presence, but not all.

"What remains?" he asked, and the pressure of her fingers in his helped him get the words out and listen for the answer. He hadn't been lying earlier: she was a comfort. "Kvanla, you said, and Heliodar and Nerapis too. Did Silane survive?"

In a sense, it was academic; nobody he'd known would still live there. At best, his father's house would stand, and those in it might have heard of Great-Uncle Amris, who'd disappeared in the war. Still, he felt his heart lift a little when Darya nodded. "Smaller than it was, but not by very much. The south did better than most—warmer, and there are those caves in the mountains, with heat and mushrooms. Kvanla, too, as I guess it's harder to kill fish and seaweed, but we were never much of a kingdom to start with. Silane and Criwath are the only real kingdoms left. And Heliodar, in fact if not in name. Nerapis is just the main city these days, and the Myrians...well, they have their towns and their fortresses. The barbarians up here—"

"Many went over to Thyran, by force or by will. Those who resisted had fled south before he and I met, or been put to the sword, at best." Amris pictured the map of the world, like a moth in shape. Klaishil had been in Criwath, with the deep forest and the nomads to the north and the Serpentspine Mountains making a western border. Heliodar lay beyond the Blue Hills to the south, in the other section of the "wing," cradled by a bay, and the Arenthan River cut it off from Silane. From there, seabound Kvanla straddled the "tail" where the mountains flattened into scrubland, and Nerapis had held the territory from the Pramath Harbor all the way up to the chain of lakes where the Myrian families had squabbled.

Nobody had gone to the far northeast, not since the battle between Gizath and Letar had scarred that section of the land. There'd always been forests and hills scattered around, claimed by one land or another but really belonging to no king or council. They'd been islands of darkness in the golden web of civilization. Now, Amris saw bigger patches of darkness around a few points, like campfires at night.

Darya's hand was a rope, pulling his mind forward into the present. "The other peoples?" he asked.

"Retreated. Mostly. Kvanla's ports trade with the waterfolk at high summer, but they've gone far under the sea otherwise. The stonekin helped Silane some, but they don't come out of the mountains."

"And we're still in Criwath?"

"In theory. Oakford is a few days' ride back, and it's only been occupied again for thirty years. We *are* rebuilding," she added. "But that's as far as we've gotten. Thyran's leftovers, and the other things, are thicker on the ground the deeper into the forest you go, and nobody has the people to spare for an expedition, let alone to try to take ground and hold it. Even the Sentinels only come on missions, and generally we get in and out as quickly as we can."

"I'm sure I'll think of more questions to plague you with. But just now—" He spread his hands, illustrating emptiness.

Doing so meant letting go of Darya's hand, which he did with surprising reluctance, then a shade of guilt about that. Neither he nor Gerant had expected the other to be celibate in times of long separation, particularly when he was on campaign, but a living lover far away was a different matter from one who was present and dead, or dead and present. Amris wasn't sure which was worse.

"I'm not surprised. In your place, I think I'd be walking into walls and forgetting my own name." With her now-free hand, she pulled out the flask of lignath, took a swig, and held it out toward Amris. "Here. Should keep off the worst of the nightmares."

He drank, then paused. "If you use this for wounds—"

"Yes," said Darya, after swallowing more hardtack, "better not kill it. It also burns very well."

"Far from startling news."

Between food and spirits, the day's exertions settled quickly on him. As Darya finished up her own meal, he pulled off his boots, stretched out on the floor, and tried to remember how best to make a pillow of his arm.

"Hey," said Darya. "Take the altar cloth." She was pulling it out of her bag as she spoke. "Not as if Sitha will mind, if you can stand the dust."

"But you—"

"My armor won't stop an arrow so well as yours, but I can sleep on it without breaking my neck."

"Sound reasoning. Thank you."

"I'm known for it—and you needn't bother snickering," she added, obviously to Gerant.

In the faint green-and-silver light, as magic and the moon blended, Amris watched Darya fold up her tunic. Her sword, with Gerant in the hilt, she lay down between them like a maiden preserving her chastity in an old tale, though Amris doubted the intent was the same.

"May I?" he asked, and reached out a hand toward the sword by way of indication, though he didn't yet make contact.

"Wha—Of course," Darya said, embarrassed. "Sorry, should have thought of that."

"These aren't circumstances any could anticipate. I hadn't thought it either, until now. And I thank you." Amris laid his fingers on the gem.

It felt as any other polished stone would have: smooth, hard, and cold. Had he not known Gerant was in there, nothing of it would have called to mind the gentle, scholarly man Amris had known, the one with nimble fingers, sure lips, and bright eyes to match the mind behind them. Yet he did know, and while it was an incomplete balm for the ache in his heart, it was balm nonetheless.

"Good night," he whispered toward the gem, and thought that the emerald shone back at him for a heartbeat.

All the world was new and strange. Yet, he thought as he watched Darya lie down and let his own eyelids slide shut, he wasn't sure there were two better people to introduce him to it.

Chapter 10

ALMOST ALWAYS, ON WAKING, DARYA'S FIRST THOUGHT was grudging acceptance: *Yes, all right. All right.* What she was allowing changed from day to day, but the feeling of *well, fine, then* was essentially the same whether she faced the breakfast dishes in the chapter house, the remnants of a previous night's celebration, or in this case, the possible end of the world.

In the light, Sitha's temple was more beautiful, and sadder. Dust motes spun through the air, and patches of green and red and blue light splashed across empty pews and an altar where nobody had stood in three generations. The smile on the carved face above it looked wistful now, though maybe it always had and Darya just hadn't noticed the night before. Sitha and Poram, the priests said, had both wept when their children fought, and since the Traitor God had never *stopped* fighting—

"Oh, yes," she muttered, "dwelling on theology's absolutely the smartest thing to do first thing in the morning."

She hadn't forgotten Amris. She couldn't forget Gerant. But her companion had long since stopped responding to most things Darya said when she woke, save to poke more-or-less gentle fun at her, and Amris's sincere "Theology?" made her jump a bit.

"Oh. Um. That." Darya indicated the carving.

"Sleeping under her gaze does encourage such thoughts," Amris said, nodding, but he didn't pry, just continued putting on his boots.

It encourages many thoughts, Gerant put in. *I've been considering it, and I think I can expand my powers enough to talk directly with Amris—though that assumes you're willing to help me.*

Happy surprises were all the more surprising. "And skip the translation? Of course, as long as I'll be in decent shape afterward. He says—" she began, turning to Amris.

He didn't interrupt her. But the incipient joy on his face let her know that he'd worked out what was happening, and after seeing that, Darya wouldn't have thought to say no even if she had been inclined.

"He always did his best work in the middle of the night," Amris said, and she laughed.

"Wizards. I've never met one that kept normal hours. Well, what do we need to do?"

First, kneel facing each other.

The floor was tolerably hard on the knees, which actually pleased Darya. It was a distraction from Amris, with his hopeful face and sleep-mussed dark hair, the clean, hard lines of his shoulders and chest, and his ability to somehow kneel in parade stance, good *gods.*

The sword goes between you, held upright. Each of you needs one hand on the hilt, and you clasp the other's.

Clasping hands felt surprisingly easy, even given their contact of the night before. Getting both of their hands on the hilt of the sword was a different matter, and required a fair amount of adjustment. Their fingers ended up intertwined there too, with each of them resting the tip of a thumb on the emerald.

Darya always felt magic before she saw or heard it. On her, it was little rivulets running over her skin, almost like raindrops but keeping to steadier and more distinct patterns, and not quite wet, though she kept expecting them to be. For this spell, they were cool and wispy, starting at the thumb on the emerald and spreading out across her skin in an orderly grid of lines like a fisherman's net.

The emerald was glowing, alternately brighter and fainter in a rhythm like a heartbeat. Darya didn't speak—she knew better than to interrupt Gerant during a spell. She watched the light illuminate Amris's face, felt the heat of his fingers in contrast to the cool threads of magic, and knew that he, like her, had started breathing to the beat of the emerald's light. He was enough taller than her that each breath stirred her hair faintly, a sensation on the pleasant side of ticklish, and Darya knew he must be able to feel hers on the side of his face.

She hoped it didn't smell too awful.

As the web of magic flowed over Darya, it took a part of her with it—nothing too large nor too vital, just a bit of what made her herself. She felt it go out, without any more pain than a gentle tug on her hair might cause, and so she knew when the web expanded to cover Amris, settling itself over his body and then farther in. Sitha wove all souls, just as her daughter cut their threads. The spell found threads in Darya and tied them to loose places in Amris: not the tightest binding she'd ever heard of, but a binding nonetheless.

Once before, she'd felt her spirit woven in such a fashion: when she'd knelt before the Adeptas, knock-kneed
and cross-eyed from a four-day vigil, and balanced her
blade on her outstretched palms while they joined her
to Gerant. This was less, and different, and to a man who
yet lived, but Darya held to what familiarity she could. It
seemed the safest path.

Breathe steadily, they'd told her in training. *Don't try to
resist. Hold back nothing of yourself. You trust the soulsword,
or you die.*

Already Amris had proven worthy of her trust—many
times, since he'd slept beside her and not knifed her and
taken the sword. Besides, sometimes she just had to jump
and hope she landed more or less whole.

She looked into Amris's eyes, waiting for him to hesitate or pull back, but he was in as fully as she was. *Of
course*, Darya thought, and she didn't let herself be flattered; of course he trusted his lover, and he had more to
gain by going through with the ritual than she did. Still,
it was nice that she wasn't an unthinkable price to pay.

The web spread outward, then inward, until it finally
knit itself completely together around Amris and Darya's
linked hands. By then, she was feeling his presence—
fainter than Gerant's, with no coherent sense of his
thoughts, but an awareness of his being that went bone
deep. If she closed her eyes and went to another room,
she'd still know where Amris was. If he was masked and
in a crowd, she would have picked him out instantly.

Hello, love, said Gerant.

Amris smiled and gaped at the same time, mouth

open and eyes crinkling at the corners. His astonishment resonated within her. So did his joy, as much keener than any Darya had experienced, as Gerant's pain had been. She thought of how the temple must have looked in the halcyon days of its use: joy, love, one human hand in another, all forming a greater pattern.

Her hand wasn't the right one. Gently she disengaged it, and then the other, leaving Amris holding her sword. "You two talk while I pack up," she said, raising the barriers in her mind. She'd done it often enough for her own liaisons. It felt odd to be the one on the outside now, but it would likely do her good, as Adeptus Brannath had said of many things. "You've a lot to catch up on."

They did, and Amris had no notion of where to start. By Gerant's silence, neither did he.

Then, rueful, *You look well.*

"Evidence of your arts, I think," Amris said. "You could exhibit me in front of a committee, if you wished."

From a few feet away, where she was sharpening knives, Darya snickered. Then she started humming a song. Amris didn't recognize the tune, and didn't know if there was one, or if it was only an obvious effort at tact.

I think I'm rather past the need for fame, said Gerant. *But thank you.*

"Did you end up at court, in the end?" It was as innocuous a question as Amris could think of.

For a while—such as there was a court. After a while I

threw myself into the magical aspects of the Order. There was enough there to occupy a man for a lifetime. Or three, considering. A moment of silence followed, where the scrape of whetstone on steel was the beat for another wordless melody. *I thought you'd perished, Amris, and within my life there was no chance of reaching Klaishil. And they needed me.*

"I understand," he said softly. Sincerely too. It had long been his job to decide where to spend men's lives, to abandon some as beyond rescue, and to go on with the larger mission. There were times when people had to put their hearts away from them, like the warlords of legend, and hope that they would still be intact when that chest opened again.

I'm still sorry.

"I know." A week before, or a hundred years, he'd have put his arms around Gerant. There was nothing to touch now, save for cold steel and hard stone, and that led to his next question. "How much do you perceive of…anything? I take it you can hear well enough."

*True, and I have some sight independent of my bearer. Smell, taste—*the hesitation was minute, but there—*and touch are far more muted. Other than secondhand, they might as well not exist unless the sensations are very extreme. I might feel fire or acid, but nothing less.*

"Ah."

There's this compensation: magic is far easier to sense in this state, and to grasp, or persuade, if one is going to be absurd about it. Amris smiled. That was an old debate, and one he'd sat through Gerant's side of on a few evenings. *You'll notice perhaps that neither the ward last night nor the expansion just now required any chanting or incense from Darya?*

"I did," Amris lied, and caught Gerant's skepticism in his head. He admitted, "Or would have, if I hadn't left half my mind a century back. Truly, it is impressive."

I had always wished for you as an audience.

"I didn't get any more knowledgeable while I was out of time, you know."

And you know that never mattered. I would rather show off for you than for the most learned mage in the world.

"And I'd rather see you conjure fireworks than have anyone else summon me a castle," Amris replied, his voice rough.

It could be worse, Gerant said. Across the room, Darya finished sharpening her last knife and started tugging on her armor. *When I agreed to this, I did think I was abandoning all hope of seeing you again, since you'd likely have moved on from Letar's realm by the time I got there. In many ways, this is an unexpected gift for me.*

For Amris, it was the opposite, but he didn't say that. Love, like so many other human ties, was built as much on the words you didn't speak. He stared hard at Sitha's carved face on the wall, slowly mastering himself enough to ask, "Did you survive long past"—*past me* came to his lips, but he *had* survived, in whatever new form this was—"that last battle?"

Longer than I should have, and longer than better people. I was eighty-eight when I died, mostly from sheer old age. The priests of Letar could heal many things, but the body wore thin over the years, until the rust outweighed the rivets.

"Good," said Amris, and meant it. But the next thing he said was, "And if we're to save the world from another such catastrophe, we'd best be going."

He couldn't ask if Gerant had been happy without him. He hoped so, truly, but he couldn't make himself say the words.

Chapter 11

THE MORNING ITSELF PROVIDED EXCUSES ENOUGH for silence at first: wrestling himself into armor again, then breakfasting on more hardtack. They washed it down with water from Poram's fountain, and Amris felt better for those few swallows than he'd done after many a feast in a lord's hall. He said his blessing again before he drank, and bowed before they left.

"If we had a week or two," Darya said, glancing over her shoulder, "I'd clear out all the temples here. Get rid of the dust and undead and rats."

Unless people resettled the city, it would only be temporary.

"The corpses wouldn't come back. Besides, everything's temporary. They deserve better."

"One day," Amris said. "And one day people might return too. If all goes well."

You've doomed us all, said Gerant, as Darya hastily knocked four times on her bow, that being the only wood in reach.

He laughed apologetically and yet was glad he'd said it—glad even for the mild heckling. After the morning, it cleared the air and lifted his own mood. With the curious vitality of the water had come a freshness to his mind, one that did not erase his sorrow but made it easier to see beyond and to take an interest in other matters.

"You're a well-matched pair," he said. "Which of you chose the other?"

"I picked Gerant for his looks," said Darya, with a sly grin. "Silver-etched steel, Nerapis-style grooves and ornamental runes, square-cut flawless emerald, excellent balance—how could any girl resist?"

And she was the most likely trainee her age—when I was ready for another bearer, that is to say—to understand the appeal of discovery. I had hoped she might develop an inclination toward more subtle methods than breaking things, killing other things, and stealing yet more things, yet here we are.

"I'm not sure whether to be flattered or turn you into horseshoes."

Have mercy on the poor horse.

Out of the temple square and back down the paths that Darya found, they picked up the thread of their journey again.

The spell coiled about all three of them. It wasn't uncomfortable, but for the first few hours, he was aware of it and thus of Darya in a way he hadn't been of anyone before. She felt much like another hand, or the breastplate on his shoulders: a presence he knew well without thinking about it. Unconsciously, they began to walk in rhythm. Even when she went ahead to scout, Amris stayed an unvarying distance behind her.

If I worked out how to expand this farther, Gerant said, *perhaps it could be of use in larger groups.*

"Not that we're generally in those. But if you can teach others, it could come in handy in war, from what I hear of that." Darya glanced back at Amris.

He ducked under a fallen roof beam, just low enough to have clipped his head otherwise. "The price might be too great to have it widespread. If soldiers feel it when one of them is injured or dies, they'd break easily, and if they didn't break, they'd be distracted. For the officers, though... It might do us good in any number of ways."

It would make your decisions harder.

"Such choices should be hard."

Darya, meanwhile, was frowning. "I hadn't thought of that. Amris's bruises don't pain me so I've noticed, and I'm guessing it goes the other way around." Amris nodded. "But would I feel it if he jumped off a cliff? And how strongly?"

I'm not certain. I don't believe the tie would be enough to kill you, or even leave you helpless if you greatly needed not to be, and I believe I could shield either of you from the worst of it, said Gerant. *But I couldn't swear to that, and I couldn't speak at all in any more detail. It's a fascinating question. Don't test it.*

"So much for my plans."

"I will do my utmost," Amris said, putting a hand to his heart, "to stay away from cliffs."

"Thank the gods we're on the ground now."

They were, and that ground was less treacherous. As they left the center of the city, the buildings became smaller, and their destruction more complete: wood and clay did not stand up to time as marble and granite did, much less to storms and invasion. Some bits of oak and stone remained to clutter the road, and a few piles of broken bricks, but the streets were largely clear. On either side, roofless walls leaned against one another, and rough indentations showed where foundations had once stood.

That was less foreboding than the huge buildings in the city's center and their shadows, but it was also sadder. Even those who'd gotten out before Thyran's army and all that followed had left their lives behind. Now there was nothing left of those, save for crumbling walls and faint marks in the earth.

The old world, the world Amris had known, was gone. At the edge of its ruin, a wilderness rose up, thick and green and trackless.

Darya wanted to cheer the first time she saw the tree line from street level. Soon there wouldn't be any more streets. Soon there wouldn't be any more undead—she was fairly sure they didn't venture outside the city—or unstable buildings or streets full of rubble. Normally she relished the chance to wander the fallen cities, but in this case, she couldn't shake Klaishil's dust from her heels quickly enough.

She settled for grinning and pointing. "There. And"— Darya glanced over her shoulder, calling the skyline back in her mind—"roughly the same place we came in."

Now to find the wasteland your horse has produced.

"I'm sure Ironhide stopped eating sometime. And he'll be rested, which is lucky for us," she said, trying not to eye Amris and his armor too obviously.

"How far have we to go before Oakford?"

"Thirty miles. Two days, more or less, given the ground." Two days before she could tell the fort's commander about the situation, send messages to the Adeptas and, well, not turn it over to them exactly— because Darya didn't think she could *turn over* the possible end of the world—but not be one of only three people who knew of it. More experienced tacticians would make decisions. People with big armies would send them. She'd do her part, and *know* her part.

When she stepped into the shade of the forest, the world felt steadier beneath her, and far more familiar. The woods hadn't produced threats from the past or companions whose good looks she couldn't think about. Under the trees, she hadn't vicariously remembered mobs and fire and blood on the snow.

Home, she thought, *or at least getting closer.*

At first, when Darya peered into the forest and didn't see the dappled-gray hide of her gelding, she thought impatience had made her misremember how close to the city she'd left him. Then, dangling from a large pine tree, she saw the loose ends of her picket line. She started swearing, but only in her mind. As silently as possible, she drew her sword.

No big cat leaped down as she approached the tree, Amris at her side. No monster sprang from the shadows, and Darya saw no motion anywhere save that of small harmless creatures.

But below the tree, and on the ground all around it, the grass was trodden down—not as a single horse would crush it by grazing, but by more beasts with more purpose—and when Darya reached for her rope, she saw that it had been neatly cut.

The pulse in her throat began to pound. She knelt and examined the tracks: there were sets from horses and from longer creatures with ten legs. All led out along the path she'd originally come on—toward Oakford.

She and Amris might not be ahead of the threat after all.

Part II

The barbarians of the north were the first to fall to Thyran and his god. Some went to him willingly, lured by the promises of power or plunder. Others bowed to superior force. Few stood against his allies, and those that did died, or worse, in large part. A handful survived to flee south with warnings. We mostly ignored them. That is our shame, and it was our undoing.

—The Letters of Farathen

Call: What are the enemies of mortals?
Response: *The dead that walk. The Twisted, once humans and once beasts. The mortal servants of Gizath, who would reorder the world in his name.*

Call: How may they be fought?
Response: *With fire, with magic, with faith, with steel. Most of all with caution and will.*

—The Catechism of Letar's
Blades, Part III, Revised

Chapter 12

"THREE HORSES, PLUS IRONHIDE," SHE SAID, STRAIGHTening up and turning to Amris. "Two big beasts, ten legs each. Do you know those? I've never seen that sort of thing with raiders, or heard of them either."

"Korvin," he said, and his mouth tightened. Darya heard the next word in advance, though she was praying inwardly not to. "A kind of Twisted. Scouts ride them. Probably one on each, though they can carry two. Human blood at close range excites the creatures too much for even the twistedmen who ride them to control them, and they don't carry deadweight well. Raiders would find them of little use."

"Scouts," Darya repeated. "Oh."

He could be wrong. Korvin could have changed since his time. Even if they were scouts, they could be from a small band. The Order and the various militant priesthoods had suspected, ever since the storms had died down enough for people to start suspecting things at all, that a few of Thyran's lieutenants had survived and gathered their own little fiefdoms, out where no mortal ventured. The Twisted, korvin and twistedmen both, could have come from one of them.

That would have been a hell of a coincidence.

"In the histories," she said, "Thyran wasn't much for simply getting the lay of the land when he sent his forces out, was he? And if he's been around for a month or two, he'd have been able to do that already, right?"

Amris sympathized, she felt, but he didn't waste time trying to soften his answer. "No, I fear, and yes. He may have changed since he's awakened, but in my day, the korvin riders always went in advance of his army, but never very far."

The muscles just below Darya's windpipe clamped down, and her own breath echoed like the sea in her ears. She looked back at the tracks, using facts to build a wall between her and panic. None of the facts were *reassuring*, but concentrating on them broke the cycle of *oh shit oh gods oh no we're dead oh shit oh gods oh no* that kept wanting to repeat at the back of her mind.

She'd known it had been bad. She'd thought they'd have *time*.

Thyran probably hadn't had a chance to raise all the forces he'd ended up with a hundred years back. He'd probably just gotten a bunch of his old chief minions to bring their separate packs together. It wasn't as though the mortal lands could field as many soldiers as they once had either. Oakford sure as hell didn't have more than a hundred, if that, the vast majority of them normal humans with maybe a year of actual fighting under their belts—and that was where any army going south would have to strike first.

"They're not long ahead of us," she said, glancing back at the tracks. Her voice was flat. Everything was flat. The world seemed to have lost a dimension in the last few moments. "Five, six hours. If I hadn't decided to sleep—"

If we'd known then what we know now, we'd be gods, or prophets at any rate, and there are reasons most mortals don't have such gifts, Gerant cut in sharply.

Amris nodded. "He's right, as he always was when he

said as much to me." He didn't touch her, but stepped closer, and the earth became more solid beneath Darya's feet. His voice, low and calm, with the words slower and more lilting than Darya was used to hearing from modern speakers, smoothed the worst of the guilt out of her mind. "And consider—if we'd come earlier, we'd likely have stumbled into at least five of Thyran's troops and their mounts, which were trained for war when I fought them. I think well of your skill, Sentinel, and likely too well of my own, but I suspect we'd have fared ill and left none to bring back warning."

"Point to you both," said Darya. "You know his armies. How far behind the scouts is the main force likely to be?"

"From what I recall, and given the land, I'd think three or four days at least. More, should he plan to attack in any great strength."

"All right." She thought of the terrain herself, planning for horses because she didn't know how the korvin coped with mole holes and tree roots, and made some quick calculations. "We can push ourselves and make it back in two, maybe three."

"Give it three, with some time for sleep and eating," said Amris. "The problem with scouts is that they're all too apt to return to their forces."

"I should've thought of that," said Darya, because it beat *Oh, good, and I didn't think this could get any worse.*

———

There wasn't much left of the road from Klaishil, just a flatter space between two hills where wide stones occasionally interjected themselves among the grass and the shrubs. Once in a while, four or five of those stones still lay side by side. Mostly, a traveler would have had to know in advance that the road was there.

Still, Darya took herself and Amris off it, into the shrubs and trees a few feet away where the hills began to rise. The going was a little slower, but not much with her gift, and Amris's point about scouts returning stuck in her mind. The tracks had led back along the old road. Thus, she knew what might be there. Thus, she avoided it.

Although he had no gift for finding safe routes, was considerably larger than Darya, and was wearing far heavier armor, Amris didn't complain about the decision or even question it. He walked when she walked, far enough behind to let her mark the trail but close enough to be at hand in case trouble did strike, stopped to eat or drink when she did, and kept the same silence. He made more noise when walking, but that wasn't to be helped.

Darya picked up a stone shortly after they started walking—round and dark, it fit neatly into her palm, and had a pleasant weight to it. She carried it for two or three hours, until movement out of the corner of her eye revealed a rabbit sitting up between two of the trees. Then she glanced, cocked back an arm, and threw.

It was a good hit. "Hold here a moment," she said to Amris—speaking softly, as whispers carried farther—and went to grab the body before another creature could.

You've impressed him, said Gerant.

"I've gotten us dinner," Darya muttered, "which will

keep us in better form to fight if we need to." Nonetheless, hearing it made her smile.

It was a good thing she usually worked alone, she thought. When she had a partner, especially a handsome one, even a handsome and off-limits one, she was far too apt to show off.

Bending to pick their future dinner up, she suddenly stopped. Her smile vanished. A few feet beyond where the rabbit had fallen, a path of blackened ferns and gray brambles slashed through the green and brown underbrush.

Shit, she thought.

She said nothing aloud, but straightened up, drew Gerant, and started backing away toward Amris.

Beyond her, like echoes in the forest, many legs skittered closer.

Stasis had largely left his body unaffected, so his muscles still worked as they had ever done, but a trek through a forest was a different matter from street-to-street fighting—or from the cavalry charges or infantry stands where Amris had spent his youth.

He was proud of himself for managing to keep up with Darya, who practically danced over the undergrowth and through the trees. She was purposeful about it, but there was a lithe ease about her—an impression that vanished completely when she started backing away from the spot where the rabbit lay.

She'd been alert before she'd fought the cockatrice and as they'd prepared to advance against the undead, ready for a fight, but this was different. Sword drawn, she retreated with taut-strung muscles, keeping her gaze fixed forward, clearly not wanting to look away from the forest. Alarm filled her and, through the spell, spilled over into him.

Dalhan, said Gerant in his mind. *One of the many wonderful new creations of the storms.*

Amris didn't recognize the name, but Gerant's voice and Darya's stance were as good as a warning shout. He had his blade out before the first set of blanched-white legs appeared from the shadows.

They had been human once, maybe, though almost skeletally thin. Some force had given them two or three extra joints in the middle and taloned, spiderlike hands at the end, then joined four of them together and plopped a headless human torso in the center. A ring of pinkish-red eyes glared out of the chest, with a snarling, fanged mouth below it, and above that the shoulders rose high, making a sort of distorted heart shape. Its arms were stunted, but one held a bone whip, more than long enough to make up any lack of reach.

Two others like it followed, all moving with insectile speed toward Darya. Amris rushed toward her side.

Chapter 13

DARYA SAW THE STUB THAT PASSED FOR THE DALHAN'S whip-arm flex, and was in the air the next second. The whip snapped through the empty space where one of her ankles had been. Its bones, the knobby remnants of something's—or somebody's—spine, rattled against each other. Darya had heard the sound half a dozen times, and it still turned her stomach.

She kicked forward and caught the dalhan right above the mouth. The sole of her boot slammed into two of its eyes. It staggered back. Darya retreated, too, pushing herself off the monster into a backwards somersault, then bringing Gerant down in a slash as she landed, one leg out low behind her.

The dalhan that had been coming up on her side swayed backward, and Gerant's edge missed the center of its torso by a hair. The stroke that would've cut through to its mouth fell, useless.

Darya let the momentum pull her downward. The whip that had been going to slash her across the face met empty air instead. She struck out low and hit one of the dalhan's legs, which split in the middle. Black blood spurted from the wound, filling the air with the smell of ashes. The plants it fell on vanished. A few drops hit rocks, hissed, and sent up acrid gray clouds.

Four legs meant the monster had some spares. It

sagged, though, taken off-balance for a few seconds, and Darya drew her leg forward, her body up, putting all of that motion behind her next stroke. Dead flesh parted under Gerant's edge, giving way smoothly up into the dalhan's torso, before a bone turned the angle of Darya's stroke. The sword came up and out through its side, the wound bad but not fatal.

Blood soaked the ground. Green light flickered around Darya as Gerant shielded her from the places where it would've splashed, spraying from the dalhan's wound. The creature reared up, chest gaping, a leg clawing at the air. Its missing leg unbalanced it, and it was falling as Darya spun away from its blood.

She lashed sideways with one leg as she did, and the whip of another dalhan coiled briefly around the tip of her boot rather than doing serious damage to her kidneys. The force of the spin let Darya shake that off neatly enough, and then she was coming around, slicing backhand at the monster that had been there when she'd started spinning. Kicking the whip away had cost her a few precious seconds, though. Gerant hit the thing, but only a glancing blow to the shoulder, giving it barely a moment of pause.

———

Always, battle took concentration, and with an unknown enemy most of all. Amris bent his focus on one of the dalhan and closed the distance between them quickly, but not before he'd seen Darya whirl in midair and land in a deadly version of a court bow. She'd slain one of them in a breath, and turned on the others in a whirlwind of steel before Amris reached the scene, but those two had flanked her, clearly with an eye—or many—to closing in.

The one closest to Amris did hear him coming. It whirled on its many legs, twice or three times as fast as any normal man, and lashed out.

Amris didn't bother stopping or turning. The whip cracked against his breastplate with bruising force. An uncanny chill spread through the metal and across Amris's chest. Both were easy to ignore under the circumstances.

He swung overhand while the whip was still out. Bone split beneath his blade, and the end of the whip went flying off to the side. The dalhan opened its mouth, showing a pair of long fangs in the middle of churning blackness, and roared with anger, then charged.

That was well.

Amris braced himself as the monster rushed toward him. It raised itself up on its back legs at the last moment, stretching out its huge front claws to grab him.

He lunged and slashed. A twist of his hips added to the strength of his arms, propelling the sword in a short, powerful horizontal arc that split bone and sliced flesh in a clean cut through the dalhan's torso just where it narrowed to join the legs.

For a moment, the thing still clawed at him, talons seeking purchase on his armor. Then they fell away. The creature's body slumped, then toppled away from the legs. Amris retreated quickly as blood hissed on his gauntlets.

The last dalhan standing didn't stand for long. By the time Amris could see the pair of them clearly, Darya had put slashes in many of its limbs, deep enough that it was moving unsteadily and unable to lift its whip. As he watched, she danced in past an erratically flailing claw, plunged Gerant deep into a spot near the base of the monster's torso, and slipped back out of reach while it collapsed.

Are you all right?

Having no breath, Gerant couldn't sound breathless. The voice in Amris's mind was weary nonetheless, and gave the distinct impression that Gerant was recovering himself in some fashion, even if not by panting and wiping his brow.

Doing the first and regretting that helmet and gauntlets prevented the second, Amris gave himself a swift inspection before he answered. The dalhan's blood had left a few pits in his gauntlets, but they appeared to be getting no deeper. His chest felt no worse than bruised beneath his armor. The cold, as clammy and oddly seeking as it had been, had vanished.

"Thank you, yes," he said. "And the pair of you?"

The wording came easily from his mouth. Battle had left him still too focused to think of the implications.

Gerant was silent, though, and it was Darya who answered, stepping carefully around the pools of black blood and hacked white bodies toward Amris. "Not too bad, thanks. I don't think we'll want the rabbit anymore, though."

———

"So. Dalhan?" Amris said.

He spoke quietly, and cleaned his sword while he did

it, but Darya saw how his gaze kept flicking back to the bodies, the blood, and the way the plants were dying around them. It wasn't horror exactly, or not all horror— she thought he'd seen things as bad as she had, or worse— but an attempt to fully understand a new threat.

The storms and Thyran's summonings left weaknesses in the world, said Gerant. *Demons took advantage of that. Gods know there were enough bodies for them to construct their own vehicles, even the lesser ones.*

"They're soul-eaters," Darya put in, feeling that she should contribute to the more practical end of things. "Probably soul-harvesters in this case. Wizards—if they're also sons of bitches—use them like that from time to time. They usually only can manage one, though. And dalhan don't hunt in packs naturally."

On their own, the things didn't attack each other, but they didn't share territory either. One of them tended to leave the land pretty unappetizing for the others, after all.

Amris spoke the thoughts she didn't want to have. "Then there's more than a slim chance they're in Thyran's service, or the service of his magicians."

"Yeah." Darya wanted to kick one of the bodies, but she liked her toes. "The Twisted, the living ones—if you can call it living—don't want them around, though, for obvious reasons."

"Sending them ahead would make all the more sense, then. As an advance force, they'd be out of the way of the normal troops and the scouts alike, and positioned well to weaken any resistance they found, or simply send back power from lower sources if they didn't meet with intelligent life. Can they do that?"

They can do that, said Gerant.

"I wouldn't mind if you stopped being right about this sort of thing," said Darya, resheathing Gerant now that the blood was off his blade. "For the record."

"It's one of my dearer wishes as well. Still—" Amris squared his shoulders, armor clanking. "These will give their masters no more power. There's some comfort in that."

It was, in fact, a cheering thought. "Does he do that a lot?" she asked Gerant.

A great deal.

"I'm not complaining," she added, starting back toward the path. "I'm just waiting for you to reassure me that I'll find us another dinner."

"I have nothing but faith in your skills, Sentinel."

Chapter 14

THEY DIDN'T COME ACROSS ANOTHER RABBIT, BUT after twilight they stopped at the banks of a small creek, and Darya quickly caught them three helmhead fish, small and violet and, as Amris recalled, delicious.

Amris built a pit for their fire while she cleaned the fish, relishing the chance to use his strength and the skills he'd learned as a young infantryman, then built the fire itself while she and Gerant put up the warding.

Darya nodded approval at the result of Amris's work, which was low and almost smokeless, and propped two sticks full of fish over the flames. "You'll want to watch them," she said, and went down to wash her hands at the creek. "I've been told I eat meat when it's practically still moving, so I don't cook to my taste when I'm with company."

Her gifts, Gerant added, *do make her a somewhat hazardous dining companion. I'm surprised you've not tried nightshade stew yet.*

"You've just given me ideas," said Darya. Her voice came back from the water, mingled with the running creek and the splashing of her hands. "Though maybe I'll wait until we've finished with Thyran's army."

"Yes, one dance at a time is best with the Lady of Flames. You might mix up the figures otherwise."

That made both of his companions laugh, and Amris

sat back on his heels and turned the fish, happy in the out-of-proportion fashion that arrived at times after great sorrow, or in the midst of it. The sun was just below the horizon in a clear lavender sky, the trees were rustling in a faint warm breeze that strengthened the scent of cooking meat, and he was with friends—and one lover, with whom the physical impossibility of that word seemed minor just then.

Had the world not been in danger, it would have been a wonderful evening. Even so, Amris whistled as he turned the spits, and shrugged when Darya gave him a quizzical look. "There's yet plenty of good in the world," he said, "and if we don't know for certain that we'll save it, that's all the more reason to enjoy what we have, true?"

You forget, Gerant added to Darya, *if we haven't been here before, we've both dwelt many years not too far distant. You know life goes on after pain, and…well, it goes on before pain, too, or around it, or generally proximate.*

Worried that the two of them sounded too much as though they were lecturing her, Amris fell silent until Darya's puzzled expression turned thoughtful, and then to amusement at herself. "I've felt that often when I risked my own neck," she said. "Makes sense to expand it… I just never had occasion before."

"You risked your neck in aid of others," said Amris.

"But if I died, the Order would send another Sentinel, and Gerant would rebind himself to another bright young thing."

Not right away. There's a period of rest, of…recalibration, you might say.

"*I* wouldn't. But thank you for not contradicting the 'bright' or the 'young.'" Darya sat with her legs folded tailor-style, elbows on her knees, and watched the fire: not brooding, just interested. "My point stands. A couple of people would miss me. A couple dozen would be inconvenienced. Maybe one or two others would die, and that'd be sad. But the world would keep turning."

"Nobody's heart would break?"

Darya glanced up, surprised, and Amris in truth wasn't sure why he'd asked. "Nah. No partner. You can't have children once you're a full and bound Sentinel, and I wouldn't know my parents on the street. A few of my teachers would grieve, and some of the other Sentinels, but they're used to the risks. We all are."

The chunks of fish were turning from white to silver. Amris watched them, unsure how to put into words the question that came most readily to his mind. "Is that so for all of you?" he finally asked.

"More or less. People do partner outside the Order, but it's rare as hell, especially long-term. And most of us are bastards, or foundlings at any rate. Once in a while, you get a legitimate fifth daughter, or a family makes some odd bargain with the gods. Most people don't want to hand their babies over to this life. Can't say I blame them," Darya added, with no trace of self-pity.

"The Order takes infants?"

"Takes in, sure. We don't go through the Forging until we're thirteen or thereabouts, and any who want can swear out before then."

Yes, Gerant added, patiently anticipating what Amris

would say next, *after being raised with the expectation of being a Sentinel. Some do stay in because of what they've been told, and don't question what they truly want—but the same is true of apprentices and cabin boys the world over, isn't it? Not to mention acolytes.*

Since Darya was waiting as well, face turned upward a trifle and body deceptively relaxed, Amris paused before he replied. He was a stranger to debate with her, as he wasn't with Gerant, and she was one of the people being discussed. Still it bore saying: "Apprentices and cabin boys don't have their bodies reshaped."

Not immediately, at any rate.

"No," said Darya calmly, "they don't. I don't say it wouldn't be kinder to wait longer or to start training older. It'd be better, in a better world. This isn't."

There wasn't much Amris could say in return.

Darya took pity on him. "What I do is necessary," she said, "and I like it better than I'd like being a scribe, or a farmer, or probably even a princess—though the feasts and the hot baths would be nice. And I like it a great deal better than the life I'd probably have had otherwise, given how it started. I've no complaints. And I think dinner's ready."

———

They ate, rid themselves of armor and boots, and lay down. The ground was softer than the floor in Sitha's temple had been, but also cooler and lumpier. Darya folded her arms behind her head and looked up at the forest through the green veil of the ward, slowly willing herself toward relaxation and sleep.

It wasn't easy. She knew every sound around her, from the chirping crickets and the running creek to the shriek of a hunting owl and the growl of a badger defending its territory. Amris's breathing was the only exception, and even that was becoming familiar, sinking in with help from Gerant's spell. Darya listened for other sounds, those she'd heard only on a hunt and those she didn't think she'd recognize, and watched the treetops for twisted shapes.

The wards would keep out most direct attacks, but a powerful enough mage could likely break them, and they wouldn't help against, say, a forest fire.

I'd warn you, said Gerant, after the third time she'd turned over, *long before any threat approached. You know that.*

"I do," she muttered, hoping she spoke too quietly to wake Amris. It made some difference, but only enough for her to try and sleep, not nearly enough to make it easy.

This, the edge beyond civilization, had been her place for a long time. She'd known its paths and delighted in what she didn't know—the mysteries that lay inside caves, the treasures of the ancient world.

That world had come back, in two different forms. Now the ground beneath Darya felt far less solid, and the patterns of tree and sky were alien.

Even Amris, ally who was rapidly becoming friend, changed things, and not only by his presence and his news. She'd never had to explain the Order and its customs before, never had to put into words why she was happy and how she could go on without worrying about her death more than the most unshakable instinct forced her to.

She kind of liked doing so.

That was another change.

And it was all better thought of over a bottle of wine and a long talk with friends from the Order, when she was safe and the war was won and she wouldn't have to wake up in four hours to try and overtake monster scouts.

Darya closed her eyes, listened to the sounds around her, and propelled herself downward toward sleep like a diver going after pearls. In the end, it was the slow, steady breathing of Amris that pushed her down over the edge into darkness.

Chapter 15

A LITTLE BEFORE MIDDAY, AS FAR AS AMRIS COULD estimate through the canopy of trees, they came to the bridge.

He knew the shape, and the blue-purple stone, from his time. Then it had been sturdy: not newly cut, but constantly renewed and maintained, with polished wooden railings to keep travelers safe. A hundred years of disuse had weakened the mortar and pitted the stones. Several had fallen down into the ravine below; they stood out of the running water in broken chunks.

"It wasn't this bad when I came out," Darya said.

Of course not. One woman is a good deal less strain than an entire scout pack.

"A pity," Amris said, "that it didn't collapse under them. Even if it would have been harder for us—and even now I have my doubts about us crossing."

"I don't know of another way over, and we don't have time to go looking. But I'll go first, and I'll throw the rope back to you after."

That had to suffice. Amris watched Darya, measuring every step of her light boots against the stone, and prayed to Sitha, who kept the world in order and loved the works of men's hands.

Darya went slowly and with care, but she never stopped until she'd planted her feet firmly on the solid ground of the other side, and Amris had changed his prayer to one of thanksgiving. Then she threw him the end of the rope: a well-practiced overhand toss that sent yards of glittering silk soaring through the air before falling solidly into Amris's outstretched hands.

"I can pray for you, if you want," she called to him, tying the other end of the rope to a tree, "but I'm probably not as good at it."

"Intent matters most," Amris said.

And if the gods have ever been inclined to answer prayers, this would be the moment most in their interest.

"You either make a good point or you've doomed us all with overconfidence," said Amris, and set foot on the bridge.

He was not such a strain as he had feared. The stones shifted occasionally, and he was very glad that he had the rope to hand, if only for his own peace of mind, but he never felt himself to be in real danger. It was almost a pity, Amris thought as he walked forward, coiling the slack rope over an arm. The weaker the bridge was under him, the more likely it would fall apart under the scouts as they returned, not only killing those creatures but delaying the army. Feeling the stones under him, though, Amris thought they'd hold together fine under more weight from above—

—and he didn't stop when he had the idea. That was never wise. But as soon as he reached the other bank of the ravine, he stepped to the side, shaded his eyes, and took as close a look as he could manage at the bridge's underside.

"You have a plan," said Darya, when he turned back to her.

"I have an idea," he said. "And a risky one."

"My favorite kind."

─────────

"You'll tell me," Amris said, looking over his shining-if-somewhat-battered pauldron at Darya, "if your gift gives you any warning, yes? One of us must live to take word back."

"Yes, I'll save my own neck purely for the greater good," she said, rolling her eyes, "what with you twisting my arm about it and all."

In fact, she had her mind focused on Sitha's blessing as much as on what she said, which likely meant that the sarcasm came out a shade dreamier than she'd meant it to. The bridge was holding under their combined weight as they walked side by side, Darya alert for the prickling, itching sensation at the back of her spine that meant the ground ahead was unsafe, Amris peering down over the side of the bridge.

They didn't go very far out before he put a hand on her arm to stop her. "Here," he said, and pointed. "Mark you the stone one layer down, the one that's almost a triangle?"

"I see it," she said. It wasn't the most damaged, but there were definitely pits enough in the surface and a deeper groove around it than the masons had intended. She checked the cords that held her sword in its sheath and tried not to look past the stone into the ravine. There was a river down at the bottom; she could see light on flowing water. It probably wouldn't help. "Gods bless our endeavors, especially the ridiculous ones."

She wiped her palms on her tunic before grabbing the knife out of her boot, and her pulse was loud in her throat and her ears. The feeling was familiar. It wasn't even unpleasant, not to her. All the colors in the world were brighter at such times. She could hear every bird calling in the trees, and the laughter of the river below as water ran past the rocks.

This was being alive.

"Ready?" she asked both of her partners.

I can shield you at a moment's notice, with all my strength, Gerant said. *That will have to suffice.*

"If you are," said Amris.

Darya knelt, then dropped to her stomach, flattening herself on the stone. One wriggle took her chin out past the edge. Another brought the stone to her shoulders. Amris's hands closed over her ankles: large, strong, solid, and warm through trousers and boots alike.

When the edge of the bridge hit her lowest rib, she started to lower herself down, clinging as best she could to the bridge for as long as she could. The smell of wet stone was strong in her nose, mingled with an acrid, chalky odor from whatever went into the mortar, which almost immediately got under her fingernails.

Amris was bearing more and more of her weight as Darya went down. Habit had her drawing breath to call and see if he was all right, but before she could speak, she realized that she knew he was. She felt, at a distance, the stance in which he'd braced his legs and the strain in his arms and back. It was present, but not overwhelming.

She crawled downward a little more, until the triangular stone was at her eye level. Amris's hands around her ankles were the only thing holding her, and the blood had begun rushing to her head in earnest.

"I'm going to be dizzy as hell, if I survive this," she said.

You could so easily have left off that last part.

"Have confidence in your old lover, hmm? He won't let me fall." Still, she braced herself against the bridge with one hand before she started digging at the mortar with her knife. Thrills were one thing; foolishness very different.

Mortar came away in chunks, crumbling beneath her knife and falling down to the river. Darya didn't watch it, but worked fast, reaching as far back between the rocks as she could manage. When she was done, she'd dug a gap around the stone—only a little wider than her hands, but clear beyond the base of the stone where it met the rest of the bridge.

"Tell Amris I'm starting the next part," she said, "and to get ready."

The hands around her ankles tightened, which was good. The next step meant putting away the knife and taking out her rope, a series of maneuvers that shifted Darya's weight back and forth so she felt briefly like a swinging pendulum.

Amris's grip never wavered.

"Good man," she muttered.

Very much so, said Gerant, *although I admit this particular skill never came up between us.*

"Don't make me laugh right now, or we'll all go into the river."

Scraping layers of skin off her knuckles and working half-blind, she wrapped the rope around the stone, crossed it, threaded it underneath and behind, and brought it around to the front, where she tied three knots. That was as secure as the damn thing was likely to get—and she sensed that Amris's strength was starting to give out.

They'd still need that strength for the next part of the plan.

"All right," she told Gerant. "Time to leave."

It was a moment before Amris started lifting her. During it, Darya stared down at the river, too tired for either fear or excitement. Her vision had started to blur from being upside down so long, and her hands had started to hurt with the irritating, insistent pain only minor wounds ever managed. She didn't want to fall, but she couldn't manage to care either. When she started moving upward again, she felt vague relief, but at a far distance.

She did rouse herself enough to take her weight as soon as she could, and the amount of strength she found surprised her. Where fear for her own life didn't do the job, apparently fairness to a companion did. Traveling alone as much as she did, Darya thought, she might have missed a few things.

It was a disconcerting notion. She didn't have much of her mind leftover to think on it, though, preoccupied as she was with finding handholds and balancing, relieving Amris of as much of his burden as she could without overbalancing herself. When she was half on the bridge, Darya's mind had collapsed down to movement, and the world was a blur in front of her.

When she made it all the way up, the world went black.

———

Amris was not a man to panic. War had taught him early to suppress many of a human's basic drives, as it did most soldiers: not much chance of charging a line of pikemen, were that not so. Fear was a series of nightmares for a week, but a distant thought at the moment when steel met flesh, or when a plan encountered complications, as plans did.

In the moment when Darya collapsed on the bridge's surface, he felt almost as much fear as when he'd lain on a battlefield and seen an ax approaching his head, or when he'd looked through a spyglass and seen an unexpected cavalry troop cresting a hill. The spell that linked them kept that fear, and the grief and guilt that threatened to accompany it, from reaching their full potential, but it took him a moment to remember that connection, and to know that what he'd taken for wishful thinking was right: she was well, only dazed.

Even with the spell, it was unsettling to see her lain

out against the stone. Every minute of their acquaintance until then, she'd been so full of vitality, so certain of herself in the face of surprise and catastrophe, that Amris had almost come to think of her body as the same steel and crystal that housed Gerant—or of Darya herself as not quite real, a spirit come to guide him into the new world.

Kneeling beside her, turning her face upward, he knew her as mortal flesh and blood, as real as any of the soldiers he'd fought with and just as capable of death. He had time, while he bathed her face and wrists with water, for that realization to sink into his gut like the dull-but-full-force impact of a practice sword.

Easy, love, said Gerant, calling to mind nights when Amris had come to bed after writing letters to the families of the fallen. *You're doing as well as any man can, particularly any man in your shoes right now. Darya's fine—and she's remarkably intelligent, not that I'll admit that when she wakes up. You couldn't have convinced her of any plan that was truly unwise.*

"Thank you," said Amris. "I'm…happier to have you here than I probably should be, considering theology."

I'd be here regardless. We may as well rejoice.

Amris laughed, and looked down at Darya. Her eyelashes lay in long fans against her cheeks—which were too red, but growing less so. He ran the wet cloth across her forehead again, and she made a pleased noise, immediately followed by a groan as she cracked open her eyelids.

"Good thing we didn't eat much," she said. "Sorry about that."

"The apologies should be mine," said Amris, and he handed her the flask he'd been pouring from. "Drink. Are you... That is, I know you're well, but—"

Darya laughed rustily. "Spell makes it hard to ask the polite questions, doesn't it?" She took a long drink of water. "I'm well enough to get off this bridge, if you'll help me walk at first. Blood was in my head too long, is all, and then reversed."

"It was good work down there," said Amris. He got to his feet and helped Darya stand, wrapping his arm around her waist; she made a pleasant weight against his side.

"And yours at this end," said Darya. "Now let's see if it bears out."

———

The rope played out long enough for them to reach the other side, and to get a few feet downward from the end of the bridge. "No saving it this time," said Darya, who couldn't resist the urge to give it a final pat. "At least it's going in a good cause."

"We can all hope our ends serve such purpose." Amris took up the end of the rope she passed him. *Just as long as they don't all happen here,* Gerant put in.

"If I was going to die on this bridge, I'd have done it already," Darya said.

Would you care to tempt fate any more? At least Amris has some sense of caution.

"The idea was mine, remember?"

And I am corrected. You're both absurd. I must have some sort of destiny.

"Lucky you," said Darya, chuckling and trying to hide the small surprised thrill she felt at being grouped with Amris.

The man in question stood right behind her, arms coming past hers, and only a little air separated her back from his chest. A glance upward gave Darya a good view of his jawline, straight and stern and faintly stubbled. A spreading warmth began to make itself known in her body, and she had the urge to lean back against him.

Darya looked quickly toward the ravine. "Ready."

"One," said Amris, on a slow breath out that Darya copied. Harmony could only help. "Two. *Pull!*"

She braced herself against the ground and yanked with all the strength she'd regained in their brief rest. Recent aches reawakened in her arms. New ones were born. Darya gritted her teeth. To either side of her, Amris's arms clenched, thick with muscle beneath his shirt. He breathed steadily, purposefully, but heavily, and a grunt of effort escaped him.

The stone shifted. Darya felt it: the jolt from below, the rope's sudden increase in slack. Sweat was starting to run down her face, but she ignored it and dug in harder, turning a little to get power from her hips. Rock groaned against rock.

More movement, and the edges of Darya's vision were going white. More still, and Amris was sounding like a smith's bellows, and she likely wouldn't have been any better, could she have heard herself clearly. One last bit of strength, and momentum suddenly took over.

The rope spun downward, yanking both Darya and Amris forward until Darya thought to open her hands. "Let *go!*" she yelled, and with that jolted Amris out of the half trance they'd both been in.

"Get back!" he yelled in return.

The rope was hissing downward, plummeting with the stone. Darya looked up from it and saw the bridge trembling. One support wobbled like a drunk. Mortar fell into the ravine, followed by another stone.

Side by side with Amris, she sprinted away from the bridge on legs that felt like wet bread. The ground below them shook with the impact of more rocks, and when Darya briefly glanced behind her, she saw bits of the bank crumbling and falling as well. She didn't witness the bridge's collapse, but the thunderstorm roar of it deafened her. It kept going well until they reached solid ground and she collapsed beneath a tree, too exhausted for relief.

Chapter 16

"How did you know to do that?" Darya asked.

They'd gotten enough of their breath back to sit up and were drinking water in shallow sips. It seemed a good time to eat, so they'd gotten more bread and meat out of Darya's pack, but neither of them had the appetite to do more than nibble just then.

Between the sweat, the strain, and the panic, Amris's whole body felt raw. All he wished in the world was to lie down where they were, in the shade of a large pine tree, and sleep for another hundred years or so. There was a certain peace in that feeling, too, though duty kept him from succumbing to it. He'd pushed his body too far for his mind and heart to keep bothering him.

"There are—were—many stonemasons in my homeland," he said, "and many of my friends were so apprenticed when I was young. And then I learned a great deal when I was in command. It is, after all, far easier to defeat the army that can't reach you, or that's just had half a hillside collapse on it. I was no engineer—but I listened to mine. Well enough, it seems."

"*Will* they be able to reach us?"

He sighed, wishing he could give her the news she would most liked. "Eventually. Thyran's troops had winged creatures among them—I cannot believe the cockatrice was the only one left—and they can carry the others over the gap. They may have magic too, and if need be, there is likely a route around, though it will take them far out of their path."

"Yeah," she said, regretful but resigned. "I halfway guessed that. If they were the sort to cut their losses and go home, they'd have done that a hundred years ago. Grudge-holding sons of bitches."

Not that vengeance isn't holy, in its way.

"Persistence is unholy in my enemies," said Darya. "Oh well. We bought ourselves more time, and I won't complain about that. It was a good idea."

They didn't only put him in command for his pretty face.

"Not *only*," said Amris. Darya's praise, and then Gerant's, brought a smile to his face and gave him a surprising amount of new strength. He took a bite of his dried meat with more enthusiasm than before, and this time he savored the taste, or what taste there was.

A bird was calling steadily in the forest beyond them, a high-pitched and slightly aggrieved sound: *What? What? What? What? What?* Other, more melodious songs joined in, but that querulous note was dominant. It was unfamiliar, too, though that didn't mean a great deal. Amris had never been the sort to learn birdcalls.

"How long, do you think?" Darya asked.

Amris calculated, wishing again for terrain maps and scouting reports—well, they *were* the scouts now, even if they hadn't been sent out as such. "It depends a great deal on their forces," he said finally, "but I'd wager we've gained two or three days. More if they can't fly and must go around to an alternate path. Fewer if they have a mage who can simply make another bridge."

Probably not. Such a spell would take a day or two itself, and that's assuming they fuel it with sacrifice. A week, otherwise. Gizath's powers wouldn't be of any assistance, unless— Gerant's mental voice fell into a speculation Amris knew well, tinged only slightly with horror—*that is, a tree might be warped against itself to make a bridge, by one who truly had both skill and power in that kind of art. Or several creatures.*

Both Darya and Amris made disgusted noises at the thought. Darya didn't stop there, but went on to invoke the anatomy of two different gods. Some of the sergeants Amris had served with could have taken lessons from her in profanity.

That was a more pleasant memory than the next to arise. "They were beginning to do that," Amris said slowly. "Nothing so large as a bridge, and I know not how long it took, but there was a battering ram at one of the last battles. Living, I suppose, though I hate to think of such life. Three or four men from the look of it, but... reshaped."

The creature had kept all of its eyes: two on the front, but the others dotted over it like knots on a log. It had walked on eight hands. Other details had gone unseen in battle, and Amris didn't want to speak even of those he was sure of. He thought the words would foul the air.

There was silence for a while, save for the birds.

"Well," Darya finally said, "even if they *can* do that for a bridge, I bet they can't do it instantly, and it'll cost them men. So to speak. Which means we've still hurt them, and that's the important thing."

You mentioned grudge-holding sons of bitches, I recall?

"Technically, I'm a grudge-holding bitch, and I don't think I should speculate about my mother." Darya brushed crumbs off her hands. "And now, if you're ready," she said to Amris, "I think we should get walking."

———

A few hours later, Darya thought they'd covered about half the distance back to Oakford. Along the way, they'd also had to duck under low-hanging branches—Amris more often than she, and more arduously, given the armor—and fight past a small legion of brambles without the small consolation of berries, for all the ripe ones had been eaten by birds. Twice, Darya's gift had guided them away from danger: a well-concealed badger hole in which one of them could easily have broken an ankle and a patch of grass hiding a mud pit that could swallow an unsuspecting person.

That would have been an ordinary journey for her, though it'd been three or four years since she'd gone that long on foot, and hers were aching properly before sunset. She was used to not talking, too, though mostly because she'd been alone save for Gerant, and they knew each other well enough to spend long periods silent.

She didn't have to keep looking back to check on Amris, which was another benefit of the spell. Otherwise, she would have been glancing over her shoulder every

few steps. As able as he was to take care of himself, there
were spiders in the forest with venom that could disable
instantly and a few creatures that could soundlessly drag
a man off into the woods if they struck at the right time
and in the right manner. But he was there and well, and
that sense became a constant for Darya, like the weight
of the sword on her hip and the presence of Gerant in the
back of her mind.

He felt more thoughtful than usual, though Darya
had neither leisure, concentration, nor privacy to inquire
more until they'd made camp for the evening and Amris
was answering a call of nature. Then she seized the
opportunity, but didn't speak loudly. The man was still
within the wards, though far enough away and trying
hard enough for privacy that she didn't get much sense of
him through the spell.

"Holding up?"

*Well enough. Better than both of you physically, since
I have no actual physicality, and…surprisingly well, otherwise. Or perhaps my emotions simply haven't gotten
out of one another's way enough for me to feel any of them
devastatingly.*

"Either makes sense," said Darya. "It's not as if it's a
situation that happens often. I—"

In truth, she wouldn't have known how to proceed,
really, if the subject at hand had been a death rather than
the sort-of-reverse. She'd never had a family to mourn.
When a Sentinel died, there was an official, rather mystic
funeral and an unofficial, extremely drunken evening in
their honor, and then the business of life the next day.

She couldn't get Gerant tipsy and pat him on the back. Nor did the respectful nod and *Sorry for your loss, sir,* that she used on civilians work.

"I hope you don't end up feeling too badly about it, in the end," she said.

Thank you. Of course, regardless, I'm glad we found him—and not only for humanitarian reasons. You work well together. It's a pleasure to witness.

"We all work well together," said Darya quickly, "or we have done so far."

Chapter 17

WITH EACH DAWN, THE WORLD AMRIS HAD KNOWN dwindled in the distance. It became memory, half-dreamed, though as yet he had little to replace it with: a forest, a ruin, tales of horror, and a deadly sylph of a woman who carried his lover's spirit. He'd known a whole world once, not long ago as he remembered it; he'd traveled its paths and seen its maps. Now he had only those few stars to steer by.

"You hunt things like the cockatrice," he said, scooping dirt over the embers of their campfire. "But you don't know korvin. Have the Twisted come as armies before, even small ones?"

Darya was sitting on a rock, braiding her hair. Her hands moved deftly, and her head not at all. "No. There've been some in packs, and some raiding parties—assuming those were all Twisted, and not other things that formed during the hard years—but nothing more organized than a band or two with a big enough bully at the head." Nimble fingers tied a leather thong tight. "They come, they go. They don't age, we're pretty sure, and they don't breed the way we do—er, mortals, I mean—although the big ones have ways of making more little ones. Did you know about that?"

"To our sorrow, yes," he said, and watched Darya to soften the memories of old horror. Nothing would banish them.

"Right. So, there were a bunch up north after the storms. They fought among each other, they fought us. Once in a while they'd work together if one was powerful enough to make the others do what it wanted. We never thought there was more to it than that."

Not precisely, said Gerant.

Seeing a woman look suspiciously at her own belt wasn't the oddest thing Amris had seen since he'd reawoken, but it was incongruous nonetheless. "What do you mean?" Darya asked.

We—the wizards, the Adeptas, the seniors—have been seeing hints for a while now. Remember that Twisted wizard we killed a few months ago, when we were retrieving that chalice a stretch westward of here?

"Sure."

We've had five or six similar incidents in the last year. They're seeking out enchanted items more and more often now. In fact, if I had to speculate, I'd say that's how one of them came across Thyran in the first place. A few of the raids lately have also been different, more focused on taking beasts in quantity than on killing people.

There was a pattern forming. We simply weren't sure what it was.

"And you mentioned none of that," said Darya flatly, while Amris stood silent, dirt specks lingering on his hands.

We didn't know for certain. We had no means of finding out more except to wait for more information, or an opportunity. You know our limits. What could those in the field have done? We don't even have the resources to reinforce all the fortresses all the time.

"We could have known." Her eyes were green glass.

Why? So you could sleep less easily at night? When have you ever needed more context to an assignment?

"There's never been more—" Darya stopped herself as her voice started to rise, sucked in a breath through her teeth, and added, quietly, "as far as I knew. All right. We don't have to fight about this now."

Amris could call to mind half a dozen similar moments in the tents of generals and the private offices of dukes: decisions made, decisions resented, feelings put carefully aside but not forgotten. He knew the reasons that command often kept knowledge from its troops, deliberately or not. At times he'd disagreed; at times he'd thought it for the best; at times the idea had been his own. He knew, too, the ire of men whose commanders had kept them in the dark when it had turned out to matter, and had felt it himself. There was no side for him to take—and no need for him to take one. Over their partnership, Darya and Gerant had clearly found their own ways of fighting and making up. They needed no help from him.

Amris was glad of it, and yet more alone for it, and neither emotion lessened the other.

He brushed his hands off, let Darya turn to packing, and bent to his own supplies, meager as they were. After a while he asked, "Which of his creatures have you hunted? Are there many with wings, for instance?"

"No. Cockatrices—I've gotten three of those. Flocks of skyrzaki, but it's not like they could carry anything heavy. There are always rumors that Thyran or another cultist managed to twist a dragon, but nothing certain."

"Any sort of dragon was only a rumor, even in my time."

They're only partly flesh in any case, Gerant put in, as deliberately calm as Amris and Darya. *I don't know that Thyran's magic, or Gizath's power in general, would have worked on them. I suppose one might be recruited, but I don't know how.*

"It may depend on the dragon," said Darya. "In all the stories I ever heard, they were like people—some good, some bad. Just different from people in the way they think. But I don't believe it's likely that they've got one."

"We have these small blessings," said Amris.

"Not much chance of others, it seems."

———

Grass bent under Darya's feet. Sticks crunched— occasionally, not often. She was good in the forest. Her precautions didn't really matter, not with Amris doing his soldierly and heavily armored best, but habit was habit. Besides, caution took her mind off her anger, which kept her from fuming as much as she would have otherwise— though not, by any means, completely.

The hell of it was, Gerant wasn't wrong.

She'd never asked for the bigger picture. The past was interesting. The present moment commanded attention, and was often thrilling. The future, beyond the next mission, was speculation, and she didn't speculate, didn't take an interest in speculating. If Gerant had spoken up a month ago and asked if she'd wanted to know what *might* be happening out far beyond the border, what the remnants of Thyran's army *might* have gotten up to since the storms, she'd have shrugged: *Get it off your nonexistent chest if you want.*

So.

There was an irritating lack of rabbits, streams with fish in them, or even decent-sized birds—though Darya expected she might be eating crow before the day was out. It would have been nice to vent herself on a target, but then it would have been nice to have a horse, and not to have a resurgent army attacking in the near future, and to have an arse-high stack of gold and a goblet of chilled wine.

She scowled at a beech.

Could she, could anyone, have done more with the information? Darya didn't know. She didn't know that they couldn't, was the point, and neither had Gerant or the rest of the Concilio Adeptas. If their theories had been common knowledge among the Sentinels, maybe someone would have had a bright idea about how to scout, or a better way to defend, or a method of assassination that would work.

Maybe she was just looking back and thinking, *If things had been different, things could have been different,* which was a typical mortal thing to do—but she *was* mortal.

That was the other part of the reason for her mood, Darya realized as she picked her way down a hillside. She was the outsider, ill-informed about the threat facing them, as well as the awkward spectator to a relationship formed, likely, more than seventy years before her parents had met. Reconciling herself to that was a light enough task when she couldn't blame anyone for it. Gerant keeping information from her was just similar enough to sting—and just different enough that she'd howled about it.

Darya started to sigh.

She stopped her breath mid-exhale, froze in place, and peered through the trees and shadows ahead of her.

There, still mostly hidden by branches, were shapes on the road. Two were horses. Five were not.

Chapter 18

DARYA HAD BEEN GLAD TO BE IN THE FOREST AND away from Klaishil. When she figured out where Thyran's scouts were heading, she changed her mind quickly. She'd have given any part of her body or soul to be back in a city, with its profusion of alleys to duck down and buildings to hide in.

Without any power showing up to make such a trade, she fell back on her own senses and searched frantically for cover. A little way back along the path, up a small embankment, plants and saplings had grown around and over an immense fallen tree, making a small and uneven wall in the middle of the forest. Darya tapped Amris's arm, pointed, then made a dash for it.

From the moment she bolted, she didn't feel a thing. It was only once she'd thrown herself to the ground behind cover, and really once Amris had settled himself beside her, that her face started stinging. Darya touched her forehead, then the bridge of her nose, then the side of her cheek cautiously, and winced each time. When she drew her hand back, it was faintly smeared with red.

Brambles, said Gerant. *I'd have warned you, but it seemed unimportant, and you were unlikely to heed.*

Both were true. Darya didn't want to speak aloud, so she nodded. Then she lay on the ground, hand on her sword, listening to the sounds on the path and trying not to breathe loudly.

As her vision cleared, she sighted gaps in her cover, spaces between the tree's branches where the plants were sparse enough to give her some view of the path. She didn't think she and Amris were visible from the path, even if the scouts did think to look up, so she adjusted her position enough to see through the space with the best view, leaving room to one side of her.

The better view we all get now, the less we'll have to explain later, said Gerant.

Without a word, Amris took the rest of the peephole. Side by side, they waited there to see what came along.

———

Amris had never been a scout and rarely a sentry. Men of his strength were more useful on the front lines; men of his size tended to be easy to spot, no matter how much training they had. Since meeting Darya, he'd spent more time hiding and watching than he'd done since he'd hunted rabbits on his father's farm, when he'd been a gawky, spotty lad and the name Thyran unheard save for gruesome tales in Heliodar.

That boy had been better suited to the task. Better dressed for it too. Amris was doing his best to ignore his armor, which hadn't been made to support his weight this way, and certainly not to do so comfortably. He used his elbows as much as he could, and even so suspected he'd be a solid bruise from neck to waist that night.

There were worse fates.

He felt the weight of the sword at his waist and knew exactly how long it would take him to reach and draw. He felt the damp earth beneath him and knew how long it would take him to be on his feet again—roll back and up, away from both the log and any weapons aimed at him, sweep a leg backward, fall into a defensive stance. He felt Darya beside him, both their bodies brushing against each other, and the lighter presence of the spell, and knew she could make it upright faster than he could.

The contact was pleasant in a more than tactical manner, too, especially with danger heightening all Amris's senses. Neither of them had bared much skin, and that was just as well; there was enough sensation where their clothed legs touched. After three days on the road, neither of them smelled wonderful, but lying close to Darya was far less of an ordeal, in some ways, than it would have been with anyone else Amris could think of.

In other ways, it was more so.

Danger stirred the blood. The body had no conscience. The rawest recruit learned both, and quickly, and with other company Amris would have been untroubled by the awareness of Darya's body and her scent, the tingling warmth where they touched, or the stirrings of his body. Such things happened, even when one's immediate partner wasn't a supple woman with gleaming hair and an intriguing curve to her lips.

That she was Gerant's partner, and Gerant was to some degree in both their minds... That had him gritting his teeth and staring fixedly forward. If the spell had revealed his arousal to Darya, or if Gerant had sensed it, neither of them reacted. Certainly they both would know, as he did, how little such things meant in their situation, but still he cringed, and thought hard about cavalry maneuvers.

Then he didn't have to.

Danger might excite, but the sight of the creatures coming down the path would have quelled the ardor of a sixteen-year-old in a tent of dancing girls.

———

The two on the korvin were twistedmen, creatures Darya had seen and fought before. Six feet high and roughly man-shaped, they were stretched, their limbs, neck, and faces all too long for their bodies. Each had a pair of outsized hands, with gnarled fingers tipped by three-inch talons, and close up, Darya knew, each would have three rows of black, razor-edged teeth.

What most people would notice first was that they looked skinned. Or they were skinned, but stayed alive without being in constant pain, or were in constant pain and that was why they hated normal people—the debates got lengthy. Darya had mostly ignored them. She knew that the twistedmen were bloodred, that she could see the ropes of muscle shifting as they moved, and that the same unlucky bastards who saw the teeth could likely glimpse veins running through and around their bodies.

Every so often, one would raid farms, stealing small

livestock and children. Less often, a band of four or five would kill and eat larger prey. It always was a matter of eating—animals didn't like them, and she'd never heard of a horse tolerating a twistedman as a rider. Thus the korvin, she guessed, though she'd never seen twistedmen bother with riding beasts before.

The korvin was a blanched-white worm, eyeless as far as she could tell, with tiny legs sprouting from each side. The twistedmen perched on a saddle strapped between a couple of pairs of the legs. Each twistedman had an ax strapped to its back, and a couple of knives at its side. They glanced around occasionally as they rode, but generally took it easy, lingering well behind the two riders in front.

Those two went on horseback, though the horses themselves weren't what Darya was used to—their fur had an oily sheen, and their hooves looked sharper than normal—and she saw no sign of Ironhide.

Like the twistedmen, the riders had two legs, two arms, and heads. They also had skin, but it was leprous white with gray splotches, and while their arms were too long for men, their legs were comparatively short— ape stock, Darya thought, and then saw the flat, wide-mouthed face of one, and thought there was likely a bit of frog in there too. As the twistedmen did, they wore leather armor, but Darya saw no obvious weapons, save for more knives at the belt.

Those are an innovation too, said Gerant, distant and dry but still obviously horrified. *Whoever Thyran left in charge, they've kept themselves busy in his absence.*

Immediately Amris started making a mental list: all the wizards capable of such creation, or all those that had been alive and free when he'd gone into stasis. It was a short list, and an alarming one.

It was also pointless just then. He knew not how that battle had ended, and had no chance to ask what Gerant knew of the people involved; neither of them knew what apprentices those living might have taken over the years, nor which other wizards of such inclination might have come up with the frog-mouthed scouts on their own. There was no good in such an organization of thoughts, save that it distanced himself from the things on the road.

No matter how often he'd fought Thyran's foot soldiers, they made his skin crawl, and they were the least—and least horrible—of his creations. Gerant and others had debated whether the horror was intentional, or whether the result of turning flesh against itself was always horrible. Amris had simply met the consequences and slain them with none of the vague sorrow that had usually come with a human opponent, only a sense of relief when a thing that should never have existed had at least stopped moving.

He didn't know if the new creations were worse. *Worse* was a word that quickly lost its meaning when the Twisted were concerned. They were unfamiliar, and that would have been a bad omen, even if they'd had the beauty of the gods themselves.

Breathing as silently as he could, holding absolutely

still, Amris waited. The creatures below spoke a few words to one another in squelching voices, but they were too quiet and too distorted for Amris to make out at his distance. He glanced over to Darya, and she shook her head.

They kept riding. That, above all, was paramount. The new creatures, the ones on horseback, vanished into the tree line. As the korvin and its occupants followed, Amris followed every step of its legs on the path. The twistedman at the front made some jest, and its companion laughed, a sound like ripping flesh.

Amris had spent years fighting them, and still the noises they made sank claws into the back of his mind and pulled. They weren't called twistedmen for their shapes alone.

But then they, too, were gone. The forest swallowed the last of the korvin's legs and its sting-tipped rear.

Darya held up an open hand, then began to fold down her fingers, one at a time: give them time to move on. Take no action they might hear.

The hoofbeats, the wetter sounds of the korvin's legs, and the occasional laughter of the riders faded very slowly. Birds began to sing again. The other sounds of the forest resumed. Through the spell, Amris and Darya each felt the other's tension—the strain of holding still, the anticipation and the dread.

Before Darya closed her hand entirely, Amris knew enough time had passed. She didn't relax, truly, but he felt the sharpest edge of her awareness easing a trifle. He stretched his legs, preparing to rise.

The leaves above them rustled, too heavy for a creature of the forest. A shape dropped just in front of Amris; before he could do more than see it, long fingers had closed about his neck with the strength of iron. The monster in front of him grinned, mouth peeling back to the sides of its gray-white head.

"I smelled your blood a league off, meatling," it breathed at him.

From his other side came the sound of a blow and a grunt from Darya. Amris got a hand around the hilt of his belt knife, but the hands at his throat were already turning his armor against him, crushing the metal into his windpipe and the great vessels of his neck. The strength was already going out of his arms as he drew. His first strike, he feared, would be his last, and even that most likely in vain.

Chapter 19

COLD PASSED THROUGH HIM. IT CAME NOT AS A WIND from outside, but upward from his guts and his heart, drawn along his spine. Then it was gone in the final desperation of his lunge.

Before his knife had so much as touched the outside of its armor, the scout burst.

No blood spurted, nor did the thing cry out. It simply fell outward into pieces, with the only sounds first the crack of bones and then the muffled thumps of flesh against dirt. One hand dropped from Amris's neck. He reached up blindly, staring instead at a lump of meat on the ground with the broken ends of ribs sticking out of it, and pried the other away. Breathing was not yet a simple matter, not with his armor broken as it was, but he could manage it again.

Full awareness took him once more at the wet *thunk* of a blade entering flesh. Drawing his sword now that he had range, Amris turned and saw the other scout falling to the ground in front of Darya, while she smoothly pulled her sword out of its chest.

The gem was dim.

His mind held only himself and Darya, one more than Amris was used to, but was still screamingly empty.

Ice went down his spine. "Gerant—"

Darya's eyes widened, but she stared at Amris rather

than down at her sword, which made him reluctantly believe her quick response. "Is fine. Will return. This happens. What about you? You sound like you've been dead."

"Have I not, in a sense?" he asked, giddy from many sources of relief and shock alike.

"This is a fine time to get metaphysical."

"Some would argue there's no better," Amris said, and then, more soberly, "but truly, lady, I think no more than my voice will suffer, and that not long." He waved a hand at the corpses. "Their fellows are a greater worry. Before long, they'll know the riders' mission failed, and come back this way."

"True." Darya wiped her blade and returned it to its sheath, then looked up at Amris with a wolf's smile. "Wouldn't it be nice of us to save them the trip?"

Amris smiled more grimly than any man Darya had met. His face was made for it, all leanness and sharp lines. The height and the armor didn't hurt either. Even amused, he always looked like he had his mind on some greater purpose—but when he drew his sword and nodded in answer to her joke, Darya recognized the anticipation in his grin.

"Shall I take the vanguard," he asked, "or be the unexpected reinforcement—or would you rather take them together?"

"Shame to waste a big shiny target and a lot of cover.

You think you can hold them off long enough for me to take a couple shots?"

"I'm certain of very little in this time and place," said Amris, with another, more ironic smile, "but *that* I'd vouch for in any company."

"Good enough for me." Darya peered up into the trees until she saw what she was searching for. "Go on ahead, then."

"And you?"

"I may not have arms like those things"—she jerked her chin toward the dead scouts—"but I manage." With that, as she'd been planning, Darya leapt up and pulled herself to the lowest-hanging branch of a nearby oak. It took her weight easily, and so did the one above it, and she didn't need or want to go higher. She had to keep Amris in her sights, after all.

Before she swung herself over to the next tree in line, and before Amris headed back up along the path, she saw him give her an ancient warrior's bow: sword in one hand, the other at shoulder height. Darya laughed under her breath and flicked a salute back at him, but she didn't have time to notice whether he saw or not.

She was off.

The forest at the side of the road spread out before her, a green and crowded road in itself. Undisturbed age had let the trees grow close together, particularly at the height she'd reached and upward. Light-footed, Darya ran down the branch she'd chosen, circled the trunk, and dashed outward along a second limb, following the course of the road back the way the scouts had gone.

Sitha's blessing was no good among the trees, since mortal hands hadn't done much for their creation. Darya trusted in her training and in being generally light and nimble. She listened for the creak that would tell her a branch was breaking, and paid attention to the feel of each one through her boots, but did so at the bottom of her mind, where it was as much instinct as actual knowledge.

Patches of sun below her glinted now and again with metal. Amris was there, moving up on the target as they'd agreed. A spare thought crossed Darya's mind: the hardship of running in metal armor, after all they'd done that day, and the hope the man wouldn't simply collapse.

All else was the moment: the smell of pine sap and the richer green scent of the oak leaves she crushed when she grabbed the next branch. Bark scraped her palms. She paid no mind to the pain. Darya looked, leapt between trees, and barely let her feet hit a slender limb that wouldn't have lasted more than a few seconds under her weight—but she used it to push off and grab the next in line, pulling herself up and over once again.

When she glimpsed the twistedmen and the korvin up ahead, the moment shifted from motion to stillness. The music paused.

Bow to your partners.

The branch of her current fir wasn't wide enough to lie on, but she could, and did, drop and wrap her legs around it—she was far enough up that they wouldn't be visible from below. Slowly, not wanting to dislodge herself or shake the trees enough to draw the scouts' attention, Darya lifted her bow from her back, brought it around, and drew an arrow.

Looking down, she saw she was just in time.

Naturally the twistedmen knew of Amris's approach well before he reached them. As Darya had said, he was a "big shiny target," and a large man in plate could never run with anything approaching silence. By the time he saw meat-red flesh and the blanched white of the korvin up ahead, they'd already turned to face him.

Awareness was fine. Suspicion wasn't. Amris froze in his tracks, then pretended to stumble backward, giving his best impression of a man who'd fled from the frying pan and only now saw the flames licking around him.

"What *are* you?" he gasped, a bit of bad theatrics that also helped him catch his breath.

The twistedman closest to him laughed in its flesh-shriveling way. "Look," it said around its mouthful of teeth. "One of them got away."

Amris barely caught the motion behind it, and was fortunate he had. The flash of steel in the air would never have been enough warning. As it was, he sidestepped just enough that the knife tore through his trousers, cutting the skin beneath but doing no worse.

A proper hit would have skewered his knee. The twistedmen hadn't lost their taste for games with their prey, it seemed.

The knife-thrower hurled a second blade, aimed

higher. Amris ducked and spun sideways again, heard the clang as it bounced off his pauldron and felt the impact as a blow to his shoulder. Rising, he saw the twistedman vault from its seat on the korvin. It pulled the ax from its sheath and started charging; its fellow dug a pair of spurred boots into the worm beast, which shrieked protest but squirmed forward with the same uncanny speed that had been the doom of many infantry during the first few battles.

Amris set his feet, raised his sword, and prepared.

The arrow streaked from the trees and into the unmounted twistedman, hitting just between shoulder and neck. If the monster had been unarmored or human, it might have been a fatal shot; as it was, the head sunk deeply into the leather and likely into the meat beneath. Force and pain stopped the twistedman in its tracks. It screamed, a sound as horrible as its laughter.

Amris dashed toward it. The armor would make him pay later, but he'd learned to put off such prices, especially in the maelstrom of battle, and the edge of his blade swept down into the whole side of the creature's neck before it stopped howling. Neither howling nor the neck lasted long: the twistedmen had thicker skin and stronger spines than mortals, but Amris was familiar with both and knew their weak spots.

He was spinning before the thing's head had finished falling, needing no noise to tell him the korvin and its rider would have changed direction as he did. With the edge of his sword, he caught the twistedman's ax in its downward swing. The korvin gave the low buzz that was its cry of alarm, and reared backward, away from Amris's return stroke. He saw a few arrows stuck in its hide, but the beast didn't pay them any mind.

———

Stupid giant worms: too many legs and hides like leather, or maybe just no vital organs to speak of. Darya might as well have been shooting a hay bale for all the good her arrows did after she hit the twistedman.

It was time for a change of plan. Shouldering her bow, she sighted down through the trees once more, noting the positions of beast and rider and Amris. This time, though, it was no arrow she was aiming.

She dropped through the branches and onto the korvin with bared steel and a scream that came from the bottom of her lungs and echoed through the forest. Only part of it was her deliberate attempt to throw the twistedman off guard. The rest, despite everything, was exhilaration.

The sound caught even Amris by surprise. He was too good to let it throw him off guard, though. His face said *what the hell* clearly, but he was still moving when Darya landed, using the moment to dash forward and lop off a couple of the korvin's legs.

Meanwhile, the twistedman got its ax in the way of her sword rather than its neck, like she'd intended. Darya's blade bit hard, but the thing didn't die or even stop fighting. It halfway turned in its seat, spine far too flexible, snarled, and took a swipe at her with its free hand. Talons tore across Darya's chest, not fatal but still painful.

"Piss *off*," she snapped back at it, whipped her sword around, and took its arm off at the elbow.

Drop hands, promenade forward.

She didn't actually drop Gerant, but she didn't try another swing because the range was too close. While the twistedman was holding up the bleeding stump of its arm and shrieking, Darya slipped a knife out of her sleeve and into her hand, then shifted her weight forward. She was inside its guard now, and while Thyran's creations were well protected, his foot soldiers had the same setup in their necks that humans did.

A quick snap of her wrist, a spray of blood that she narrowly avoided getting in the face, and *that* job was done. She scooted forward and knocked the dying creature to the side with shoulder and hip—she'd stopped hoping for dignity five years back—then kept moving up. "Where's the brain on this thing?"

"It has none!" Darya couldn't see Amris, and his voice sounded muffled, but then the korvin reared again, remaining legs pawing the air. She grabbed at the saddle, holding on tightly as the thing crashed back to the ground.

It went still. She blinked, clearing her vision, and saw Amris withdrawing his sword from the monster's side.

"The heart," he added, "is the vital spot."

Chapter 20

"HE'S ALL RIGHT," DARYA REPEATED.

She was wiping blood off her sword, and Amris, unsurprisingly, was watching her while trying to look like he wasn't. "The deadly blessings, they're like casting spells—though the sword-spirit doesn't have to have been a wizard in life, and Gerant says there are other differences." Darya waved a hand, bloody rag flapping with the gesture. She'd known what the power of her sword could do, and what happened after. That had always been enough for her. It'd have to be enough for Amris, at least until Gerant woke up again.

"But they take the same sort of effort, though the caster has no body left?"

"More or less. I can't explain it, but then, it's not as if magic uses anyone's muscles to begin with. And they don't sleep, Gerant says. They go…not to Letar's halls, but elsewhere, or to a different part of this world, a place that's not a place. I'm sorry… I wish I'd listened more."

"No blame attaches to you, or no more than ever did to me. In such conversations as these, Gerant would resort to drawing figures for me more often than not." Amris got on with such cleanup as he could manage, and really did sound reasonably casual when he asked, "How long will he be so away?"

"Usually a few hours." Darya resheathed her sword

and wiped as much of the blood from her own person as was possible. "The cold doesn't usually kill like that, though, and never when he's hitting two at once with it. Either having two of us connected helped, in which case he might be back sooner, or he pushed himself harder than he thought he could because your neck was on the line, which means later."

The worry line on Amris's brow reappeared. "If he drew on such reserves, are you certain it did him no permanent harm?"

Darya tapped the emerald. "This would've chipped. Cracked, if it was really bad, though I've never heard of anything that severe. They're a lot harder to hurt than we are, even with magic."

"Does the reverse hold true? That is, should the sword or the gem come to harm, would the spirit within feel it?"

"Not the sword. They stay sharper longer than the normal sort, and they're a little tougher, but they still have to be taken care of, and most of them don't see active service for more than a couple decades without needing major repairs. A lot like their wielders, actually."

"Had the Threadcutter's martial servants chosen a different name for themselves, your order might have been Blades."

"Best not to compete with them, though. Brr."

"A fine assessment, though from a woman who spends her life with a disembodied spirit."

"Gerant's mortal. Obviously. Death changes your outlook, but I don't think it gives you a god's perspective. Not that I'd know, but... Well, you've met the Blades."

Tinival's followers were knights-errant. The Sentinels were hunters and, at need, guardians. Letar's Blades were another matter entirely: few and far between, plucked from the trainees for the more common priests, they'd all been grim and silent in Darya's experience, stripped of anything except their goddess and their mission. If the Sentinels were weapons, the Blades were vessels, and the goddess of death and vengeance was a terrifying thing to contain, even just a little bit.

Amris prodded the cut on his leg experimentally, then looked back along the path they'd traveled. "Perhaps we should see to our own welfare. Is there water ahead?"

"A spring, not so far off," Darya said, relieved when her memory brought it forth. The claw marks on her chest were indeed beginning to sting, and though cleaning them wouldn't do much for that, it would keep her from adding worry to irritation. "And we'll have to wash if we're to get anywhere near the horses."

She wasn't at all sure she wanted to, having seen the "horses" in question—but they had four legs and they'd go faster than she and Amris would afoot. If she'd ever had a chance to be finicky about her mount, this wasn't it.

———

Amris muttered an apology to Poram as they approached the spring. Twistedman blood had an acrid, burnt stink and an unpleasant pallor. Given the choice, he'd have introduced no such thing to any innocent body of water, but given the choice, he'd have also not introduced it to his skin, or the world at large. He'd put enough of it into the soil in his day, gods knew, and would likely do so again before much time had passed, given what he assumed was happening somewhere in the north.

"We've delayed them again," Darya said, and for an unsettling moment he wondered if the spell had her reading his thoughts too—but no, he'd been looking off in the direction that had sent them Thyran's forces in the past, and from where they'd surely come again. "A little more expensively than with the bridge, though. Next time we'll lose limbs at this rate."

"I'll make no jokes about things costing an arm and a leg, if you were setting me on a course for that."

She laughed. "Wish I had been. Too tired."

Perching on a rock near the water, she shrugged her pack off and removed her boots. Amris did likewise, unstrapped himself from his armor, and then hesitated.

The knife wound was across the back of his leg, below his knee. Rolling up his trousers would be sufficient, save that the fight had gotten blood all over his clothing. With his troops in the field, that would have been cause enough to strip and swim, using only a little of the time they'd purchased by eliminating the scouts.

A good many of the soldiers he'd led, or fought beside, had been female. Modesty didn't enter into it.

Yet Darya sat there on the rock, eyes like the light shining through the leaves and body as supple as one of the saplings nearby. With the heat of battle still in his blood, Amris saw every strand of her hair, every graceful inch of her long legs. Even guilt couldn't stifle his awareness much, or for long—and with her presence searing into him, the thought of being naked together made him feel as dizzy as looking down over the bridge had done.

"You go first," she said, with an abrupt, rough clearing of her throat. "One of us should stay armed and on watch. In case."

"Ah. Yes. Wise."

Amris turned his back to her and began to undress, quickly and far more clumsily than usual. As he lowered his trousers, he asked, by way of distraction, "Was there much danger out here before?"

"Nothing too horrible." Darya cleared her throat again. "That's to say, mostly natural. Bears and wolves, though they usually have better prey. Greycats do think we're tasty, and they're around every so often."

Water closed around Amris's legs and up to his waist, blessedly cold. The scratches he'd received without knowing stung from the contact, while the cut on his leg sent a sharp pain all up and down the outside of his thigh. He muttered an oath.

"Chilly?"

"That as well." Holding his clothing in a bundle, he ducked under the water, stayed as long as breath and temperature would allow, and then shot back to the surface. Even that brief submersion, without soap or sand, felt thoroughly cleansing: Poram's pure water counteracting Gizath's filth, perhaps, or perhaps simply the joy that came with ridding himself of three days' sweat.

It reminded him of the cold that had destroyed the scout, and he turned back toward Darya. She was still on the rock, looking off in the other direction. "Keeping watch" was the most practical interpretation, but Amris suspected not the only one, and not only out of his own vanity. She, too, had fought recently, and nobody had suggested the Sentinels had become celibate.

Well, his question was far from lascivious. "Is the lethal blessing always cold?"

"For me. Or for Gerant, really." The line of her neck stiffened, and she added, in a more brittle, preemptive voice, "It was Poram's power long before the storms."

"So it was." Amris tried to sound calm but not patronizing. "Indeed, I know not if Thyran had intended the cold specifically, or if he even knew entirely what he was about. Not, that is, that I had opportunity to ask him."

"Didn't exactly seem like a tea party you were having," Darya said, reverting back to herself. "Sorry. You get enough warding signs when they think you're not looking, you start…trying to get out ahead of it, you know?"

———

On the other hand, Darya had thought she'd gotten used to the sidelong glances and the awkward questions. Any of the Sentinels dealt with a certain number of those. The ones with powers that governed cold or flesh took a greater share. Normally she was only glad she'd avoided the rare powers that read, or influenced, minds and hearts. This time, she'd bristled as soon as Amris had mentioned the cold.

It had been a long few days. Gods knew she had plenty

to be on edge about. And if she wanted him to like her—this competent man that her partner had loved and loved still—that was reasonable.

She went on, not looking over her shoulder to see how the water clung to his bare chest, beads catching in the dark hair trailing down the center, or the muscles of his back flexing as he turned to rinse his clothing again.

Not looking more than once or twice, at least. She wasn't made of stone. That was a different blessing, and another one she was usually glad she'd avoided.

"The lethal gifts are really gifts for the sword-spirits, not for us. Gerant says I stabilize him, and that gives more force—like pushing off the ground when you jump—but he's the one who actually sees how to do it and reaches for the power. Mortals…our flesh is an obstacle, as I understand it. And so the swords generally go to Sentinels who get their major blessing from the same god, but sometimes you get differences. There was a man I trained with, blessed by Tinival, who carries a blade bound to Sitha. He can cause earthquakes and then leap clear out of the way."

Behind her, Amris wrung his clothing out and spread it on the rocks. Darya heard the run of the water, then the thick slap of cloth against stone. She watched the forest. You never knew what might come out of the trees, inclined to find bathers tasty.

"Everything look all right?" she asked, realized how that could sound, and added, "I've got a little more of the lignath, and we can heat up a knife if we need to, but we're within a day, day and a half of Oakford unless we have more mishaps. When I left, they had a Mourner, though a junior one, and a couple herbalist healers."

"Likely I'll be fine without magic or hot steel, but the lignath would be a useful precaution, if you've enough to use on yourself."

"Plenty. I won't need much for these."

She didn't turn around at the footsteps. She knew what they meant. That was Amris getting out of the water. The rustling was him rummaging through her pack. Then came a popping sound, and a splash, and then he hissed.

Darya chuckled. "Can feel it doing you good, hmm?"

"On second thought, I'm not certain cautery would have been less pleasant. Still—" He replaced cork and bottle. "No point in regrets."

"There are bandages in there too."

"You prepare well."

"I have to. It's generally just me out here."

"With nobody to stand guard while you bathe?"

"I'm not generally long enough in the wilderness. Or in need of catching horses."

"Or engaged in pulling down bridges and fighting monsters, I suppose. Not in the same day."

"I generally leave the stonework alone. It's never done anything to me." She remembered the falling wall in Klaishil, and added, "Mostly. And it's usually not its fault, when it does."

Amris chuckled, but gave no other answer, just the sounds of dressing and then his footsteps as he came around the rock.

With that warning, Darya did prepare herself. She

didn't flush like a girl. She didn't stare at Amris's bare chest, nor the way his damp trousers outlined the smooth firmness of his thighs. She was fairly sure she sounded casual when she asked, "My turn?"

"Just so. I think I can ward off anything natural without plate—gods know I managed it when I was a boy with a sling."

"I'm not sure I enjoy being compared to a cow," she said, heading toward the water.

"Pig. They're smarter, if that's a comfort."

"Some."

The water *was* cold, which helped Darya in one sense, and also made her bath speedy: duck herself and the clothes, scrub until both were as clean as mere friction could make them, wring the clothes out and lay them on rocks, then pour water over the cuts on her chest a few times. They were already starting to close up and healing clean—almost all Sentinels' wounds did, though intentional poison would trouble anyone but her.

Still, she touched the last of the lignath to them when she got out of the water—and then made a face, not only at the sting but because certain logistics had just announced themselves. Namely: bandaging her wounds would be a good idea, both for their healing and so that she'd smell less like blood to anything around, but doing that would go better with another pair of hands.

She sighed. "I'm going to have to ask a favor."

Chapter 21

HALF-NAKED, FROM BEHIND, DARYA BROUGHT TO mind birch trees—the same straight slenderness, the same pallor crossed by scars—if a man was trying to keep his mind vaguely elevated. Amris was doing his best.

He unwound a strip of bandage across her back and passed it under one raised arm so she could take it with her free hand, the one not holding the other pad of cloth against her cuts. The inevitable moments in the process when the back of his hand brushed against the side of her breast were moments he fought hard to ignore, as he was fighting hard to ignore the curve of her neck up toward her jaw and the firm roundness of her backside in wet trousers, so close that he needed only to shift his weight forward to make contact.

Hard was both an appropriate and an unfortunate word.

The years had taught Amris discipline. War had taught him to bear with physical discomfort. His first lover had been many years ago; a woman's body was no less familiar to him than a man's. He tried to let his experience make him jaded and to concentrate on the process: wrap close to the body, keep the bandage flat, hand off promptly, take it again without hesitation, and finally tie a good, solid knot in the back.

Then he tucked the ends of the bandage into the top.

His fingers brushed over a long scar, a jagged dip surrounded by smooth skin, and he heard Darya's breath catch.

"Not too tight, I hope," he said, because it seemed vitally important just then to say *something*, as though words would be a shield.

She shook her head, and a strand of her hair fell against his withdrawing hand.

The soft contact froze Amris where he stood. Not knowing that, Darya turned.

Facts burned themselves into his mind very quickly. He knew that her face was full of high color, and her lips parted. He knew that her breasts rose uncovered below the bandage: small, soft, and curving upward, with nipples the color of cherries against her pale skin. He knew that she began to speak, and stopped before she could get more than a syllable out of her mouth. And he knew that no more than a hand's breadth divided her bare skin from his.

He didn't know which of them closed the distance.

———

Desire swept all thought out from under her.

Darya forgot what she'd been going to say. It might have been a joke, a reminder about the need to get back on the road, or just a word of thanks. It had washed completely out of her mind, and she didn't care.

Amris's hands bracketed her waist, low enough that his smallest fingers skimmed the top of her arse. The calluses rubbed against her skin with every slight movement, sending shivers of sensation in all directions: down through her arse and legs and up to where her hard nipples grazed the thick hair on Amris's chest, where one expanding spiral of feeling met another and fed into it.

The ground was rocky under her bare feet, and the pressure of her chest against Amris's made her cuts ache in a not-so-pleasant way, but those small pains were distant. Darya could ignore them. She couldn't—or wouldn't—ignore the hoarse sounds from Amris's throat, or the hard muscle of his shoulder, tense beneath one of her palms as she wound her other hand through his hair and brought his mouth harder against hers.

His hands tightened, pulling her closer, and the truly impressive length of his cock did more than nudge against her thigh: it strained toward her through Amris's wet trousers, rubbing tantalizingly close to her aching sex. Starting to rock her hips in response was as natural and as inevitable as the tides.

Everything felt more instinctive than Darya remembered from past lovers. It wasn't just that Amris gave and took with equal adeptness, kissing her with the same deft force she remembered from seeing him fight but responding eagerly when she took the lead. He seemed to sense just the time to slide his hands downward and cup her bottom, just as she knew that dragging her nails down the back of his neck would make him groan and shudder, and the precise force to use.

It was the rush of new energy that came with an unfamiliar lover, but the expertise in one person's preferences that even the most skilled courtesan couldn't manage without knowing their partner well. It was feeling a shadow of Amris's pleasure when she touched him, and knowing what he most wanted next because an echo in her body wanted it too.

It was the spell.

Gerant.

Shit.

The spell *didn't* extend to mind reading, but they could both draw conclusions. Even as Darya swore silently, Amris dropped his hands and stumbled backward, shaking his head.

"I—" he began, and then stopped, breathing hard.

"Yeah," said Darya, looking at her feet so that she wouldn't notice the flush on his face, or the bulge in his trousers. "I'd better get my shirt."

While Darya dressed, Amris stared at the pool. He could have retrieved his own shirt then, but their clothing was laid out close together, and it was best not to take any chances, best to stare at the spring, each rivulet and rock imprinting itself into his vision, until his lust and the throbbing manifestation of it subsided.

"That's me done," Darya said, finally and awkwardly. "I'll, um, keep watch while you finish dressing. Unless you need a hand with your armor."

"No. Thank you."

He could have used one, but it wasn't absolutely

necessary—and the kiss had taught him that it was better not to take risks. A drunkard could resolve to stay at one glass, a gambler to only wager a few pence, and all such vows would be for naught in the moment. Best to avoid temptation altogether, or as much as he could manage given the circumstances. Besides, the clammy shirt and the clumsy process of rebuckling his own armor were useful distractions.

The neckpiece was too badly crushed to be useful. He wondered that he'd been able to get it off, and touched his neck lightly, then winced. There'd be black bruises there, if there weren't already, and he could feel the line of a cut closing.

An hour back, he would have asked Darya to inspect it.

At last he turned to face her, unable to put it off any longer. She sat on the rock once more, dressed and armored, hands folded in her lap and face grave.

"I'm sorry," said Amris.

"My fault as much as yours."

The memory of her enthusiasm made that impossible to deny, and was still, even with his guilt, far too pleasant. "You have no pledged lover, you said, and certainly none only a night's rest away."

Her eyes flashed. "I have a partner. And a friend. That's as much of a tie—more, really."

Again, he couldn't say anything in the way of denial, not even to assuage her guilt. "Will he know?"

"Not from the spell. And not from our bond." Darya sighed. Her hair was in a neat braid again, but she made as if to push it back nonetheless. "You can tell him if you want."

"Will you?"

She shook her head. "It was an impulse. After a fight. We stopped. In a day and a half, less if we get horses, we'll be at Oakford, and we won't be alone together after battles, so this won't happen again. Telling him would just make him worry over nothing." Darya paused, and her mouth twisted sideways into a rueful smile. "And I realize how much of a hypocrite I am right now, yes."

"You're not wrong," said Amris. "I… Gerant and I…"

The trees were a green wall behind the rock where Darya sat. Beyond them was a road that Amris had known well, once. "Had this happened before, I could have told him or not, as the whim took me, and he'd have thought nothing of it. Not that you're not—" He felt her assent, her total lack of affront. That made it easier to go on. "We knew what we were to each other."

"He didn't talk about you much," said Darya. "Not a subject for light conversation. But when he did…I didn't get the impression any other person could've changed what you had."

It was good to hear, but painful: the flame of Letar, who governed love and death alike. "Time may have," Amris said. "It's a question we've not been in any place to answer yet, or even to ask."

Chapter 22

THEY MADE THEIR WAY BACK TO THE ROAD. THE HILLS got steeper and more forbidding as they approached Oakford, and she was almost glad they'd run into the scouts when they had. Now they *could* take the road, and save a scramble up and down among roots and rocks.

Now they could also ride, in theory.

The horses weren't near either of the battle sites, as Darya had expected. "They're a little big for us to have missed," she said, "even in a fight. My guess is they hitched them a way up, then swung back through the trees. They *thought* they'd be coming back."

It still made her smile to say that, even to think it. *Spiteful creature*, Gerant would have teased her, though with no real reproof behind it.

The thought of him made Darya grimace. She didn't think Gerant would be angry if she told him about the kiss. Things happened in the moment after a battle. He'd retreated from her mind for her liaisons often enough in those circumstances and had made a few comments about the body in the wake of danger that suggested he'd understand.

Understanding was one thing. Pain was another. She knew what Amris meant. A night or two far away, when your lover would be in your bed again before long, might be easy to ignore or even amusing to hear about afterward. If you had no bed and no body for him to return to, that was a different matter—to say nothing of having to work with the third party.

Looking back, Darya thought she could have probably managed the bandage on her own, just more clumsily, or just ignored the cuts until she reached Oakford. If they'd gotten inflamed, the Mourner would've dealt with it, or one of the herbalists would've slapped on a salve that burned but did the job, and the cuts probably wouldn't have bled enough to really hurt her. Looking back, she could have kicked herself.

This was what a life of impulse did.

Cursing at herself, she walked on, and watched for sight of the horses.

———

"There," said Darya, pointing to a glimmer that Amris could barely see. "Thank the gods."

A few steps forward, the glimmer became shapes: the scouts' two mounts, greenish-gray horse shapes with a sheen to their coats like that on a vultures' wings. One of them swung its head around to regard the intruders with a yellowish eye and flared nostrils half the size of a true horse's. In truth, its whole head was smaller than a horse's would have been, out of proportion to the blocky lines of its body.

"They'll grace no nobleman's carriage," said Amris, "but they'll serve, if they *will* serve."

"Only one way to find out."

"Let me," said Amris, stepping forward a pace. "Plate might be some protection against their temper."

So it was—against the first strike, at any rate. He approached from the side, carefully judging how the horses were tied up and how far they could get around to kick. The one Amris had his eye on shifted, snorted, and laid its ears back, but acted otherwise no worse than a number of mounts he'd had in the army. It was only when he reached for the rope tied to its bridle that it whipped its head sideways and snapped at him, showing more and sharper teeth than a grass-eater would ever need.

Those teeth grazed the metal of his gauntlet, making a screeching sound that set Amris's teeth on edge and drew a low obscenity from Darya, but did no harm to the flesh beneath. "Very well," he said, and left the rope alone for the moment.

Darya was following him on the other side, watching what he did and how the horses reacted. "There was another Sentinel blessed by Poram," she said, her voice lower and more soothing than the words would have required. "Could talk to animals. I never was jealous of him before now."

"Talking might not aid us a great deal with these, no more than it does with some people."

Quickly, Amris placed a hand on the horse's withers and swung himself up onto its back. The saddle was made for a creature with shorter legs and of little help; he held on with his thighs as the horse snorted and bucked. Indeed, he thought, any speech from the beast would most resemble the string of profanities he'd heard from men he'd had to pull out of tavern fights, a declaration of hatred for the entire world and most especially the part meddling with them.

He felt a hair more pity for the horse, who had neither enlisted nor ordered a dozen pints of bad ale, but that changed nothing of the situation.

Out of the corner of his eye, he saw Darya mount the other horse, which liked the process no more than his had. He had a moment of concern, thinking of her lighter weight, but she stayed on, showing no more signs of distress than a few hissed breaths and some more muttered oaths.

As a boy, Amris had seen men break horses by the simple expedient of mounting and then staying on until the beast grew tired enough to accept the weight. Those who knew better—his first commander, among them— said it didn't result in good mounts, but they had no time just then, and Amris wasn't certain anything could gain these creatures' trust. He hung on and waited.

Bad-tempered or not, these *were* broken to saddle, and it didn't take more than a few minutes for them to accept their fate. As Amris's mount settled itself, snorting and blowing, he looked over at Darya. "Be ready," he said, drawing the knife from the belt.

"On it," she said, and cut the rope tying her horse to the tree.

━━━━━━━

Once they had the freedom to move, the horses didn't act like they cared who or what was on their backs. It took some tugging on the reins to get them to go the right direction, but the land was an ally there: so close to Oakford, the hills were steep on either side and thick with trees, terrain no sensible horse—or sort-of-horse thing—would risk.

That didn't make the ride pleasant. The saddle wasn't made for human proportions: the stirrups cramped Darya's legs, and bits of leather poked her in the tailbone. Farther down, the "horse" felt as if it'd grown extra bumps on its ribs, maybe as a defense against being stabbed or just to aggravate any human trying to ride it. The animal smelled like wine going to vinegar, too, and its natural gait was swaying and unsteady.

On the other hand, it covered ground faster than she and Amris would've managed walking. That was the important thing.

"And you're both mares, thank the gods," Darya said to her horse's ears.

"No interest in fresh blood for the local stock?" Amris joked from behind her.

"Isen would nail my head up over the stables if I introduced this"—she waved a hand to indicate smell, sharp teeth, and all—"to his mares. And I think the farmers would come after me in a mob if their draft horses caught pregnant with this line." She thought of the hooves and the teeth, as well as the odd bone structure. "For a start, I don't know that a normal mare would survive."

Amris made a sound of revulsion. Glancing back, Darya saw his upper lip curled, and he shook his dark head with considerably more disgust than she'd expected—not that the subject was pleasant.

"Much of the farm boy remains in the man," he said after a moment. "I'd never have called us sentimental about our stock, and I've long since been used to their deaths in battle, but this..." Amris shrugged, his armor clanking. "It calls forth the shade of my father in me, perhaps."

Because the mention of his father didn't seem to sadden him further, Darya felt free to smile. "You'll like Isen, then. Practical man, but damned if he doesn't think our horses are worth more than our own skins. Especially the breeding stock. If Ironhide hadn't been a gelding, I don't know that I'd have the nerve to tell him about the loss."

She still wasn't eager for that conversation—or many others. Oakford itself—in the form of beds, baths, and food, not to mention being in company less attractive and less forbidden than Amris's—sounded as good as it had all along. She'd thought about the good points, Darya realized. Conveniently, she'd forgotten, not the news she was bringing, but the ways she'd have to deliver it.

The road ahead looked less promising in that moment.

Chapter 23

In Amris's youth, Oakford had been a cheerful bustling crossroads of a town, thick with traders and travelers and the places that met their needs: taverns, inns, brothels, smithies, and a market square full of noisy peddlers. Luxury had been the province of Heliodar in the south and Klaishil in the north, as had culture and scholarship, but for cheap goods from a distance, a night or two of merriment, or a horse of dubious origin, Oakford had been more than sufficient.

Often, he'd been able to hear the town before he'd seen the first house.

He still could, but mirth and even trading had little to do with it. Save for the white towers that had once belonged to the lord's residence, all of the houses were hidden behind a palisade of stout logs, their ends sharpened to points, planted in a mound of earth as high as a man's chest. At each end of the wall facing Amris, where it formed a corner with another, a tower held torches and two men with bows. Four others, armed with spear and shield, stood guard beside a gate. The road leading to it was too narrow for more than one horse to travel abreast.

At the sight, Amris's mind, or perhaps his heart, split in two. Half of him mourned the changes and the picture they painted: a town on guard, anticipating no revelry or trade from the north, only threats. The other half reckoned how long the gate would take to close, how well the palisade would hold off a siege tower and how well the wood would burn; it noted how the guards talked idly to one another and how unscarred their faces were; it thought of what would come out of the forest in a few days, and knew that Oakford wasn't wary enough.

———

"Evening, Aldrich," Darya said to the chief of the men on duty, and raised a hand in further greeting: *See, you know me, and I'm not here to knife you in your sleep.* Given the horses, going out of her way to be harmless was probably a good idea.

Sure enough, the guards were staring at her and Amris's mounts in surprise and revulsion. It took a second for Aldrich to snap his gaze up and focus on her face. "Sentinel," he said, giving her a quick on-guard bow—a gesture that combined courtesy with the need to keep hold of his weapon. "What are those? And who's he?"

"Amris, this is Corporal Aldrich. Aldrich, Amris," said Darya, hoping she didn't sound unfriendly but talking rapidly enough to forestall questions. There'd be enough of those in time. Giving out the answers was neither her duty nor her place. "And these... Might as well say they're horses. We found them out in the forest."

Aldrich peered at the slick coats. His nostrils flared at the scent of bad wine. One of his men looked at the teeth and forked the sign of the gods' protection in front of him. Aldrich, less observant in any number of ways, laughed. "Horses. More like horse-isn't."

Two of the men laughed along with him. The others groaned. Aldrich shrugged it off—the man was even-tempered, you could say that for him—and added, "Well, they're in your care and not mine. Go on in. You both look like hell."

"Much obliged," said Darya dryly, though she couldn't be offended by the comment. Glancing behind her at Amris, she saw the same acknowledgment on his face. Cold water made a poor bath, and it had been days since either of them had spent the night in a bed.

They passed through the gate. The main road grew wider there, and Amris rode up beside her without any problem.

"Well," said Darya, gesturing around. "Here we are. Welcome to civilization—or the closest you'll get for a hundred miles."

———

The broad street running from the gate to the manor was much as it had been in Amris's day, but the buildings along it were far fewer. Oakford didn't have any ruins that he could see, but trees grew on the site of the tavern where he'd gotten his nose broken at sixteen, and sheep grazed where he'd shod his horse before riding off to meet Thyran's forces at Klaishil.

What shops and dwellings there were had become patchwork creations. Amris saw log cabins with thatched roofs and first floors made of stone, and houses where timber beams had propped up failing stone walls.

Scavenging had clearly been the order of the day in the past, when the usual routes for goods had failed, and the living had taken what they needed from those who could use it no longer.

Amris thought of the fallen tree he and Darya had hidden behind, and the plants that had grown over it.

Life went on, however it might manage to do so.

Two taverns yet hung out their shingles along the main road, and an upper story on one, as well as a rough picture of a bed below the sign of a wolf baying at the moon, suggested rooms to let. A short ways down, a smithy sent up clouds of smoke and the smell of hot metal; a fat brown gelding outside snorted and neighed restlessly as Amris and Darya passed on their uncanny beasts.

The market square was empty, though the ground bore the marks of feet and wagons. "Do people yet come here to trade?" Amris asked.

"Not constantly. There are"—Darya gestured vaguely—"market days and things. Probably. I got rations and equipment up at the garrison."

The manor had become a fortress, then, though one that showed it little on the outside. The delicate wrought-iron railings he remembered were gone, though, buried behind another wall of logs. Only the gates, with their abstract swirling designs, remained.

"What became of the lord?"

"Gods, I don't know," she said. He felt her astonishment that he'd even think to ask turn to gentleness when she remembered his reasons. "Was he a friend?"

"No, nothing of the sort. I doubt we ever spoke. When first I came through, our ranks were far too different." Amris remembered lights in manor windows, carriages with noble crests, tall, handsome figures on fine horses. "I was only curious."

"Commander Hallis might be able to tell you, or some of the men. Most of the garrison, the regular army, comes from around here. And there are probably records. Sorry. There are only a few ways I ever bother learning the history of a place. He didn't leave any treasures, curse the place, or become a revenant, so..."

"No," he said. "No reason to do so, I suppose."

The last light of the sun shone on Darya, drawing rainbows across her skin and bringing out the sheen in her dark hair. She sat the not-horse she rode with as much grace as anyone could have managed, and neither the bloodstained and torn armor she wore nor the clear signs of long travel could greatly blight her appearance.

In that moment, Amris realized she was not just comely but beautiful...and felt her more a stranger to him than at any time since he'd woken to stare into her eyes and find that his life had vanished.

Chapter 24

ENTERING THE GROUNDS OF THE GARRISON ITSELF was easier than the village had been, since Amris had never been there in his own time. When he'd come through at the end, leading men, he'd had no time to stop for more than a few hours; when first he'd been in the then-town, he'd been a gawky youth in ill-fitting armor with barely a coin to his name, and most decidedly not the sort of man to dine with nobility.

Outwardly, the years hadn't wrought many changes in the manor itself. The white and tan stone of which it was made had lasted centuries before Thyran and had held its own well against storms and scavengers alike. A flat, featureless parade of ground stretched in front of the gates where gardens had once blossomed, and smaller outbuildings had mushroomed farther back; that was all.

There had always been footmen in front of the manor. Now there were guards, but it wasn't so dramatic a change. They were only outfitted differently: pikes and short swords, and businesslike leather armor rather than the livery Oakford's servants had worn, all silver buttons and lace against purple cloth.

The pair of guards at the manor doors were young—just old enough to enlist, to Amris's practiced vision. They gawked at the horses and Amris even more obviously, and for longer than those at the village gates had done.

"Tell Hallis we'll meet him in his office in a quarter hour," Darya said to them. "Literally life or death, sad to say."

The guards went pale—paler, in the case of the tow-headed lad on the left. He swallowed and stepped forward, extending a hand. "And the…horses, ma'am?"

Darya shook her head. "That's why the delay. We'll take them 'round to the stables. Best nobody else try and touch them without armor."

The boy retreated, trying and failing to conceal an expression of profound relief. He and his fellow didn't give Amris much scrutiny after that. Compared to odd beasts and unexplained news, one stranger in armor wasn't much excitement.

A small flagstone path took them around the side of the house. In the back, the stables stretched out in a long, low row of solidly constructed wood, with several paddocks occupying the space between the building and the dark line of trees where the forest resumed. A few horses sported in the larger one; the others were empty.

As Amris and Darya rounded the corner, a girl in rough clothing paused in the act of forking manure from a stall, goggled, then popped her head back into the building. No more than a minute later, a man stepped out of the door nearest to the main house and strode toward them. "Those are *not* replacements," was the first thing he said, "whatever else they may be. Ironhide was a damned good horse."

"I know," Darya said, and ducked her head apologetically.

This, then, must be Isen, of whom Darya had spoken earlier. He was a tall, thin man in the same rough clothing as the stable hands, with close-cropped brown hair and apparently more than his fair share of problems, of which Sentinels and their unexpected finds were currently the largest. "What happened?"

"Tracked the cockatrice to ruins—no place for a horse." As she spoke, Darya dismounted, and Amris followed her lead. "I left him on a loose tie outside, with water and plenty of grass nearby. While I was in the city, he got stolen."

"By what?"

"I can't tell you until I tell Hallis. I'm sorry."

Isen blinked rapidly. "That bad?"

"Probably worse."

The yard was silent save for the horses, who didn't know enough to speculate or eavesdrop. Isen sucked in a breath, puffing out his cheeks, and then blew it out in a sigh. "I should have expected it. I'd just gotten a foal from Seafoam. What are these things?"

"Amris," said Darya, with a slight smile and a gesture toward him, "and…twistedmounts, I guess is the best name for them at present. I wanted to get their gear off and give them water, whatever they are."

"Good plan. I'll do it." Isen raised a hand before either Darya or Amris could object. "You don't have to tell me they're vicious. And I know a damn sight better than you do how to handle temperamental beasts. Give."

He held out a hand imperiously. Almost by instinct, Amris put his reins into it. He fought the urge to salute.

Tired from the journey, the horse did no more than take a half-hearted bite at Isen's hand, one which the stable master—Amris assumed—dodged easily, and countered with a light smack on the neck and the first of a sharp series of whistles.

"Come on," said Darya. "He won't know we're alive until they're dealt with, and we need to be in Hallis's office by then."

"I heard that," said Isen, but he didn't look away from the horses.

Amris started toward the path, but Darya caught him by the arm, then dropped her hand quickly. "Short cut," she said, and gestured toward a door by the stables that Amris had overlooked—and no wonder, since it was far smaller and plainer than the double doors at the main entrance.

It also wasn't guarded or, as Amris shortly discovered, even locked. Darya simply opened it and led him into a low hallway made of rough stone. Torches on the walls gave off dim light and much smoke, more akin to the bonfires of wartime than even the farm of his youth, where tallow candles and oil lamps had been fit for peasants.

Even *light* was different.

Amris's armor was heavy on his shoulders, and the hallway endless and featureless. Strictly speaking, there were doors, and smells and noise beyond them, but they were far away, perhaps not even real.

"All seems worse the closer it is to being over, doesn't it?" Darya asked. "Don't worry. We'll get cleaned and fed before the world ends."

———

The problem with Hallis's office was that it was up two flights of stairs.

True, Darya had never complained about that, or even noticed it, on her previous visits to Oakford. True, she'd climbed higher in the ruins of Klaishil without minding the ache in her feet and the strain in her thighs. But when she'd been climbing around in the ruins, she hadn't already been climbing around in the ruins—a concept that made sense to her weary mind—much less running, fighting, sleeping rough, and riding an oddly shaped horse-thing for three days.

Now that she was out of immediate physical danger, the supports were falling out from under her body. Danger was still out there, and she still had things to do, urgent things, but that didn't matter. Bodies were stupid. Even willpower could only do so much with them.

She *smelled* like the horse now. Sweat had matted her hair to her head and her breeches to her legs. It stung the cuts on her chest, which were aching of themselves. Amris was limping slightly, though Darya suspected that wasn't the cause of his set face.

There was nothing she could do about any of it. If she turned her own mind away from injuries and weariness, from the immediate need to put one foot in front of the other, the new direction it took would be worse.

Up two flights of polished granite stairs they went, passing servants who stared at them nervously and backed up, soldiers who tried to disguise their nerves, and Katrine, a tall, rangy blond Sentinel who gave Darya a sympathetic look but was too wise to try and stop her for conversation.

After the landing, Hallis's office was at least not very

far: second door on the left, past a tapestry of an elven hunting party. She'd admired it the first time she'd been stationed at Oakford, and noticed it with some appreciation after that. Now the colors blurred in her vision.

Lifting her hand to knock was a matter of intense focus. Thank the gods, she only had to do it once.

The door opened nearly under her hand, and then Hallis was staring up at her. *He* hadn't changed: still short and blocky, still dark-skinned and gray-haired, still wearing rumpled clothing beneath his green sash of office. "What the hell is wrong with you?"

"Many things," Darya said. "I can explain a couple."

"Both of you, come in. Sit."

Darya was glad to, as soon as Hallis opened the door, and she suspected Amris was as well, though he kept up a facade of blank good discipline. The office was no fancier than became a bachelor commander of a remote outpost—dark shutters at the window, no carpets, a few candles, Hallis's own wood carvings for the only ornaments—but it was comfortable, with a low leather couch rather than chairs in front of the desk. She sank down with a murmur of relief and closed her hands around a flask Hallis pressed into them.

Drinking was blind reflex. The drink itself was cool, and tasted of mint and orange, with a powerful hint of spice behind it: fuiroig, a liquor the Criwathani used for energy. Two swallows and Darya no longer felt in danger of falling asleep, or like it was going to be too much effort just to move her mouth to talk. She passed the flask over to Amris.

He was as good a place to start as any. "Sir," she said, "this is General Amris var Faina."

There was more, but Hallis broke in, frowning, "I'm calling the Mourner, Sentinel. You've been out there too long. You, sir, what *is* your name?"

"The lady has it right," Amris said, "incredible as I realize it is. I'll swear it so, under whatever oath you'd like or in front of a dozen priests of Tinival, but we have no time to explain in detail."

It was good that Hallis was also sitting down. His mouth opened and his hands clenched tightly on the arms of his chair. "You died a hundred years ago."

"No. I'm no ghost, Commander. A hundred years ago, I faced Thyran and, with the help of an enchanted object, cast us both outside of time. Then came storm and ruin, and I stayed as I was while the world moved, until Darya came seeking her prey and found me."

Despite the couch, Amris sat straight-backed, his hands folded before him. In profile, his nose was sharp, his jaw clean; he could have been the face on an old coin, shining through tarnish. He didn't even slur his speech as Darya knew she'd done from weariness.

A more worthy and high-minded person might have sighed with admiration. Darya felt the urge, and partly as a result also wanted both to kick him in the shin and to drag him off to bed. Thank the gods, neither was an option.

Hallis sat back in his chair, staring at Amris. The office was warm and smelled of woodsmoke. A carving of an owl watched everyone from the mantel. Darya swallowed, tasted the last traces of mint and orange, and waited.

"Found *you*, you say?" Hallis asked eventually, and Darya could see him approaching the question as she'd approached the horse-things, ready for the sudden kick or bite. There was no avoiding it this time, though, and she could see by Hallis's face that he knew as much, only hoped in this last moment to be wrong. "*You* stayed in place? And you faced"—his voice dropped, veteran that he was, and Darya thought he wanted to look over his shoulder—"Thyran."

"Yes," said Amris. "For just this reason, we demanded your presence so urgently. Thyran is active once more, Commander. I know no reason that he wouldn't have all his old strength and malice. I know that he *does* have an army, and that already they move this way."

Outside, the sky was turning purple with evening and the smell of cooking meat was heavy in the air. People called to one another from elsewhere in the fort. The couch was soft under Darya's thighs, the floor smooth beneath her boots.

All of it felt like the mirror in her pack: pretty, unreal, and very easily broken.

Part III

Nature is change, and change is nature. Even the rocks shift, given time. Mortals and gods have the gift of directing their own transformations, and the perilous task of influencing the way others change.

—The Lessons of Poram, Part II

You yourself, Your Grace, have met with those who pursued fleshcrafting as a magic and those who sought its results. It has the dangers of any new craft, particularly one so tied to the body. What Thyran did to his forces—and to himself—was a different matter. Whether he worked with the help of the demons from outside the world or the power of Gizath alone, he stripped away the best parts of those who came to join him. They became mockeries of those they once were, and their spawn mocked all life. Worse, most of his closest servants chose that path.

—The Letters of Farathen

Chapter 25

HALLIS RAISED ONE OF HIS HANDS. FOR A MOMENT HE seemed about to make a point, or reach for something on his desk. Then he stared at his own hand and put it back down, clutching the chair harder.

It had been bad enough when she found out, Darya thought, and she'd gotten to do it in stages. She wouldn't have said *gotten to*, like it was a privilege, until she saw Hallis get it all dumped on him at once.

"How—" he began, and it was the gasp of a drowning man. "How far are they? How many?"

"I'd say between two and four days out," Darya said, after some quick and uncertain calculation and a glance at Amris. "No real idea how many. Sorry. But we ran across a few of their scouts on our trip back, and it seems like the monster I was hunting was a part of the army."

Briefly, she described the collar on the cockatrice, then the party of twistedmen and frog-mouthed creatures, and mentioned she and Amris had destroyed the bridge. "That might have done some good. There's a lot I don't know. Too much."

"Thyran was ever a creature of dark impulse," said Amris, "but he'd never move against us without a fair-sized force."

Hope crept back into Hallis's face. "Maybe he's not doing so. The scouting party could've only been his creatures making sure *we're* no threat to *them*."

Darya shook her head, though she hated to do it. "They already know that. You have raids here every, what, two, three years? And I was the first person to get as far north as Klaishil since the storms."

"Besides," Amris said, "forbearance was never in Thyran's nature. Neither would he have learned patience in our time outside of time, for it was as if we slept." He sighed. "No, he'll be angrier, if anything, and with more of a mind for vengeance. And if one of his underlings woke him, as I believe to be the case... Well, that suggests they wished for his leadership again and have the strength to back him."

"It could've been a lone fanatic," said Hallis, and shook his own head slowly. "But we can't count on that. All right. He'll attack here, then. There's no other route." He glanced at the map on the wall, which showed the hourglass-center where Oakford stood between the northern forest and the lands of civilization, with high mountains to the east and the sea on the west. "Not unless he has an army of winged beasts, and then why send out horses? No, he'll strike us."

Slowly, showing every year of his age for the first time Darya had seen, Hallis rose from his chair and crossed the room to kneel before a dark chest, which he opened with a silver key that had been hanging around his neck, under his shirt. Darya heard quiet clicks and thumps as Hallis lifted and replaced hard objects, the whisper of cloth, and the fluid ringing of metal.

He came back to the desk with a small box, this one silver and ivory. Inside, nested in green velvet, were three robin-sized birds, each carved from light-blue stone swirled and flecked with white.

To Darya's surprise, the sight of them made Amris smile—and despite more than a trace of wistfulness about it, despite the circumstances, seeing *that* made her want to smile back.

———

The messengers were yet in use. More than that, they were much as Amris remembered them, if obviously rarer from the care with which Captain Hallis had stored his. For Amris himself, they'd been pretty common-place, first flying to and from his commander's tent and then, as his career had progressed, bearing messages to him. Some had been nuisance requests for information, or demands for the impossible; others had informed him of reinforcements or alerted him to a change in situation; a few, toward the end, had taken messages to and from his friends.

He and Gerant had sent one back and forth every few nights.

Less pain accompanied that memory than Amris would have expected. He wasn't certain whether that made him resilient, callous, or just numb from weariness. Nor did he have time to consider the question, for Hallis moved quickly, opening the shutters and then taking the first of the birds in his cupped hands.

"Captain Hallis greets you and requests aid," he said, carefully pronouncing every word. "Reliable witnesses report return of Thyran and approach of Twisted army to Oakford. All available reinforcements needed."

Hallis spoke a few more words, even more careful with those than with the message. The bird lit from within, so that the aventurine of its body became transparent and it cast blue-white shapes on the wall behind it. Spreading stone wings, it launched itself from Hallis's hands into the clear night sky beyond the window.

The next two birds carried the same message and followed the same process. When the third had flown off, Hallis closed the shutters and sat back down, dropping his weight into the chair somewhat more heavily than he'd done before.

"If I might ask," said Amris, "where do they go?"

"Affiran, which is where we're likely to get aid from if any comes in time, though they'll be half a week at best." Amris nodded, recognizing the capital city of Criwath and glad to hear that it still was a potential source of reinforcements. Hallis went on. "Silane, which will try, but they're farther away. And Heliodar, which... I'll not even dream it."

"Do they care so little?"

"Yes," said Darya.

Hallis made an equivocating gesture with one hand. "They're unlikely to believe any story like ours without ten or so witnesses in person, and the ruling families won't want to risk their soldiers for a possibility."

"That's why you get the command post," said Darya, shaking her head. "You can be a diplomat without spitting afterward."

Amris suppressed the urge to chuckle. "What are—" He paused. "Forgive me. I've no rank here, and no right to question your plans."

"Plans." Hallis barked laughter. "The plans that come to mind are drinking ourselves into a stupor, slitting our own throats, and setting the place afire, or first one and then the other. You can't know how—" He shook his head. "But we must make a stand, and if we're to do so, I'll want your thoughts above all, General. You've fought him and lived."

———

"He is mortal," Amris pointed out gently, and then had to amend his own statement. "At least, he's no god. He can't see save through his own eyes, his attacks take time and strength, and he *can* die."

"Can he?" It was a serious question Hallis asked—no childish seeking of reassurance, but a military man's need to know about his enemy.

Still, his fear was real and obvious, and Darya didn't blame him at all. She'd grown up as a Sentinel-in-training, knowing about timelines and battles. She'd been able on some level to see Thyran as a petty, spiteful man, no different from the tavern wench throwing plates at the head of a faithless lover or the child breaking his toys rather than sharing them. Still she was terrified.

For most people outside the Order and *maybe* the priesthoods—even for old soldiers like Hallis—this news would be like hearing of a mountain about to fall from the sky. *Drinking ourselves into a stupor, slitting our own throats, and setting the place afire,* Hallis had said, and she could only hope they hadn't just caused thousands of people to start doing exactly that, once the birds brought their messages.

There was a tightness around Amris's mouth that suggested he was having some of the same thoughts. He answered carefully. "If my knowledge yet serves, yes. His death would be harder and more dearly bought than that of any man. He has spells and armies both at his command, and he's reshaped himself with more care and skill than he spent on any of the creatures he made—but it can happen. I used the spell I did, not because it was the only possibility, but because it was the only certainty. Or so it seemed then."

Hallis nodded. "What were his numbers, at the end?"

"At a rough count? Five thousand, going in, but we accounted for a fair few of those before the end," Amris said, and showed his teeth in a smile. "I could say at least half and not think myself vain."

"We've killed a few hundred since then, over the years. Some of them might have killed each other," Darya added, paraphrasing her lessons. "I don't think they get replacements as fast as we do."

"Better not to underestimate, even so," said Hallis. Darya saw the look on his face, the narrow focus that sliced away all panic and fear and left only the situation and the next steps. "Call it three thousand on their way here. We have a hundred and twelve trained soldiers on hand. Say another hundred or so peasants we can stick up on the walls with spears and hunting bows, assuming they don't all bolt when they hear the news."

"Mages? Priests? Healers?"

"One army wizard. A priest of Sitha, a Mourner, and a couple herbalists here. I think the village has a midwife, maybe someone to see to sick goats and whatnot. One of Tinival's knights was stopping here for a few days—I counted him in the hundred and twelve, though he's worth three or four normal soldiers in a fight."

"So are we," Darya put in, touching the hilt of her sword reflexively, though she knew Gerant wouldn't answer. "And that's not vanity either." It wasn't, but she was glad to have something to say. Here, with Hallis, Amris was speaking not as the man in the woods, displaced from his time, but as a commander—and she, who'd almost always ridden and fought alone, didn't know that language nearly as well.

When Amris smiled again and said, "You speak truly, if you're any measure—and of matters beyond my experience," she felt ridiculously proud of herself.

It's the end of the world, Gerant would've said, *and you're still showing off for handsome men.*

At least, he would have said it if the handsome man on the other end of the sofa had been anyone else.

"Good," said Hallis, "and glad to hear it. I haven't seen your people in action very often, Sentinel, but there are three others here at present. I'd counted them among our ranks, though I knew you had…" He hesitated over the term, which clearly wanted to come out *uncanny powers*, and finished with "abilities we lack."

Darya didn't protest. Yes, everyone had abilities the next person lacked, but not everyone had the sort that'd come in handy in a fight, particularly against twistedmen and whatever other monsters Thyran was going to throw at them. This wasn't a situation for humility.

"The high ground and the fortifications are ours," Amris added, "and I'm sure you know the use of them well. That will count for a great deal. Thyran ever struck from ambush and at the unguarded when he could."

"There's that. And with the warning you've brought, we can prepare a few more defenses and get the civilians to safety. Speaking of which…" Hallis frowned. "We've no chance of keeping your return quiet, and I've already heard of your mounts. I'd thought to put the official word about tomorrow, but it might be best done tonight. I'm not sure."

"Spare no time, I'd think," said Amris. "The further in advance people know the truth, the more distance those fleeing can put between themselves and this fortress, and the less rumors will spread."

Darya shook her head. "Normally, you'd be right. But it'll be full dark when the news gets out, we're on the edge of enemy territory and in the middle of nowhere, and the roads out here are piss-poor even by day. The messengers would probably manage well enough, with lanterns and whatnot, but you spread the word now and you'll get a bunch of old folks and children running off. Half of 'em will break their legs and get eaten by wolves, or worse."

Briefly, Amris wore an expression that Darya was getting used to: a combination of surprise and sorrow that translated to *I hadn't realized how shitty the world had gotten,* though she knew he would have said so more politely, and only if pressed. "They could leave tomorrow, and use the time to pack their belongings," he said, but he didn't sound convinced. He'd been a farm boy, and he'd led men. He knew people, even when he didn't want to admit it.

"Some might," said Darya. She softened her voice, sorry that she had to make him confront one more bit of horror tonight, but not sorry that she was doing it. As with being humble about her gifts, this wasn't the time. "Lots wouldn't. And bad news is always worse in darkness. There are other ways of running."

"A moment," said Hallis. He rearranged the scrolls on his desk, regarded the resulting unsteady pyramid, and then said, "I'll call those within the fortress together and tell them tonight. Even the servants here are in the army— new enlistees and those on punishment—and there's not much chance for anyone to be alone long. Tomorrow, I'll send wider messages. Among other things."

"Only tell me," said Amris, "how I may best be of service."

"Right now, you can both go get yourselves fed, watered, and brushed down," said Hallis, who drank with Isen in his off-hours. "Even if you want to be present for the bad news, it'll take at least an hour to get us assembled. General—"

"Forgive me the interruption, Commander, but just now I hold no rank. Make it Amris, I beg you."

"Amris," Hallis continued, after a second of hesitation. "I'll put you in with Olvir, our other visitor. He's the knight I mentioned. Sentinel, you're where you've always been."

"So to speak," said Darya.

Chapter 26

"WHICH HELL DID THEY SCRAPE *YOU* OUT OF?" ASKED Emeth. She'd turned her head and cracked her eyelids when Darya walked in, but she didn't make any motion to get off her bed or even sit up. Her dark hair flowed loose over her folded arms, and her bare feet, crossed at the ankles, sent slow trails of smoke up into the air.

"I don't look that bad."

"Maybe not for someone who's been dead a week. Have you? Should I guard my neck?"

Darya shucked off her boots with a sigh of relief and started on her armor. "If your blood's as sour as you are, you're safe from any undead walking."

"You hurt me, moss-head. You really do. Want a hand?"

"Nah, I'm half done already. As the soldier said to the dancing girl." The innuendo came without thinking, as much instinct around her friend as the proper lunge and strike were when facing an enemy. Darya dropped the torn and filthy leather on the floor and wrenched her tunic over her head.

Emeth opened her eyes all the way, gaze sharpening when she saw Darya's bandaged chest. "A little near the important bits, isn't that?"

"Stop staring at my breasts, you lecher. It's not bad."

"Only you could say that after getting clawed by a cockatrice."

"Wasn't a cockatrice." Darya kept her voice neutral as she undid her trousers and was glad of the excuse to bend her head, so that her face didn't show. "We ran into twistedmen on the way back. Couple of new and unpleasant scouts too."

"And you can't tell me more, right?" Emeth said after a short pause.

"Right."

"'We' means that living statue Katrine saw you with, or have you picked up a troop of entertainers on the road?"

"Just him." Darya rubbed her eyes. "Where is Kat, anyhow?"

"At the bathing pool, where you should go," said Emeth. Swift as a leaping flame, she sat up, grabbed a frayed tan robe from among the bedclothes, and tossed it to Darya. "Probably either out or half a raisin by now."

Darya laughed. "Good thing for her that you've always liked fruit," she said and began to pull the robe on, with a lighter heart than she'd brought into the room. Even with doom hanging over her head—all their heads—it was good to be back among her people.

———

A page with a recently shorn head and ill-fitting green tunic showed Amris down the hall. From the very first, they kept darting curious glances at him, and the questions began after no more than a minute. "Where are you from, my lord?"

"I was born in Silane."

"But you met the Sentinel around here?"

"A few days' walk to the north, yes."

The child paused, then headed down another track. "It was you two who brought those horses in, wasn't it? Not horses, really. Were they yours?"

"Not originally," said Amris, "but now they belong to your commander, for all the good he'll likely have of the poor brutes."

"Poor!" The page blinked up at him. "Ugly, they say, and mean too."

"So they've been made to be, broken and bred to it, and without the wit that lets men change themselves."

The page fell silent to absorb that information, to Amris's relief. Trying to squash the curiosity of youth wasn't to his taste, yet he had no wish to start more rumors before Hallis could break the news—nor, in truth, did he have any desire to let the page know what was approaching. Their voice and build suggested a girl no more than fifteen, or a lad a poorly grown twelve at most; there'd been drummers and squires as young in Amris's commands, but he hadn't missed the sight of them.

Gods willing, Hallis would send the pages off with the refugees the next morning. If not, Amris said to himself, he'd see to it, despite his oath not to interfere with the other man's authority. The soldiers could manage their own chores for a while, and what would come was no training the young needed.

They stopped at the end of the hall, by a narrow

arched window that let in a pale shaft of moonlight. The page knocked at the wooden door in front of them.

"Please enter," said a cheerful voice from inside.

It proved to belong to a tall, broad-shouldered man with dark-red hair and pale skin. He'd been sitting on one of the narrow beds and taking off his boots, but he stood and bowed when the door opened, pressing the heel of one hand to his heart. It should have appeared ridiculous coming from a man with only one boot on, and the other dangling from his free hand, but the grave courtesy in his face tempered any urge Amris might have had to laugh.

Tinival's knighthood still trained its members well, it seemed, even after a hundred years.

"You must be Sir Olvir," he said, returning the bow. "Amris is my name, and I'm pleased to make your acquaintance. The commander tells me we'll be sharing a room."

"The pleasure's mine," said Olvir. He had a wide smile and big, dark-brown eyes. Amris had been a farm boy, once, but this young man looked fresh out of the fields. "Pip, does Commander Hallis want me?"

"No, sir," said the page. "I'm just the delivery. I'll drop off fresh clothing for you in two shakes, sir," they said to Amris. "Robes and towels are in the chest at the foot of the bed, and the bathing pools are in the basement. Dinner's over, but there's plenty left, and we'll send that up too."

"Can I trouble you to add fresh bandages to that load?" Amris asked. "And calendula ointment, if you have any."

"Jars and jars, for after training. But if you're wounded, we've a Mourner too."

Amris shook his head. "Only scratches. Thank you."

"Oh. Yes, sir." Pip bowed and left, closing the door behind them. They didn't sigh, but they were also too young to conceal an expression of distinct disappointment.

"She had frighteningly high hopes," said Olvir.

"Her age was ever one for blood and gore, if she's as young as she looks," Amris said, chuckling as he thought of his younger brothers. "Wounds gained in high adventure are better still."

Olvir smiled briefly. "I haven't known many children. But she's asked me enough questions along the same lines. Can I help you get settled?" He'd pulled the second boot off while Amris and Pip had talked.

"A hand with the buckles would be most welcome," said Amris. "As would directions to the armorer, once I've mended myself a touch."

"I won't ask children's questions, but it does look like you've been through the wars."

"Truer than you know, or than I can explain just now." He took off his armor with Olvir's help, pushing through the urge to simply throw it on the floor and be free of the weight, and piled it neatly by the foot of the free bed. "Most recently, Darya and I fought twistedmen—three, and their mount."

"Darya—oh, the Sentinel." Olvir sat back down. "I haven't fought any myself, but I've heard stories of twistedmen. They're always nasty foes."

"That part of the stories, at least, is true." The robe was where Pip had said it would be. Amris disrobed and folded his clothes neatly, though he suspected Hallis or the fort's servants might recommend burning them. A wash in the river couldn't get rid of blood completely, particularly not that of twistedmen, and then there was the other grime of three days' hard journey and rough sleeping.

While Amris undressed, Olvir politely kept his gaze averted, but when he did look back, he focused on the bandage near Amris's knee. "More than a scratch, I think."

"Somewhat more, perhaps," he said, "but I want to see how it fares before I ask the Mourner to use his strength."

The powers of the gods resembled the magic that Gerant now used: they themselves had few limits, but they channeled their might through their mortal servants, who could only take so much of such use. Under ordinary circumstances, it would take little effort for a Mourner to mend a simple leg wound, but Amris thought of the approaching army, and couldn't bring himself to spend even that slight amount of force carelessly.

Olvir lifted his gaze from Amris's leg to his face. His brown eyes were calm, level, but keen, and his young face was somber. "I guess that's part of what you can't explain just now."

There was no accusation in it, barely even a question. When Amris nodded, Olvir's jaw tightened, but he pressed the point no further. He sat back on his bed, looked at the sword hung on a rack beside Amris's and the armor on a nearby stand, then at the small window at the end of the room. "How soon will more word come?" he asked.

"Your commander will give it to you tonight," Amris replied. "I cannot in good conscience speak before he does."

"Of course," said Olvir, understanding military formality as only Tinival's servants could. "You'd better go and bathe, then, and see how the wound's healing. I'll make sure Pip leaves the supplies on your bed."

"Thank you," said Amris. "And I'm glad to make your acquaintance." He meant it—he liked the other man already—but when he left the room, he was also relieved to be out from under the scrutiny of those mild brown eyes.

As Emeth had said, Katrine was in the bathing rooms. Wet-haired, she lounged on the edge of the pool, with her feet dangling in the water. Beside her sat another woman: short, with bronze-gold hair and an ample bosom. For a moment, Darya wasn't sure whether she was a Sentinel or one of the keep's other soldiers. Then she shifted her weight, the shadows and steam fell away from her, and Darya saw the stripes of copper running like seams up her arms and legs.

"Branwyn," said Katrine, "this is Darya. She's been wandering around in the forest. Darya, Branwyn. The Adeptas sent her up here to cover for me at night."

"Still glowing?" Darya asked.

Katrine gave her breasts an exasperated glance. "Less, but yes. I've got no complaint about them otherwise, but they mean I'm no damned good at stealth. I can name my fee if I let a fleshcrafter or two ogle them, though. It seems they've never done this sort of work on a Sentinel before, and there's a, ah, fascinating pattern of magical interaction."

"At least they're fascinating." Darya shrugged off her robe and stepped into the pool, groaning in a mixture of pleasure from her sore muscles and pain from the various cuts, major and minor, lacing her body. "Nobody's ever complimented mine in words of more than one syllable."

"Seduce more mages," Branwyn suggested, with a slow smile and a husky voice.

"I have magical theory enough from my sword, thank you. Though he doesn't talk about my tits." Darya winced as she thought of Gerant, and then of Amris, but she was reasonably sure she passed it off as a reaction to the water.

When Katrine handed over the soap, Darya scrubbed vigorously, feeling the dirt of her sojourn practically peel away in strips. The cut on her chest was almost healed, with no redness and not much pain when she prodded it experimentally. Everything else was just scratches, and some truly spectacular bruises on her back, according to Katrine. "It certainly looks like you weren't bored."

"Ruins aren't the best place to run around. Even for me."

"Which ruins?" Katrine asked.

"Klaishil."

"Truly?" The other woman's eyes widened. "I wish I'd gone. What was there?"

The handsome warrior my sword-spirit was in love with. The end of the world. The usual.

Hysterics would spread the word too much. The Sentinels were discreet, but there were limits. Besides, one never knew how sound carried.

"You'd be amazed," said Darya, and sank down under the water.

───────

The bathing pools at Oakford were underground, and the light on the staircase and the passage beyond was dimmer than it had been in the servants' passage. Too weary to trust his feet or his reflexes, Amris made his way carefully, trailing his left hand along the wall as a guide.

Still, Darya seemed to come from nowhere. A door opened and she slipped out into the hallway, wet hair hanging down her back, skin radiant where her slim arms and legs emerged from a short, sleeveless robe of the sort Amris himself wore. Her mouth opened in surprise when she spotted him, letting out a surprised "Oh!"

The sound Amris made was similar, but he thought it was further from any precise word. He cleared his throat and remembered that he was a rational man with a vocabulary. "We had the same thought, so it seems."

"Great minds. Or sweaty people." Darya laughed breathlessly. Her gaze dropped to the open neck of Amris's robe, and though she quickly brought it back to the level of his shoulder, Amris couldn't resist his own look in return.

The robes didn't conceal much—modesty wasn't valued nearly as highly as fabric in a military outpost—and Darya's showed everything from the curve of her long neck into her square shoulders down to the sides of her breasts, shining with the heat and moisture of the baths. The hem fell only as far as was essential, exposing most of her sleek thighs, and when she shifted her weight, it only revealed more. It was like the stream all over again, but without cold water close at hand, and Amris's own robe did very little to conceal the way he was responding.

Keeping a clear head in the face of danger had always come easily to him and was second nature by now. Doing so when the danger was so damnably pleasant was new, and far more difficult.

"I..." he said hoarsely, and then had to remember what he'd been going to say. "I shouldn't detain you from food, or rest."

"I do need both," Darya said, and still it was a moment before she started to move past him, or he started to get out of her way.

The hallway was narrow, and each of them went the wrong direction at first. Darya's shoulder bumped lightly into Amris's chest, and reflexively he put a hand out to steady her. It fell low on her waist, and for only a second he gave in, spreading his fingers and letting himself feel all the yielding firmness below his palm. She gasped, not in shock—the woman, as far as Amris could tell, was unshockable—but in obvious desire.

Another few breaths and he'd forget their weariness, forget how public the hallway was, forget that he and Gerant still needed to have a long and awkward conversation. He'd have her up against the wall, legs locked around his waist, nails digging into his spine. Amris could almost feel them.

He dropped his hand to his side and lunged for the door.

Chapter 27

SLEEP EBBED AWAY SLOWLY. FIRST DARYA KNEW THAT she was conscious again, not drifting in the murk of dreams that had been just short enough of nightmares not to wake her. Normally, remembering the frog-creature's dead eyes as it dropped down in front of her, and seeing what might have happened differently, would have at least brought her awake enough to realize she'd dreamed, curse, and turn over. She'd been too tired for that.

She'd been too tired to do anything. When she woke, the light from the window was the deeper gold of early afternoon. A tray by her bed held bread, cheese, and fruit. She vaguely remembered that from the night before. *I'll eat in a minute*, she'd muttered into the room, *just want to lie down first.*

Then, dreams.

Now, the room, after at least fourteen hours of sleep, with untouched food and a glass of wine nearby, and the quiet flick of someone turning pages. Darya pushed herself upright and saw Branwyn sitting cross-legged on another bed, bent over a small book.

We both pushed ourselves considerably harder than usual, didn't we?

Gerant's voice in her head sounded like it usually did. It had never been absent for so long, though. As confidently as she'd told Amris that he was fine, Darya felt an instant and consuming relief—the spiritual equivalent of unknotting a muscle in the back of her neck—as she looked over by the side of her bed and saw the emerald in her sword glowing.

"Damn straight," she said quietly. "But we're here. How are you?"

Branwyn nodded a greeting, but didn't ask questions. That was one of the reasons Sentinels roomed together when they could manage it; they were all used to what sounded like their comrades talking to themselves.

Well, now. And intrigued. If I'm not wrong, spreading the connection to Amris gave me a wider power base to work from. That's why I could target both of those creatures at once. I'd give a good deal to research further, if we have time.

"Pretty useful, in the circumstances," Darya agreed. She took a sip of the wine. Neither warmth nor exposure had made it worse. It was wet, and better than the lignath, which was all she needed. "Time... I'll figure that out."

"Three hours past noon," Branwyn said, not closing the book, "more or less. Hallis wants to see all of us at five. I was going to wake you beforehand, if you hadn't managed it on your own."

"Hope it hasn't been an inconvenience."

"No." Branwyn glanced down. "I wanted the chance to read this again, anyhow. It'll be a good memory."

"Hallis made the announcements, then?"

"Both of them. If I hadn't known the hunt myself, I'd be surprised you managed to sleep through"—she raised her hands, fingers splayed slightly outwards, and then let them fall—"everything that followed."

The fort wasn't, as far as Darya could tell, on fire. That was a start. "Sorry I couldn't tell you before."

"You had orders."

She wanted to apologize for more, as though bringing the news back had made it happen, but that wouldn't have helped. She washed and dressed instead, pulling on her remaining clean clothes—her best on the road, since Sentinels rarely got invited to state dinners. "Desertions? Suicides?"

"I haven't heard of any," said Branwyn, "not that I necessarily would. All the pages *are* being sent off with the other civilians today, but that was Hallis's call, not theirs."

More likely than not, it was Amris's suggestion, said Gerant. *We tried to send the young away from the front lines, when we knew where they'd be. He won't yet be used to the way things are now.*

"You could go your entire life not getting used to that," Darya muttered. Because of Gerant, she didn't say a word about how short the rest of that life could be, given the circumstances.

He is well, isn't he? I assumed you'd have told me otherwise.

"I would've. He was fine when I saw him last night, so unless we've been ambushed and Branwyn's not saying anything about it"—Branwyn smiled and shook her head—"or he choked on a lump of cheese, I'd say he's fine, if tired. Got a nasty cut on his leg when we took out the twistedmen, but nothing that won't heal."

"If he died from cheese," Branwyn put in, "it would have been within the last few hours. He was there this morning when Hallis broke the news to the town."

"Now I just feel lazy."

Not inappropriately.

Darya stuck her tongue out at her sword, getting a knowing laugh from Branwyn, but added, "We can go find him. He was worried about you, too, when you went quiet."

"They knew each other?" Branwyn asked, gesturing to Darya's hilt and then toward the door to stand for Amris. "Or simply got along very well on the journey?"

"Both, really," said Darya. "It's a long story. I'll need more wine to tell it, and you'll need more to hear it, I'm fairly sure."

———

Secrecy isn't important to me, Gerant said out in the hall. *And I doubt it will be to Amris, though you can ask him yourself.*

"No," said Darya, and waited for a pair of men to pass by before she spoke again. Both looked gray, stunned. They walked silently. When they'd gone into one of the other rooms, she added quietly, "But 'he went to sleep a hundred years ago and didn't age until I woke him' isn't a simple conversation."

You're likely correct.

Hallis's office was a hive of people. Darya glanced into the doorway, saw no trace of Amris, and decided not to add to the man's problems. She passed onward, footsteps soft and regular on the stone floor.

We didn't deliberately choose to keep you in the dark,

Gerant said. *Or I didn't. Not you personally, or even*—He stopped, and **Darya** got the feeling of a sigh. *I suppose we didn't want to think about it any more than we had to.*

Darya stopped on the landing going down, turned right, and paced slowly over to the window. It wasn't much more than a slit in the stonework, but it gave her a reason to face away from the hallway and spectators, and the journey let her delay answering. "Don't worry about it," she said, trying to sound normal around a large knot of guilt. "Honestly, now that I've slept—and now that I've talked to Hallis—" She broke off and shrugged. "You might have been right. Or not. But I know you thought it was the best call at the time. We should all do that well."

You're generous. Not to mention troubled.

The window glass was thick and greenish, bubbled in places. Through it, Darya could make out figures in the courtyard, distant and dreamlike. Wagons unloaded barrels of grain, fruit, wine, and water. Soldiers stacked wood in the corners and inspected the walls for weak points. Five youths passed through the gate and spoke to the sergeant on duty; they wore the plain clothes of peasants, and Darya could see, even through distance and cloudy glass, the way duty warred with fear in their bodies.

"There's a lot to be troubled about, wouldn't you say?"

I wish I could argue.

———

At the outer gates of the palisade, the old, the young, and the incurably unfit for combat fled Oakford. Merchants' wagons, full of families and what belongings they'd been able to pack in a few hours, rumbled out. Others followed on horses, mules, or their own feet. Amris watched as a young woman kissed a towheaded child and set him on horseback in front of an old man. All three were weeping; the adults only did so quietly. The woman kissed the man on the cheek, smacked the solid draft horse gently on the rear, and then turned away and walked over to Amris.

"Where do I go to train, sir?" she asked, her voice still choked.

"Make your way to the fortress. When last I saw Corporal Valerin, he was...making his presence hard to miss, but if you need further guidance, he's roughly my height but rounder. He has long black hair, and he wears a brown sash."

Over the course of the morning, he'd repeated the same instructions nearly a score of times. Although he was a stranger and wore no sash to indicate rank, the folk of Oakford chose Amris to answer their questions. He wasn't entirely surprised, and that wasn't entirely vanity: of all the armed people in the town, he looked steadiest on his feet. Many of the soldiers were positively green. Even Olvir and Katrine, making themselves useful as he was, had a lost air about them; they moved as though they weren't quite sure the world around them was real.

For them, of course, this duty was new. For Amris, it was sadly familiar—but as he watched the young woman jog off toward the fortress, he doubted that was all the explanation.

He'd watched that morning when Hallis had broken

the news. The faces in the crowd might have been from
his own time, his own commands, in their fear and con-
fusion, but there was an element of disbelief that Amris
didn't recognize from so far back. He'd seen it on Hallis's
face, though. It had been less present on Darya's—
because she'd discovered the situation piece by piece,
because she'd seen him locked outside of time, or simply
because the Sentinels lived intimately with magic and
threats—but present nonetheless.

In Amris's day, Thyran and his army had been bad
foes, and their reputation had grown over the course
of the war, but that had been all. Now Thyran was the
architect of a hundred years of ruin, of death and priva-
tion that had driven people to the most desperate acts: a
name to conjure with. *Known to bad children and old wives
everywhere*, Darya had said.

The folk of Oakford faced not just a threat, and a bad
one, but the upending of the world they'd known—of
time itself, in a manner, for Thyran had been safely dust
and legend before Darya and Amris had come in and
dragged the past bloody-handed behind them.

Thus, Amris answered questions, gave directions,
broke up the occasional argument, and helped to get run-
away stock or children into the care of those fleeing the
city. He wouldn't normally have known either the land or
the people as well as the rest of the soldiers, but just then,
he knew *everything* better than they did.

He turned from pushing a barrel back upright on a wagon
and caught sight of Darya headed toward him through the
crowd. Even in the chaos, many drew back from her.

"You're making me feel lazy" were her first words when she reached his side.

Like him, she was clean and cleanly dressed, itself a dramatic change. While Oakford had done the best it could by Amris in the way of one man's second-best tunic and another's spare pair of breeches, Darya clearly wore her own clothing, and wore it well. Sea-green wool served her for hose and for the laced doublet that cinched tightly over a light-brown shirt with wide sleeves and a low neckline.

Many of those avoiding her touch were staring surreptitiously all the same. Amris would have been among them, had he not seen the glowing emerald in her sword hilt and heard the cheerful voice in his head as Darya got closer. *She's only halfway lying, love. I wouldn't have expected to find you on your feet so soon, much less out here—except that I know you.*

"You're awake," he said, drawing close enough that— hopefully—nobody would notice the warmth in his voice, or think it strange for apparently addressing a woman he'd known all of three days. "And you're well?"

*Very well, considering the circumstances—and very interested in what I managed to do, now that I had the link to both of you. It was as much instinct as logic just then, you understand, but—*Gerant broke off and laughed at himself—*I am so glad it worked, and that the creature didn't harm you seriously.*

"Not seriously, no." Amris touched the bruises on his throat gently. Necklines were lower in this time, and his did nothing to conceal the marks of the previous day;

that might well be working to his advantage as a figure of authority. "And we made short enough work of the others."

I would've expected nothing less from the pair of you.

"I've more or less filled him in on what happened," Darya said, with a sidelong glance that meant she hadn't been forthcoming with *all* the details. "I'm meeting with Hallis soon. He's moving quickly, I see."

"Not him alone," said Amris, gesturing to the refugees, "but yes. Already he's gathering what supplies are in reach. More will be coming soon, and soldiers to go with them—with any luck."

"And you're the voice of reason in the middle of it all?" Darya took in the fleeing townsfolk and the soldiers struggling to do their duty. "I don't think I could help— somehow, I'm not the sort people ask for directions— but damn me, you don't get a minute of rest, do you?"

He hasn't in years.

"Life hasn't allowed it," Amris replied. "Though some might say I had a hundred years of rest."

Yet it hadn't felt like rest. He'd been in the midst of battle one moment and facing Darya the next, with a strange sensation between that had been more similar to a long blink than sleep. When Darya responded with a dismissive laugh, he didn't argue the point.

"I should go and hear my fate," she said, and bit her lip before going on. "I'll find you afterward, all right? Grab a spare sword from the armory, give you two an hour or so to talk. I'd do it now, but there'd be questions."

And I should be at the meeting as well, said Gerant. *Afterward, though—I'd be glad of the chance. Thank you.*

"That's most generous of you," Amris added with a slight bow, and hopefully no sign in his voice of anything but gratitude. He *was* grateful, and he'd take Gerant's presence with a joyful heart—but he realized, in that moment, that being close to Gerant now meant being close to Darya, with all the temptation that implied.

He thought she had come to the same conclusion. The way she'd caught her lip between her teeth before making the offer, and the uneasy shift of her weight while they spoke, implied as much. They each loved Gerant, in their own manner, and as much as that kept them from acting on their urges, it would also keep them from maintaining the distance that would make such restraint comfortable.

"I'll see if I can find some decent liquor," said Darya. Her voice implied that she'd need it. Amris silently agreed with the sentiment.

Chapter 28

DARYA BROUGHT NO DRINK LATER WHEN SHE MET Amris in the spacious, many-windowed room that was now the dining hall for the fortress. She carried her soul-sword sheathed in her hands, while a plain sword of the same make hung from her waist. Emeth came with her, the hilt of her own sword glowing with dark-red light. Both were in dark clothing and had donned armor again; Hallis had found Darya a whole, unstained doublet, evidently.

"Sorry," said Darya, "but duty calls. Hallis wants Emeth to establish scouts."

"And his conscience would trouble him if he sent me alone to do it," Emeth said with a roll of her eyes.

Darya shook her head. "I don't think any of us should go out alone until this business is done," she said, "even the Sentinels. And this is me talking."

"Sobering," said Emeth, eyeing Amris's mostly empty plate, "more so given that you could eat fresh pork and new bread if you stayed."

"Likely there'll be plenty left for you," said Amris. "Best, they thought, to get the stock killed and salted before the siege."

Sausage is easier to stack than pigs, Gerant added in his head. *It smells a good deal better, too, and is far less noisy.*

Not being a Sentinel, Amris didn't want to speak

aloud in response while they were still in the main room, but he smiled as he'd always done when his city-bred lover had made such comments. Gerant wasn't wrong, but he always had preferred animals as meat.

Darya, who had more freedom, laughed. "If only we could breed 'em straight to meat, huh? And you don't even *eat* these days." She passed the sword to Amris, carefully and hilt first, though it was still in its polished leather scabbard.

"Will you be all right?" Amris asked, setting the blade across his lap. "With an ordinary weapon—"

"I've still got better reflexes and endurance than most people in this fort." Darya spoke quietly, evidently not wanting to brag too loudly in front of the soldiers, but she also tossed her head just a little, its dark braid bouncing with the motion. "And I've been training for longer. Besides, Emeth's with me, and I'll hide behind her if things get rough."

"Try to shriek and clutch your bosom too," said Emeth. "Might as well have some fun before Thyran's hordes rip our throats out and eat our bones."

"You think that'd be fun for me?"

"No, for me." Emeth sketched a bow in Amris's direction. "A good evening, sir. And may I say that you're in fine shape for your age?"

Darya winced and shot her friend a truly annoyed look, but Amris couldn't get very upset. He knew the rough edges of humor in the days before a battle. "I'll treasure such a compliment for the rest of the evening, madam. Best of luck surviving in the woods—I hope the insects are less fierce at twilight than they always were in my day."

Before the two of them left, Emeth gave him a nod of respect. Darya's face was considerably harder to read.

―――――――――

"You're touchy on his behalf," said Emeth. "Touchier than you've ever been for yourself."

She'd waited until they were far enough outside that Amris wouldn't hear, gods be praised for small blessings. "I've never spent a century outside of time. And if I did, I wouldn't have nearly as many people to mourn."

"Your heart wouldn't break for me? I'm wounded, truly."

"Keep this up and I can arrange it."

"No, you wouldn't. I'm a tactical asset. Gods, are those the beasts?" They'd rounded the corner to the stables, and the non-horses were standing in their own paddock outside, quite visible. "Last time I saw something that ugly, I was eighteen and she'd looked wonderful the night before."

"Tell me again how you, of all of us, ended up with a lasting partner?"

Emeth chuckled. "I have great legs. Or so I'm told. And a wonderful…sense of invention."

The stable hands were waiting for them, with real horses saddled and ready. The older of the two looked up at Darya for a long minute as she mounted the bay. "Sentinel," he said, "will the things coming all be riding the sort of creatures you brought in?"

"Not all," said Darya. "I don't know how many. Even they won't bear twistedmen—those have other mounts, and I don't know how many of those either." The boy couldn't have been more than eighteen, and his hands shook as he gave her the reins. "Sorry," she added. "I wish I could tell you more, and better."

He nodded, bowed, but didn't speak again. Darya wondered if he trusted his voice.

Upstairs, in private, Amris settled himself on his bed, with the sword across his lap. "An odd way to talk," he observed, "though I'm sure I'll grow used to it."

You have a great deal to grow used to, Gerant said. *How is it sitting with you?*

"More easily than I'd thought, in truth. It might well have been harder in peacetime, but war is still familiar, for good or ill. Or it's so heavy itself as to make other burdens seem light."

I'd be inclined to the second. I slept beside you for a while, after all.

"You were very kind."

Among other adjectives. Gerant's mental voice held an echo of lust, or the memory of it, as faint as a drop of wine in a flask of water. Then it vanished and he went on, sympathetic. *Even when you didn't wake, you rarely looked easy.*

"I dreamed less when I was young." Fear in the moment had been sharper then, and starker, but command strained the nerves with an unrelenting pressure. "The fighting was easier too, and not only physically." Amris thought of the woman he'd given directions to earlier, and the fear on her child's face. "If someone's already a soldier when you come to love them, you know the risk you're taking, and a child of such parents grows up with it, but when war comes to civilian doorsteps... It will be very sudden to those we're training, and to those who love them."

I never had the heart to take up with another warrior, after you, Gerant said. *In those times, that wasn't much protection, but you're right. I had the choice.*

The moon shone in through the tall windows, making narrow lines of silver on the floor and across the thin beds. "I hope," said Amris, breaching the topic gingerly, "I hope you *were* happy, after I vanished. You said you were past eighty when you died, and—"

That would be an ungodly length of time for grief-stricken chastity, yes. And I was happy, as much as the circumstances would let anyone be. I found someone five years later—but you only have to know as much of that as you want.

Amris leaned back and thought about it. "The lecture notes," he said, a joke between them that his tongue still knew well.

In his head, Gerant laughed softly. *Well, then. He'd been a potter, and a sculptor, before the storms. He helped to craft a few statuettes that I needed for magic. We stayed lovers until I died, he perished a few years later—we were of an age—and we raised his sister's children. She didn't survive one of the storms.*

"Ah," said Amris.

Yes, I miss him, said Gerant, who'd learned to read his silences far too well. *But I miss many people. It's a part of my state. I expect the list to grow until my work is done—if it ever is. I'm glad,* he added, *that I can stop missing you for a while, however different our circumstances are now.*

"I'm glad I didn't have to miss you," said Amris, still on unstable ground. He hastened to clarify. "Not to say that I wouldn't have you back in your body, had I the choice, or have spent more time with you then. But you're here. Your form doesn't change my love."

Nor mine, said Gerant. *You know that I never stopped thinking of you, or loving you, even with Dominic. It just took different shapes. Love always does.*

"It does indeed. Now—" He raised his head to take in the bare room and the moonlight outside. "I'm only starting to find my way here, though gods know I may not have time to do more than start. I'd have been utterly lost without you. I don't wish to part again, not more than briefly, if we all survive. Still, I don't want to hinder you and Darya about your duties."

I won't leave you either. Darya... Gerant thought it over. *She does work alone, generally. Unless I count. Most men have no chance of changing that. You might be the exception, and not only because you're tied to me.*

———

"Things shaped like we are," Emeth told the owl. It perched on her wrist, fluffing violet wings and listening with that particular owl tilt of the head. She gestured with her other hand, pointing to the north. "But coming from that way."

Her voice was higher and sharper than normal, though not enough so that a stranger would have been likely to notice. Darya had noticed at first, but now took it as fact, and accounted for the sound and its echoes as she listened for others.

At night, the edge of the forest was still loud, as bugs, bats, and birds all tried to mate with or eat one another. Darya knew those noises well, though. Different ones would stand out.

Her horse, placid and plump, continued munching nearby leaves as Emeth spoke to the owl again. "Come this way when you see them." Another wave of the hand indicated the direction they'd come. "Big stone place. Find a person. They'll find me."

With her free hand, she stroked the owl gently on top of its head. The multicolored eyes blinked in contentment, and the bond that made the animals remember her request set itself. Darya had seen the same process with a badger and a fox already that night.

As the owl flew off, she said, "Pity you can't get them to fight for us."

"If there were wolves or bears nearer here, I might," said Emeth, with no trace now of her earlier teasing, "or if we met a greycat by chance and it didn't kill us before I could talk. But they won't come to my call, and the smaller creatures will hide from anything as large as the Twisted, not fight."

"Smart of them," said Darya.

"If you only think about the moment. Now," and her voice dropped, became whuffly and braying, *"everyone stand still and be quiet."*

The horses froze. Darya froze. Emeth was silent as far as human ears went, but she threw her head back in the pose of one calling out, with her mouth open wide, and Darya saw the muscles of her throat moving.

She stopped and sat upright. Darya began to speak, but Emeth held up a hand, and that was when Darya heard scores of small wings flapping above them. She tilted her own head up and saw the colony of bats just as it descended.

They perched on any and all convenient surfaces. That meant Darya too. Tiny claws clung to her sleeves, her boots, and her hair. She looked sideways into a black-velvet face with tiny eyes. Individually, the bats were cute, which didn't keep her from feeling like a statue in the middle of pigeons. Her horse, which didn't care anything about cuteness or missions, was shifting uneasily beneath her as Emeth's instructions struggled with its instincts.

Talk fast, Darya thought at her friend.

━━━━━

"The Order has done well under your guidance," said Amris, "though I never expected that guidance to be so lastingly personal."

Gerant chuckled inside his head. After the initial

melancholy had passed, it had done them both good to speak of his life after the storms, though they'd avoided the most immediate aftermath. Instead, they'd talked of the politics of mages and the struggles with gardening, once the weather had shifted, and over an hour had relaxed into the comfortable conversation Amris had once known well.

It would have been better to have such conversation with Gerant draped over him, his breath warm and his heartbeat soothing, but that absence didn't hurt as much as it had five days or so back. This was the way they were now, and it was better than many found after a war.

None of us did, at first. I can't take credit for the idea either—that was Ayleen. Do you remember her? She was a tall lady, and I believe her hair was still red when you left, though it went gray very quickly. Extremely fond of dogs.

Amris called to mind a tall, spare figure in dark robes, frequently present alongside a cup of tea and a tray of pastries when he'd come home from training. Once, she'd arranged the pastries in a half circle to make some point to Gerant, with a lemon scone as the focal point.

He wondered if anyone made lemon scones anymore. Or tea.

He'd liked the dogs. He supposed he'd liked Ayleen, too, though they'd had little in common aside from that.

She focused on the properties of rocks and metals, as a rule, and she always had more than a slight penchant for necromancy. All ethical, of course—she thought about bringing back one of her dogs, she said, but she decided they had bad enough breath when they lived.

"Practical lady," Amris said, laughing.

I do seem to find their company, don't I? Though Darya's practicality takes very different forms.

"She'd be a strange sort of wizard, or scholar." It was difficult to be careful while sounding as though he wasn't. "That's no slight to her intelligence, of course, but she seems ill-disposed toward theory—toward much that doesn't progress in one direction or another, in fact."

True. Though she's excellent at stillness to a purpose—well, you've seen her hunting.

"Yes, with a variety of prey." He thought of her descent, arrow-like, onto the korvin's back, prevented his mind from going on to their encounter at the stream, and ended up remembering the fire in her face when she'd spoken of her bond to Gerant. "It's well that the two of you found each other, and not only for my sake. She cares a great deal for you."

I'm very fond of her as well. As I said, I seem to have a taste for the ridiculous and valiant.

While Amris was laughing, the door opened, and Olvir stepped inside. His earnest face turned immediately perplexed at the sight of his companion laughing in an empty room, a Sentinel's sword on his lap, and he started to step backward. "Apologies for the intrusion."

"No, no. It's your room too. Er—"

By all means, tell the poor lad. Before he thinks you've cracked under the strain, ideally.

"You know, do you not, about the Sentinels and their swords?"

"The spirits?" Olvir asked. He closed the door and

crossed to his bed, and Amris became gladder that he'd insisted the younger man stay. He looked pale and drawn, and his hair was plastered to his head with sweat. The day had been hard on them all, and the knight might have gotten the worst of the training—or pushed himself deliberately to avoid thinking.

Amris had done as much, in his time. "Aye, just so," he said. "Well, the spirit in Darya's sword is my lover. Or was." He made a face. "There's…some difficulty about describing it. Beloved, still, and always, but—"

"But he's a spirit in a sword," Olvir finished. "And unless I'm in error, that makes you considerably older than you appear."

"True, in a fashion." Briefly, Amris sketched the situation and was more than a little surprised by Olvir's relative lack of astonishment.

That must have shown, for Olvir gave a slight, sad smile and a shrug of his broad shoulders. "Thyran's returning, sir. Once I've got my mouth around that, any news after is easy to swallow. Besides, it's not the first oddness I've had close at hand."

"Ah, I should have expected as much from a knight," said Amris, and laughed. "Still, it's a great comedown for me as a figure of mystery and excitement."

There's nobody like Tinival's servants for keeping you honest, after all, Gerant pointed out.

Chapter 29

AN IMPORTANT THING TO KEEP IN MIND, GERANT SAID to Darya, and Darya said to the small audience in the mage's tower, *is the physical enhancements of the twisted-men leave scars, magically speaking, or holes. Their flesh is far harder to affect than yours or—well, than mine some forty years ago.* He laughed, Darya grinned, and the mages produced a couple of smiles between them.

The army wizard was a small person with bronze skin and a cap of dark hair, close cut to their skull in the style a lot of wizards sported; working around candles did that. By their side was the square-built old midwife who, Hallis had told Darya, apparently was known for a side trade in fortune-telling, good-luck charms, weather-witchery, and maybe the occasional curse, though nobody had come right out and said that. Third in the line was a gawky, spotty, towheaded lad, with a squint that spoke of nearsightedness and ink-stained fingers from writing: an apprentice with no master, just a lot of old books and experiments in his father's barn.

Other than what the gods might do for their servants and the Sentinels might manage in partnership with their swords, those three mages were all the magical power at Oakford's command, outside of healing.

All of them watched Darya with varying degrees of awe and unease, as they'd done from the start. It was well

known the Sentinels kept the dead in their swords—
which dead, and how dead they had to be beforehand, was
the subject of youthful rumor and parental threat—but
hearing the proof was new. So far, Tebengri, with their
military background, had taken it the most calmly of the
three. Gleda eyed Darya as though she were a good hunting dog that still might go for a hand at any moment, and
young Eagan gazed at her with all the curious wonder he
probably brought to pickled young mermaids and stuffed
gryphons.

The smiles might show they were following the lecture, if they hadn't just been responding to her expression.

But their spirits are more vulnerable, Gerant went on,
and thus so did Darya. *A bolt of lightning or an aetherstrike
might leave them still standing, but it is possible to exploit
one of the holes and yank their spirits outward into the
earthly astral. That will leave the body disoriented, at least,
and if you can sever the connection, they may both collapse.
It is, however, very individual work and perhaps best used on
their officers, such as they have.*

"Ma'am...sir?" Gleda asked, gaze moving uncertainly
between Darya's face and the gem on her sword. "What
about striking at their minds?"

*Good question. Possible, possibly effective, but very dan-
gerous. I have seen twistedmen made to turn on their foes, or
groups to fall to their knees from phantom pain—but getting to that point means touching their minds, and that's not
always the sort of contact a mage can stand and retain their
own wits.*

"I'd think not," said Tebengri, the wizard with the most

experience with Thyran's monsters. They grimaced, as if at a memory. "Better to focus defensively, then. Alroy will already be strengthening the walls, unless he and Hallis have both lost all sense, and there's not much we can do directly there. I'd wager the three of us can prepare the field beyond, though—gods know there are enough rocks and branches there normally—and start the long-term encouragement of rain and fog. That will help with the walls, too, and we might be able to get a few more barrels of water out of it."

"Is that important, your honor?" Eagan asked.

"Most important of all," Tebengri said. "Hunger and thirst are the chief weapons of any siege—especially since I doubt the forces coming will manage treachery."

Hunger, thirst, and gold, Amris used to say, Gerant added to Darya, and then added, *and likely is saying now.*

───────

"They likely won't have gold," said Amris, facing the ranks. Four hundred eyes stared back at him, set in faces of all genders and ages from fifteen to fifty, and that moment was another that might well have come from his past. Some, particularly among the career soldiers, watched him with suspicion: Who was this stranger from outside the ranks, and why was he leading the training that day? Others, particularly among the rawer recruits, had more wonder in their expressions. Rumors had already started about Amris's origins, and not all were far from the truth.

All were afraid, and all tried not to show it.

Amris went on. "And you all would know better than to take it, if they did, or any other bribe they might offer. If you've not read the histories, I'm sure you've talked to those who have. You know what they'll do if we don't stop them here, how much wealth will avail you, and how long any safety they offer you or yours will last." He searched the crowd, focusing on faces at random for just long enough to make them flinch, then moving on. "If you know not, there are many who can tell you. Believe them."

The crowd was quiet. Thyran had done this much of their work for them. No human would betray the fortress, save perhaps one whose mind was a match in hatred for Thyran's itself.

Hallis stepped forward. "We're already working against hunger and thirst. The well's in no danger of going dry, thank the gods, and we have some stores here already. When you're not trading or getting the walls ready, you'll be stretching your muscles by lifting and carrying, or you'll practice your knifework butchering pigs or goats, or you'll help build rain barrels. No job's below us. Not any of us. The civilians are gone, and there's no rank here that isn't the army's or the gods'."

As many in the crowd glanced—some subtly, some failing at subtlety, some not bothering—at Amris, Hallis added, "For orders, Amris, like the Sentinels, the mages, and the priests, is a first lieutenant. They're not regulars in this army, but they're experts about what we're facing, and you'll listen to them unless I say otherwise."

Some muttering arose from that announcement, but less than Amris had feared. Classing him with the mages and priests had put him on known ground. He saluted Hallis, right hand pressed in a fist against his shoulder, and then did the same to the assembled soldiers. The woman who'd gotten directions from him was there in the crowd, he saw, and so were Isen and two of his stable hands.

"First watch," Hallis went on, "recruit training, groups of twenty." He rattled off a list of five names—the officers who'd supervise. "Stay here. Second and third cohort, you're with me. We'll get the landscape out front ready for our guests. Fourth and fifth, you join Amris on the walls. Outer, then inner. Dismissed."

He strode off, and forty soldiers broke from the crowd to follow him. Amris went the opposite direction, found the pile of prepared supplies, and picked up one of the great barrels. It reeked of fat, and the weight was almost more than he could handle. That was all right—that was, indeed, encouraging.

"Two to a barrel," he told his troops, "and any empty-handed when those are gone, pick up spears or arrows. The Dark Lady gave us fire and steel, and it's best we be generous with Her gifts."

Chapter 30

ON OTHER NIGHTS, NIGHTS THAT NOW SEEMED A HUN-
dred years ago themselves, Darya had sat in the Lonely
Wolf's taproom. The other patrons had mostly given
her wide berth, but sometimes she'd gone with another
Sentinel, or soldiers worldly enough to approach friend-
ship, and often there'd been a minstrel, though the skill of
those had ranged widely. There'd always been spirits, and
their quality had been a constant—rougher than you got
closer to the cities, but clean and sharp.

The spirits were gone, taken up to the walls in case their
defenders needed to start fires or doled out to the herbalists in case they ran out of salves for wounds. Most of the
furnishings had vanished too. The owners had taken the
curtains, the candlesticks, and the flatware. The army had
grabbed the tables and chairs, moving them into the stack
of potential emergency firewood. War stripped buildings
with the efficiency and thoroughness of a good hunter
butchering prey.

But beer was actually useful for very little in war, and old
Colton hadn't been able to get the barrels onto his wagon. His
son was in the army and had issued a general invitation—"If
we empty the kegs, we can use 'em for other things, so we'd
truly be doing a good deed, aye?"—and so Darya, Branwyn,
and Katrine sat cross-legged on the tavern floor, soldiers
around them and crude clay mugs of beer in their hands.

"It's a bit sad, isn't it?" said Katrine, looking around at the bare walls.

"We've all drunk in worse places," said Darya.

"But we didn't remember any of them being better," Katrine replied. "Or I didn't."

"No," said Darya, "no, you're right," and thought of Amris's face as the two of them had walked through Klaishil. She sighed, not wanting him in her mind, and looked around at the local talent.

There was a slim honey-blond man by the door who looked a little like an assassin, which had its appeal. A new recruit across the room was older than most of his fellows and had an impressive mane of black hair and a damned fine chest, from what she'd noticed walking by him at training. The knight was a strapping young man, although she'd always found Tinival's sworn irksomely earnest.

She wasn't without choices.

That might make a good experiment, if we have time, Gerant said, completely confusing Darya. She looked blankly from her waist to the other Sentinels, and Katrine, reading her face, laughed.

"Those of us with our minds above our belts," she explained, "were talking about whether two of us could—link?—as you did with Amris. It'd be a four-way tie, of course, since we'd both have soulswords."

"Yathana says she's willing to try," Branwyn added, "but she'll need detailed instructions, since she…ah, never was much of a scholar." By the other woman's face, Darya thought that was probably a tactful translation.

Gerant laughed in her head. *I've never minded an opportunity to lecture. Just ask...ah, Amris!*

Darya wasn't sure if he'd truly seen the figure across the room before she had, or if she'd just avoided the knowledge. Once Gerant spoke, though, the words locked her focus into place. Every detail about Amris stood out: his tousled hair, his straight back and slim hips, the faint but gentle smile on his lips as he spoke to Olvir. It wasn't just heat that ran through Darya's body at the sight, but pure sensation, awareness as bright as sunlight on her first steps outside a ruin.

She wished she were alone so that she could start swearing.

———

"Ah," said Olvir, helpfully, "there's the Sentinel who brought you in!" He raised a hand, which, given his height, was hard to miss, and beamed a far-too-engaging smile in Darya's direction.

She was sitting on the floor with two of the other Sentinels, long legs folded neatly beneath her and a mug of beer in one hand. As Amris turned to regard her, she laughed at some comment and waved her free hand, dismissing the suggestion or the speaker. The firelight flickered over her, and the shadows welcomed her when it faded.

Amris couldn't have avoided her, not without rousing Olvir's questions or offending Gerant—and he didn't really want to do so, only thought he should. He was old enough to know the difference.

However the top of his mind might protest, whatever he knew of temptation and risk, he couldn't be displeased that Olvir had called his attention to Darya, nor hers to him. When she turned, not only Amris's body leapt to attention—though that was certainly a factor, and one which made him glad he still wore armor and a long tunic.

He raised his own hand and thought resolutely of troop numbers and defensive preparations. The soldiers in the tavern laughed. A few of them had already started singing, and a few others were groping in corners, seizing what might be their last few hours with vigor.

Amris looked away quickly and let Olvir lead him over to the group of Sentinels.

"You haven't died from recruits yet?" asked Darya, with a determined smile. "Good to see it."

"In my day, I've trained far worse. And in my turn, I'm glad to see that you returned safely from your mission. I hope the same holds true for your friend."

"Oh, Emeth's fine, thank you," said Katrine, "only she has to wait in our room in case any of her creatures return with warning. She's far from thrilled about it, but I've promised we'll drink with her later."

"It's a noble sacrifice," said Olvir, and Amris introduced him around. He bowed low over the Sentinels' hands and smiled earnestly.

He is egregiously adorable, said Gerant, laughing. *If he weren't a knight and they weren't Sentinels, at least half of them would be carrying his picture next to their hearts.*

"You're not wrong," said Amris, thinking of the way

most of the women and some of the men in his squad had watched when Olvir came up the lines. "And I now have many questions I can't ask, you know."

I wasn't thinking of that, but it is an unexpected gift.

Amris laughed, started to make a face, and then caught himself.

"It must be a very strange situation," said Branwyn. "We're all used to it, and it's just one more odd thing about us where everyone else is concerned."

"You do look normal otherwise," Darya added.

"My thanks," he said, with a slight sardonic bow, and then, to Branwyn, "It is, but little about this isn't—for all of us, I expect."

"Is that how you're climbing the ladder?" asked a slurred male voice from behind Amris.

Olvir turned his head toward the speaker, and the three Sentinels, all in a position to see without turning, looked up: Katrine with bland curiosity, Branwyn with her eyebrows arched in quiet challenge, and Darya with tightened lips and narrowed eyes. Amris himself didn't move. The drunk was too far away to be an immediate threat, and ignoring him might yet prove fruitful. He shook his head slightly at his friends.

They *were* his friends, albeit on very short notice— Branwyn and Katrine on the strength of only a few conversations, words passed when Katrine left the chapel as he was entering, or when Branwyn mended armor on the manor steps. Still they'd welcomed him, and if some of that had been for Darya's sake, or Gerant's, he couldn't be unhappy about that either. In the barren taproom,

Amris felt an unexpected tie binding him to that time and place, one which was more than necessity, and he smiled because of it.

"Oh, you think that's funny?"

Ah, the drunkard. He was closer, and there was muttering behind him. Amris sighed and turned. He hadn't even had the chance to sit.

The speaker was a washed-out blond man with an aristocratic lift to his chin—and lack thereof—that went with his voice, as well as a silk doublet and a fine linen shirt. Jewels shone in the sword at his hip, but Amris would never have mistaken him for a Sentinel, even without knowing there were only four in the keep. His friends, two women and three men, were also dressed richly. All wore sashes of rank.

"I assure you," said Amris, "I desire no promotion. Should we leave this alive, I'll eagerly relinquish my rank."

What he'd do then, he had no idea, but that was a matter for another day.

"Is that what you told Hallis? Or did you *tell* him anything?"

"Sirrah," said Amris, "that is flagrant disrespect to your commander. I advise you to rethink both your words and your state of mind, and do so speedily. We have far worse things to face than one another."

"So *you* say," said one of the women.

"Yes." Amris regarded them one at a time. They didn't want to believe what was coming. He was the one who'd brought the news. "I will not fight you, if that's what you hope to achieve. Insinuate anything else about

Commander Hallis, and I'll see to it that you spend tomorrow morning doing the worst work in the keep, ale-head or no. That's all."

"And," Darya added, "he's not the only one who's saying it. Any of it." She hadn't yet stood, but a coiled-spring tension in her body suggested she could be on her feet with blinding speed.

"Ah, yes"—another of the men chimed in—"*you* witnessed the invasion. It's an emergency. So your gang of aberrations put your tool in place instead of those born to the responsibility."

"Says a fellow who couldn't put his tool in place with both hands and a diagram." Branwyn's voice was low, almost seductive, and a smile played over her lips. "Or that's the word in Affiran."

The man flushed an ugly red and made a move toward the knife at his belt, but Olvir put a hand on his arm. "This will do none of us any good," he said, and touched the silver crescent around his neck. "As a servant of the Silver Wind, I give you my word they speak truly, no matter how much any of us might wish otherwise."

"Doesn't make it all right, stealing a man's command," the first man muttered, but his friend stopped reaching for his knife, and all of them dropped their gazes when Olvir kept looking at them. His eyes were as mild and brown as ever, but Amris felt a presence behind them, one miles and years beyond the peaceable young man who shared his room, and yet not completely separate from him.

Amris sensed the Sentinels and Olvir watching him,

waiting to follow his lead. It wasn't a matter of direct command—they, of everyone in the room, were least obliged to take his orders, and they, unlike everyone else in the room, might actually know more about their foes in some aspects than he did—but he had led men more times, and in greater numbers, than any of them. This was his terrain, and they would follow him as he'd followed Darya through the forest and into the underbrush.

"Take heart, then," said Amris, with as easy a smile as he could muster. "Many an officer doesn't survive battle. You may yet climb to glory over my body."

"Morbid bastard," said the woman who'd been quiet until then. "Come on, Brynart. There's still a fair amount of beer to go around."

They headed over to the barrels, making a good show of walking slowly and never looking back. Amris took that into account and sat down anyhow.

"She's not entirely wrong," said Branwyn. "Though I'm sure your parents were very respectable."

"They were wed when I was born, at any rate," Amris said. His oldest brother had been a little "early," but still well within the realm of legitimacy, especially for farming folk.

"Prolapsed arsehole," said Darya. "Wouldn't have blamed you for breaking his nose."

Yes, you would, said Gerant. *You'd have said Amris should start with the kneecaps.*

"Or the bollocks. Yeah." The other Sentinels, clearly guessing the gist of things, laughed only a second or two after Darya.

"We need every able, warm body we can get," Amris replied, "in as good condition as we can be. And that"—he gestured toward the nobleman and his friends—"was as much nerves as it was temper. Once we've had a battle or two, they'll most likely settle down."

"I think," said Katrine, "that we should all have another drink or two."

They did. There wasn't enough to get most people really drunk—Darya suspected that the inbred shitpile and his friends had been using it as an excuse more than anything—and Sentinels held their beer well, anyhow, she more than most. Still, after a mug or two, she was pleasantly relaxed and lounging on the floor, resting her weight on alternate elbows and absently cursing the lack of cushions.

"There were very nearly wars over flowers," Amris said. He sat up straight, even after beer, with his legs folded neatly under him and his hands light on the firm length of his thighs, which Darya was trying not to notice. "When first I found employment in Heliodar, it was with a noblewoman—guarding her prize roses by night, lest her rival send agents to steal cuttings."

"Sounds like a euphemism," said Branwyn. "Were the lady's roses lovely and fragrant?"

The crowd laughed—and it *was* a crowd, if a small one. Their circle had opened up, letting in soldiers. Tebengri's head was in Branwyn's lap, where the Sentinel idly played with their hair—*Good thing*, Darya thought, *that army mages get their own quarters*. Katrine and Emeth were enough to deal with secondhand.

Of the men she could have had without guilt, both

of the appealing ones had vanished, one into the darkness of the bar, and the other off with a pleasantly curvy redhead. Darya had seen him go when the potential fight had died down, but she didn't want to cut in on anyone else's good time—assuming she could have managed it. The blond man had been gone entirely.

That left Olvir, who was listening to Amris and laughing like the rest of them were, as though he wasn't freakish and god-touched. So was Darya—but stopping a fight with a word was, somehow, far more unnerving than killing things.

"They were," said Amris, "but the lady herself was well into her eighties and not a pleasant woman."

Her niece, however... Gerant added, making Darya laugh harder than the others.

Amris's attention fell on her again, as it had done several times that evening, and he smiled as though he knew exactly what Gerant was saying to her. She grinned back and lifted her empty glass, trying to act as if her whole body hadn't responded to the brief glance.

She was ridiculous.

Conversation broke out in spots again, the crowd dividing, and Amris rose from its center. He seemed like he was going for more beer, but on the way he diverted to talk with a young blond woman and the stocky man who had his arm around her. Darya watched him nod, watched them both stand a little straighter at whatever he'd said, saw the flash of his smile.

"This sort of thing is his ruin," she said, mostly to herself.

"Is it so hard on him?" Olvir asked, frowning. "He hides it well, if so."

"Oh. No, not like that. But"—she sighed—"I'm better in cities that were than cities that are. Climbing buildings, looting, breaking and entering. This"—Darya waved a hand that only wavered a little—"this is to him what that is to me. His...his place. His gift."

Oh, yes, said Gerant, in a voice that would have gone with a wistful smile, if he'd had a body. But then, if he'd had a body, the smile wouldn't have had to be wistful.

"Some people wield weapons, and some wield people, but he does both."

Darya peered at Olvir. "Are you drunk at *all*?"

"No, not really."

The beer was gone. In twos and threes, or fives or sixes for those with little carnal luck or inclination, the soldiers had begun drifting away toward the barracks, or the converted houses that served the same function for the new recruits. Darya looked back toward Branwyn and Tebengri and found them both gone.

Amris stepped back from the small group he'd gone on to talk with after the young couple. A few of them bowed. One, barely fifteen at best, wobbled on the way up. His older comrade caught him by the arm. He flushed and darted a glance at Amris, who put on a good show of not seeing a thing.

Maybe we should have had the younger ones swear their age to Tinival, Gerant said.

"Too late now," said Darya.

"We'll try to keep the youngest behind the lines," said

Olvir, following Darya's gaze and making a decent guess. "They can bring fresh supplies or carry the wounded. It won't keep them completely safe, but it'll help."

"If we can keep them out of the front."

"That's part of the duties of command," said Amris, drawing back into speaking range. "And as with Byrnart and his friends, many of the young will likely change their thoughts once the first wave breaks over us. 'Judge no metal until it sees the forge,' they said in my land."

"Can't argue with that," said Darya, touching Gerant's hilt lightly.

Amris laughed. "I hadn't intended the new meaning, but it applies. And I think, to change the subject, that I should be going. Those who're left will want to celebrate without too much authority to dampen the mood, and there's no danger of them needing it."

"We both should, then," said Olvir.

"All of us." Darya stood. If Amris was too much in command and Olvir was too much a servant of the gods, she was too much a... What had Byrnart's friend called her? Aberration? It had more syllables than the names she usually heard from drunk men, she'd give him that. "Besides, I *think* my room is quiet by now."

Chapter 31

OUTSIDE THE DOORS, THE AIR WAS GENTLE AND JUST A touch cool: almost high summer. In the forest, the night would smell cool and green. The fort mostly smelled of woodsmoke and horse dung, but that wasn't unpleasant in its way. Side by side, the three of them—four, really—walked up the road toward the inner gates and the fortress beyond.

All three had been in the field for a while, and none was particularly drunk, so the young man who approached from one of the houses didn't catch any of them by surprise. Darya noted him as a few essentials: short, square, no unsheathed weapons, not staggering or singing. That was all she needed to know, though she kept a wary eye on him as he approached. Men could always surprise you.

This one bowed to Olvir. "I'm sorry to interrupt, your honor," he said, "and I hope I'm not inconveniencing you. Only, my friends and I were hoping you had time to say a few words over us tonight. In case we don't have a chance for it when the moment comes, I mean."

It was the sort of request that would have made Darya suspect a trap—but she wasn't the kind of person anyone would ask for spiritual aid to begin with. Olvir, who'd had years of practice with lies and truth, simply smiled. "It would be my honor," he said, and bowed to Darya and Amris. "Please excuse me."

"Of course," said Amris, and Darya nodded right along with him.

No soldier would dare ambush one of Tinival's servants right before a battle, Gerant said as Olvir walked away with the man.

"Might be leading him off," Darya muttered, once they were far enough away that her voice wouldn't carry, "so they can try and ambush *us.*"

"In which case, good luck to them," Amris said. They fell into an easy pace with each other, footsteps crunching an unhurried rhythm in the dirt. His voice was a deep, smooth melody to that beat. "I doubt any would really try it in such close quarters, where all would know— but if they did, I have no worries that we'd come out the victors."

"Especially since they're too drunk to be subtle," Darya said as they passed through the inner gates. A line of a song floated out from a window in the barracks, slurred but enthusiastic:

"The captain's daughter, she was there, and had them all in fits…"

"That," she added, "sounds like someone's been keeping a personal flask back. The herbalists wouldn't be pleased, if they knew."

Not necessarily, Gerant said. *Two pints of good ale will make more soldiers merry than they like to think— particularly the young ones.*

"Nerves, too, are their own kind of liquor," said Amris.

"Oh, it's all the ladies back," the singer went on, *"with their arses to the wall—"*

There were deep voices in the chorus, and the high ones could as easily have been women as young men, but it was hard to tell. And yes, there was an edge to it that ale or even spirits couldn't explain—the high spirits that came with being desperate not to think.

"I'm glad you're here," she said. She wasn't too drunk to look at Amris while she walked straight ahead, and the sight of him, thoughtful and clear-eyed despite the ale and with no reforging to account for it, was comforting. "It's not just that you know what we're facing out there, but you know how these things work, and what they feel like. I don't think anyone else here does. I know I don't."

The keep's staircase was more or less deserted. The barracks were on the lower floor, and Hallis and the others were in either their rooms or someone else's. Dark—there were no servants to change the torches, and the torches themselves might be more useful elsewhere—and empty, it seemed like another ruin to Darya in that moment.

"It does me good," Amris said, "to know you think it worth your while to have brought me back."

He was joking, with his eyes crinkling at the corners and his mouth almost straight but curling up just enough to give it away. Darya laughed under her breath. "Oh, definitely," she said, "you're at least as good as a candlestick or a mirror. Better, as I don't have to carry you."

"Only wait a few days. Battle changes any number of things."

"So you've said."

At the top of the stairs, Amris paused and turned to

face her, no longer joking. "You would've defended me back there," he said, "and I thank you for it."

"Of course," and the next words, the lighthearted ones about him being useful, or Gerant killing her otherwise, wouldn't come. He looked too grave standing there, and there was a softer expression on the clean-cut planes of his face than Darya was used to seeing from him. She'd found his presence comforting, but he'd been actively comforting people for the last two days, and he knew enough to fear more than most of them. "Any of us there would, you know. Branwyn. Even Emeth, if she'd been present. Olvir, certainly—Olvir *did*."

"Olvir likes me well enough, but he has a duty to his god. And I thank him for it, but—" Amris shrugged. "It meant a great deal to have people angry on my behalf. Selfish as that may have been."

"I think you're allowed a little selfishness, considering," said Darya.

He smiled, and it was the loneliest thing she'd ever seen. Impulse, ale, and her own set of nerves drove her forward and reached her hand up: his hair was too short to push back, but she stroked her fingers through the dark curls and down the side of his face. "This is a hell of a thing for you, Amris. Even aside from us all maybe dying. I–I wish I could make it easier."

"You do." He spoke quietly, and his voice was thick. Beneath her palm, his face was warm and faintly rough with stubble.

Gerant was silent, and the sword at Darya's hip was a weight in her mind as well. She dropped her hand.

Already, she wasn't sure how much she should apologize. So far, it had been just a gesture, not much more than what might pass between close friends, but she wanted too much more to escape guilt. "Sleep well," she said. "We'll all need it."

Spearpoints skewered hay bales, left holes as the soldiers pulled their weapons back and thrust forward again. Amris walked up and down the lines, repositioning a shoulder or nudging a foot back, calling out verbal advice, and clapping his hands between times to set the pace. Sweat dripped down his face. It hadn't been very long since his own morning training, facing off against Olvir and Emeth in the yard, and he hadn't given himself time to rest.

He had to keep distracted, after all.

Amris had never been one to take himself in hand in shared quarters. The previous night, not knowing when Olvir would walk in, he'd set his teeth and ignored the heavy fullness in his groin when Darya had left him. She'd meant the touch for kindness, no more, but he'd sprung to life nonetheless, and all of his possible partners had long departed—

—and he couldn't truly turn to any of them, regardless. He was the commander to most. A few of those left were to his taste and might be amenable, but as Amris took to his solitary bed, he'd realized that a night with any of them would only be a substitute for what he really

wanted—a shabby trick to play on a bedmate who didn't
realize it, and not a situation to enter in limited company,
even if he'd wanted to explain his situation.

The morning, thus, had been an exercise in working
himself ragged, to the point where Emeth had raised her
eyebrows at the end of the bout and advised him to save a
bit of himself for the Twisted. She was right. Amris wished
otherwise, and he could justify more effort when training, for his exhaustion mattered less than the skill of fifty
others.

Working them too hard would be worse, though, so
he brought the exercise to a halt with no hint of the reluctance he felt. Amris dismissed the men, turned to find
the nearest butt of water, and felt Darya's approach.

The spell was going to be the death of him—a more
pleasant one, granted, than Thyran or his troops probably had in mind.

He lifted his head from the water, turned, and saw
her approaching, once more in green and with her hair
down around her shoulders. As always when she had a
clear destination in mind, she moved like a fired arrow,
all purpose and speed, but as she got closer, Amris felt
her trepidation. "Is all well?" he asked as soon as she was
close enough.

"Relatively speaking," said Darya. There was color in
her cheeks that her walk didn't account for. The bond
didn't tell Amris all of what she felt, and he didn't want to
pry, but he sensed that not all of her discomfort was bad.
Some was embarrassment, some the effort not to hope.

Amris brushed water from his face and ran a hand

through his hair to push it back. He kept silent, not wanting to rush her.

"Gerant and I were talking." She was withdrawing her sword, still in its sheath, as she spoke. "This morning. Had some time alone."

I'll handle the rest. Gerant spoke too quickly for Amris to get much sense of his emotions.

Set against the background of Thyran's invasion, being nervous about what Gerant might have deduced and how he might react left Amris more than a touch abashed. That didn't make him any calmer. Facing Thyran again had been endurable because Gerant was with him too. If that was about to change—

He took the sword automatically as Darya handed it over. "I'll be mending armor in my room after dinner," she said, and swallowed. "If you want to talk. After."

Without another word, she turned on her heel and left.

Amris watched her, bracing himself for whatever Gerant had to say.

You are both—the words came in a tone of far more teasing affection than he ever could have hoped for—*the most idiotic creatures I've ever met, particularly for your advanced age.*

———

All the gods be praised, Amris had a free hour. "How do you mean?" he asked under his breath, making his way quickly toward his room.

I mean, Gerant replied, *that I don't need eyes to see that*

*the two of you want each other. And I'm under the impression
that you've refrained from acting on it, so far, for my sake.*

"Ah," said Amris. He would have elaborated, had he
not been on the stairs. In truth, he knew not exactly which
of several possible responses he'd have chosen, so there
might have been good fortune in his enforced silence.

Gerant certainly seemed to think so, for he went on,
with a tone of voice that, in life, had always accompanied
an elaborate roll of his blue eyes. *Very chivalrous, I assure
you. Very loyal. Top marks for both qualities. But I have no
body, in case you haven't noticed, and as Emeth observed,
you're in remarkable form for a man who's seen more than
a century. Did you truly think I expected you to live the next
forty years as a eunuch?*

"There's no certainty that I'll live forty years more,"
Amris muttered as he hurried down the hall, "and I could
at least choose a less... Well, a person you didn't know so
well. One you weren't linked to, at minimum."

The room was blessedly empty, Olvir being off at his
own duties. Amris made it to his bed and then let his
knees give out as Gerant went on, tender now rather than
hectoring.

*But it would be worse that way, I think, for me to be so
cut off from a part of your life. Not that I would be present, necessarily,* he added as Amris lifted his eyebrows.
*I've been accustomed to depart when my bearers take lovers,
among other things. Still, if it were you and her, it would be
two people I care about. Two whom I love, each in your own
fashion. I'd be part of both of your lives.*

Amris blinked down at his hands. Mechanically, he

began to strip off his armor. He was likely overheated, in addition to everything else.

I'm not saying I would've suggested it on my own. Matchmaking never had any appeal for me.

"So I recall," said Amris, with a hoarse laugh. "I can't promise we would remain lovers, you know, even if we became so involved."

Gods, I wouldn't want you to promise anything—not on the strength of a week's acquaintance, even such an eventful week. That kind of promise is asking for trouble at the best of times. But I know you both. If you part, you'll part as adults, and if nothing else, that'll be far better than having the two of you walking around like storm clouds of thwarted passion.

"That's quite a turn of phrase."

Katrine reads bad poetry aloud.

Without the armor, with his neck and arms exposed to the air and the rest of him covered only by a thin tunic, Amris felt invisible iron bands loosen from around his chest—or perhaps that was the conversation.

"You… Truly, it won't hurt you?"

No, said Gerant. As before, he sounded kind and loving, but there was a distance in his voice now that there hadn't been before. It wasn't unspoken pain— Amris knew the sound of that—but a fundamental difference between the spirit and the cheerful young scholar who'd been his lover. Between the spirit, perhaps, and any mortal. *Once… I don't know any longer what I might have felt, once. But I had my life, beloved. It was a good life, despite everything. I loved some wonderful people, and I did a few things I'm proud of.*

"Thank you," Amris said, his throat sore. "You mean you're content?"

In part. In part, I mean that life is over for me. Living is over for me. I love you, I'll always love you, but— Living, Gerant would have thrown up his hands then. *It's not being uninterested in the physical, or not wanting a companion, not the way a living man might be.*

Amris nodded. He'd known a few such people in his time. "Then—"

I'm further away, even when I'm with you or her, even when I'm observing, and not only because of the vessel. I can't see the future, but a part of me is always in it. It— He sighed. *It doesn't go into words. I promise, I'm not hurt, nor will I be.* Gerant paused. *And though I hate to think it, you're right. You may not have forty more years. Nor might she.*

"You counsel decisive action?"

I counsel a bath first, but yes.

Unable to take Gerant in his arms, Amris settled for projecting the feeling of warmth as strongly as he could, hoping it came through the link. "I would have died happily as an old man with you, if things had been different."

And I you. But happiness is never only one thing. All three of us might find it in another form, here and now.

Chapter 32

BLOOD NEVER REALLY CAME OUT OF LEATHER. DARYA didn't know much about laundering clothes, but since she'd entered the field, she'd been able to count her kills by the marks on each doublet, until they got too torn up to mend. The one she'd worn to Klaishil wasn't there yet, though the rents across the chest weren't helping. She squinted, punched another hole with her awl, and tried not to speculate about Amris.

She'd nearly choked on her ale when Gerant had spoken up that morning: *You really should take him to bed and be done with it.* Darya had started to apologize then—if she couldn't control her feelings, she could have at least been less obvious about them—but Gerant had cut her off. *I mean every word of it, and I'm not being snide. Nor will I get my nose out of joint, particularly since I don't have one.*

The discussion that followed had left her stunned, and wanting to be glad but not daring to. Gerant was fine with her and Amris; that didn't mean Amris would be. What some people defined as loyalty was strange, and, hell, maybe knowing that she wasn't off-limits would kill any desire he'd had for her. Amris hadn't struck Darya as the type, but she was no great judge.

She drew a string of rawhide through the holes she'd made, careful not to yank it. The damned things snapped easily. The light was fading outside the window.

Amris was in the hall outside when she felt his presence. Darya put the armor aside quickly. If she tried to keep mending, she'd muck the whole thing up. That meant she had no way to look casual when he came in, but she didn't care. He could tell through the spell that her heart was racing, and she knew that his was.

Still, they stared at each other for a long time. The setting sun lit him from behind, and he became a tall, columnar shadow of a man, which made it easier to speak. "You talked to Gerant?"

"Yes. I gave him into Olvir's keeping. He said he'd no wish to intrude on our speech."

If it wasn't only Darya's imagination, Amris had hesitated a moment before saying "speech." He was unarmored, and his hair was wet. As the light shifted outside, she could see that his borrowed white shirt was almost transparent, with the shadow of dark hair visible beneath.

She swallowed and stood, mostly for the need to act. Lust was beginning to tighten her groin, but she didn't dare focus on it yet. This might be a rejection in person. "So…" In the end, she shrugged and retreated to the blunt speech she knew best. "I'm up for it if you are. No obligation."

In answer, he crossed the room and pulled her against his body, tight enough that she could feel every inch of his rigid cock. "Does this resemble any obligation you've heard of?"

Darya laughed, wound her arms around his neck, and kissed him.

═══════════

Long, wonderful moments passed before Amris lifted his head and looked down at the woman in his arms. She fit very well there, her breasts soft against his chest, her waist and back toned muscle beneath his splayed hands, her head just enough below his that he could pull back from kissing her and see the red flush on her pale cheeks, the darkness of her parted lips.

He made a sound in his throat without realizing it, a sigh of appreciation, and she smiled: hot, sweet, looking more intoxicated than she'd ever done the night before. "Well," said Darya, sliding the words out on a warm breath against Amris's neck, "consider the sentiment returned. With interest... Ahh."

Amris had lowered one of his hands, tracing a light trail down her spine to a spot just above her backside. He felt her shiver against him, and the rapid rise and fall of her chest. "Mmm," he agreed. "Just so."

In response, she brought her mouth to his again. As their lips met, Darya insinuated her own hands under the hem of his shirt. Her callused fingers were hot against his bare skin, her short nails providing just the right blend of sharpness and pressure when she dragged them up his stomach, and Amris groaned.

"Do we have the room for a while?" he managed to ask through the haze.

"Don't know." Darya punctuated the short sentence with a lick up his neck to the spot behind his jaw. "Don't care. They'll leave if they come in."

He ached for her, and gods knew it wouldn't have been the first time he'd taken his pleasure heedless of potential spectators, but still Amris hesitated. It had been a while—rank had its privileges—and even in the midst of desire, he had no wish to deprive anyone else of rest.

Darya circled her fingers around one nipple and added, "Always the wine cellar."

"Mmm—the—what?"

"Wine cellar."

"Explain," he said, inadvertently falling into the deep voice he used to command.

Darya shivered again, the motion mind-stopping when it meant her thighs trembled against his erection. "Yes, *sir*," she said with a grin. "Not much wine there now. But it's where the soldiers go to have a good time, if their mates are trying to sleep in the barracks or whatnot. If—"

At that point, she stopped talking. Given that Amris had taken her earlobe gently between his teeth and wound one hand into her hair, he would have been disappointed if she hadn't. "If?" he said nonetheless.

She laughed again, glorious as she'd been the first time she'd kissed him, and reached down to cup the pulsing ridge of his cock. "If you can make it that far."

"For that," Amris said, trying not to pant the words and failing, "I should carry you there over my shoulder." With an immense effort of will, he let her go and stepped back.

"I wouldn't try it," said Darya. She spun toward the door, then looked back over her shoulder at him. "You'll need your strength."

———————

Darya thought they made it down the stairs and into the kitchen with a bit of dignity—at least, compared to a number of other couples she'd seen or been part of. They didn't stop to kiss, and neither of them kept a hand on the other's arse. Nobody passing tried to talk to them, though, and nobody asked why they were both wearing cloaks, so Darya suspected a few conclusions were getting drawn.

She didn't care. Hunger was twisting between her legs, her breasts felt every minute motion of her shirt when she walked, and she would happily have taken Amris up against a wall like a drunken guard and a dairymaid in a joke. She resisted for his comfort, and because Hallis would likely have had her head for it afterward. That was all.

In the kitchen, she opened the small door downward to a narrow staircase that smelled of stone, wine, and old oak. There was no light, and she didn't care. Amris couldn't see in the dark, but he followed her with no hesitation, closing the door quickly behind them.

On that staircase, in the darkness, he followed closely enough that Darya felt the heat of his body behind her, and closely enough for her to smell the clean, sharp scent of his body fresh from the bath. She wanted to sprint forward and find the nearest stable surface, but she trusted her feet far less than usual.

Finally, after what felt like a week, they were at the bottom, surrounded by racks of casks and nothing else. Darya had already been undoing her cloak. As soon as her feet hit a flat surface, she cast it onto the floor, turned, and reached for the neck of Amris's.

"Trust," he said, catching her wrist gently in his off hand, "that I'm as prepared as you are. Not to mention eager."

With his other hand, he spread his own cloak down on top of hers, and the two of them descended in turn.

Darya had thought the first time would be quick and hard, and upstairs hadn't weighed against that impression, but once the darkness had closed in around them, it was like there was no time. She lay on her side, head pillowed on Amris's bicep and one leg twined around his waist, and nibbled up the side of his neck. Beneath her shirt, he toyed with her breast, cupping with his palm and then lightly tweaking the nipple until Darya gasped and squirmed.

It was all exploration down there, all mystery, even though the subject in general had held very few secrets for Darya since midway through her fifteenth year. She stroked the tense muscle of Amris's hips and thighs, savoring both the firmness beneath cloth and hand and the way he hissed and thrust against her, aware of every second as though it were new, and not only to them.

She was wet and open for him long before he slid her pants down over her hips and cupped her sex. When he slid one large finger into her, then another, she arched and groaned and begged for more—but there was none of the desperation of that point with other men, only sureness. By the end, Darya would have what she wanted. There was time to enjoy the journey.

As far as she could tell, Amris agreed. He hissed when she undid his laces and wrapped a hand around his straining cock, and her name left his lips like a prayer when she started to move her fingers, but *his* hands never stopped. The man had discipline, no question—but the extent of it, and the echoes of the spell around them, suggested that he felt the same confidence Darya did, the lack of any need to grasp or hurry.

Neither of them undressed more than they needed to—the air in the cellar had a chill edge to it. Amris's tunic grazed against Darya's thighs when he entered her, an additional point of delightful friction, and hers rucked up above her breasts. Her trousers were halfway down one leg and completely off the other, the one draped over Amris's hips so that he could thrust his full, thick length inside her slick passage.

Back arched, she looked straight into his face. His mouth was slightly open, his eyes half-lidded: the picture of a man in rapture, and it excited her further. Darya was the one who began to move, unable to contain the urge, and she was by far the first to go over the edge, in a steady ascent made wonderfully almost unbearable by the flexing of Amris's hips, the pressure of his fingers on her arse, and his mouth on one nipple, tongue teasing through wet cloth.

She let herself scream at the end. She so rarely got to do that, and this time, of all times, it felt right.

Once again Amris followed her lead. "Gods— Darya—you're so lovely, so—" and then a sound between a groan and a roar, one that almost echoed in the empty cellar while he jerked and pulsed inside her.

She almost wished it had. It was the sort of noise she could stand to hear for a while.

———————

Darya's eyes shone in the darkness. In all other regards, she was a shape: warm, firm, and comforting in the lassitude that followed physical enjoyment. Amris listened to her breath near his ear and felt her heartbeat against his chest. He wouldn't have traded the hard floor beneath him for a featherbed with anybody else living.

"Thank you," he said, running a hand slowly down her side and back.

In the dark, he couldn't see the lift of her eyebrows, but he knew it was there. "You're, um, welcome. But I don't think either of us meant it as a favor—unless I'm wrong."

"No, not at all. But thank you for speaking the offer. My courage might have failed me at the last, with matters so sudden."

"You can't tell me you've never propositioned anyone before," she said. Her laughter was sweet to his ears and warm over his neck. "Even bluntly—you were a soldier for years."

"I was mostly younger, and often had strong liquor to give me courage. And for the most part, I didn't believe that I'd see them again. Wagering is easy when you have little to lose."

"That does help." Uncertainty surfaced through the comfort pervading her. "This is the first time there've been stakes for me, really."

Hearing that, even indirectly, sent a thrill through him. He tightened the arm around her waist. "Then you're simply more daring than I am. I'm far from surprised."

"Better at leaping before I look. Not sure it's the same thing. Glad I did."

"So am I." Darya fit his arms easily, her weight against his chest a comfort. "And if you wish to continue as we are," Amris said, "I would greatly desire that as well, and not only because we have Gerant in common."

The thought caught her off guard, he could tell, and so did her own enthusiastic reaction. "Me too. Not that I'd ever keep you two from each other, even if you and I don't last. But…I like this. I like you. Not just in bed, although that was damned good."

"Understating the case," he said, and kissed her. Had he been twenty years younger, he would have wanted her again almost at that minute. He *did* want her again, for that matter—but the body would take a while, and with his most immediate desire satisfied, Amris could no longer put off duty.

"I fear," he said, pulling away reluctantly and beginning to employ a handkerchief in the service of certain necessary duties, "I had better return soon."

This time, her "me too" was a sigh. "Stupid Thyran. Stupid army."

"Gods willing, we'll have longer in the future. Perhaps even with light."

"You and your luxuries," she said. "Gerant didn't tell me you were *degenerate*."

"Clearly he wished to leave you some surprises."

Amris reached out with his mind, trying to signal that it was all right for Gerant to come back if he wished— welcoming him, if he wanted to join them. He got only a vague sense of connection, no thoughts or even emotions.

"He's a little too far away to talk," Darya said. "Stone doesn't help either."

"Then we have quite the evening's conversation in front of us."

"A pity there's no more wine."

Amris dressed mostly by guesswork, hearing the sounds of Darya putting her own clothing on and seeing vague movements in the shadow. He was checking as best he could with touch when she said, "You look fine."

"Wha—oh. My thanks. I'd forgotten the dark is no hindrance for you. It's quite an advantage in a lover."

"I have a lot of advantages," she said and donned her cloak with a theatrical swirl.

They were laughing when they started to climb the stairs. When Amris put his hand to the door handle, Darya shook her head. "We'd better look sober," she said, "or have some story to hand."

"And not simply let people think what they will?" he asked, surprised to hear it from her.

"Might be a problem for you, commanding. You remember last night."

"Such people as they were already—"

There was shouting above—not close enough for Amris to make out words, but it was several short syllables. Without any further speech, he opened the door and they rushed out. His hand was on his sword hilt, and though Darya didn't have her own sword, the dim light of the kitchen suddenly gleamed on two shorter blades in her hands.

From the halls beyond came slamming doors and marching feet. Another shout went up from outside the kitchen, by the stables, and it was to that door Darya went, plunging out into the cool night air with Amris behind her.

One of the new soldiers, a middle-aged man with a fringe of red hair, met them as he headed back to the keep, walking so quickly that he almost ran into Darya.

"Careful, there!" Amris said, as Darya sidestepped neatly. The man turned, and Amris saw that his face was gray-white, his eyes wide but only just now seeing Amris—and that only barely. There was no need to ask what was happening, only to get confirmation. "Close, are they?"

"Crossed the sentry line a quarter hour ago. The dark-haired Sentinel just heard it. I... Gods help us. Gods help us all."

Part IV

A great deal was lost when the Traitor was exiled. He governed the connections among people, between things, even within flesh. Thus there are aspects of control over these things that are unmastered and treacherous, or subject to his influence.

Yet the other gods did what they could to fill the gap. Poram upholds the rhythms and bonds of nature. Sitha teaches the crafts that bring civilization out of chaos, weaving her Golden Web between all. Letar brings blood and flesh together with healing and joins people in love—or vengeance. The youngest, Tinival, provides the words that let us reach out to one another, the truth that permits trust, and the honor that binds warriors when they seek to defend a noble cause.

—Meditations of Lord Marshal
Dravarhan, High Priest of Tinival

All else from this point is theory, my lady. The chaos of war covers much, and after the war, a great deal more was lost in darkness, cold, and death. We move from what is known to what we speculate, and in that movement I can only say that the world we once knew is gone, irreparably so. Our comfort must be that the man who destroyed it is gone as well, as we heard no word of him once the storms struck and his troops scattered into the north. The gods have some mercy, in the end.

—The Letters of Farathen

Chapter 33

THE FIRST ATTACK CAME IN THE DARKNESS, AND THE twistedmen were even more horrible in the flickering, waving light of the torches. Most were the skinless bastards Darya knew well, but there were plenty of the frog-mouthed creatures and gaunt figures whose heads were only beaks full of teeth. At irregular intervals, wearing shining armor over elaborate robes, she saw things that looked almost human in form, except their faces were melted and, if you watched too long, the melted bits moved independently. The mage she'd killed a few months back over an enchanted chalice, in what had apparently been an early sign of all this, had been one of those, which was a moment of recognition she could have done without. There were plenty of the korvin, carrying a couple passengers each, and near the very back, orange and gray standards flapped in the wind.

An accurate count was impossible, but it looked like thousands. Soldiers moaned in terror as the first ranks came out of the forest, or called on the gods, and even Darya felt fear dry her throat and wet her hands. *Oh, bugger, this is really happening.*

Amris assessed the approaching horde, then slowly turned his back on it and faced the troops on his section of the outer wall—including Darya, who crouched on the highest tower. "Our foes are many, yes," he said, his voice pitched to carry to the ranks, "and terrible. I'll not deny that, nor will I make promises. But think, now, not only of what faces us. Think of what—and who—wait behind us. Think of those who depend on us."

Faces pale with fear stayed pale, and tears still ran down some cheeks. But jaws set, and shoulders squared, and a far-off look came into most of the weeping eyes, like the minds behind them were picturing familiar, well-loved faces.

I'd never heard him speak like this, Gerant said. *I was always well behind the lines. I would've envied his troops, had I known.*

Over on the other section of the wall, Hallis was speaking, though Darya couldn't make out the words. Amris glanced over to him quickly, then delivered his final statement. "We'll give them as much chance as we can buy, by the gods. Now, archers ready—"

He hadn't even looked at the twistedmen as they started to advance. Darya supposed he'd seen it in the reaction of the soldiers he was addressing. She lifted her bow and nocked an arrow.

"—draw—"

A hundred arms went back: some with twenty or thirty years of expertise, some with the shaking hand of the new recruit.

"—loose!"

The arrows flew.

Height gave them distance, and the plummet down toward the advancing army added to their lethal force. No few found targets in strange flesh. Darya saw one of the twistedmen hit through the eye and topple, another groan and fall back as it got hit in the shoulder, and a korvin squeal and rear, throwing its riders.

Even the ones that weren't lethal right off did more damage. The herbalists knew plenty of ways to harm as well as heal, and Darya, impervious to poison, had spent a few hours coating arrowheads with the most lethal mixtures they could manage. She noticed a toad-thing fall back, shriek with pain, and begin to tear at its own flesh, and she smiled.

There was little time for joy, even cruel joy. She was nocking another arrow before Amris could give the next order, waiting only to shoot in unison with the others. Gerant was silent in her head, but that didn't bother Darya; she knew he was directing all of his attention to the magics that would protect her, should the need arise.

The dance had begun. Though there were more partners than usual, still the steps remained.

As Amris had suspected, the arrows took their toll, but not nearly enough to stop the advance. Across the field they came, filling every inch of space with warped flesh, barbed teeth, and eyes full of malice. When their comrades fell, most of the twistedmen left them, or walked over them. A few, farthest from the scrutiny of their commanders, stopped to wrench off a limb or pluck out an organ; an army marched on its stomach.

He heard a few of the soldiers being sick. Best they do

it quickly. Amris didn't remonstrate, just kept up the pace of draw and loose, draw and loose again, until he saw the ranks of the twistedmen halt and caught motions from those just behind the front.

"*Down*," he shouted at the top of his lungs, and suited actions to words as a volley of crude arrows arced up from the ground.

Some flamed as they went. Those didn't fly as high or hit as hard, but Thyran's generals doubtless didn't intend them to. They struck the outer walls, where wood normally would have sparked to deadly life. Instead, most sputtered and died as they struck the fresh animal skins draped over the logs, kept damp by the efforts of mages and young men.

A few places did begin to spark. Tebengri made a quick gesture and, one by one, the bits of light sputtered and died.

Amris heard cries of pain—the scouts were shooting from the ground, and the soldiers had ducked in good time, but an arrow or two almost always seemed to find flesh, no matter what the advantage on one side or another—but the cries sounded like those of pain and surprise, not true danger. He spared a glance, saw a young man with an arrow in the shoulder being helped down by a friend, and nodded.

"Archers ready," he began again, picking up his own bow and reaching for an arrow. Archery had never been his strong suit, and he was far from a match for Darya, but every set of arms helped.

"Draw—" The timing was almost instinct, save for the

need to watch the twistedmen and adjust as needed. The rest of it *was* instinct by now: the breath came up from deep in the belly, the sound formed in the chest, and the word released on the breath out, just before an inhale to repeat.

A commander kept a steady volume that way, and a steady pace, to keep going without losing breath or voice. In time the throat would feel the pain of such work. When battles went long, Amris had often come back to his tent unable to talk at all.

He watched the arrows strike, and watched the twistedmen advance regardless, some hiding behind shields, some ignoring wounds that weren't deep enough for the poison to take effect, and some merely coming in fresh to replace the fallen. Amris couldn't see the ground between the bodies as they squirmed forward.

This was going to be a long fight. He *wanted* it to be a long one—his throat be damned. Delay was their only chance.

———

Bodies made decent walls. Behind them, or atop them, the twistedmen dug in. Korvin cut deep trenches in the earth, swallowing soil and spitting it back out. Troops with hands stacked logs, stones, and flesh, giving themselves cover from arrows while dozens of them got hit and died, screaming.

Darya would have cursed them, but she didn't want to waste the strength, not even to think it. Besides, they

were plenty damned already. She just kept firing, target-
ing eyes on things with too many and necks on whatever
had them. Sitha's blessing let her edge far out onto the
tower, and from there, she tried to target the back ranks,
and the creatures that she thought served for officers.

That was hard to tell. Many twistedmen wore jewelry
of sorts, mostly bone or organs, some gold and gems.
There was no official sign of rank for them. The beaked
figures were a clump of their own and stayed at the back.
Their arrows carried farther than the others, one or two
barely missing Darya as Gerant's magic deflected them.
The scouts likewise stayed back and kept shooting, sty-
mied by the newly cleared ground.

Others weren't so lucky. There was more screaming
on Darya's side now. She didn't look to see who, but she
smelled blood and the ranker stink of death. That mingled with smoke and oil, then became unnoticeable: just
the way things smelled, like darkness and teeth were the
way they looked.

An arrow sped from her bow and caught a toad-thing
in the side. It started to writhe, and Darya reached back
for her quiver, then saw a glint from behind it—the robe
of one of the tall figures with the running faces. The shot
was clear.

Quickly, not waiting for orders, she nocked, drew, and
loosed. It was a good shot. Her aim was true. The arrow
went too fast to dodge.

It crumpled.

When the point had almost reached the robed figure,
the shaft warped outward into a circle. The point curved

around and drove itself through the wood, and the whole thing dropped to the ground.

Fifty feet down and far across ichor-covered, corpse-strewn ground, the creature raised its face toward Darya. Moving white specks glistened there; they looked like maggots, but she thought they were its eyes, and she thought that it saw her. Pain scraped across the tips of all her fingers and under the nails, like splinters shoved deep.

It was gone in an eyeblink.

"Tell the others!" Darya panted.

Done, said Gerant. He had no breath to pant with, but his own mental voice was short and faint.

The spell between the three of them must have let Amris know she'd been in pain. She couldn't see his reaction, but his orders stayed as consistent as ever, and his voice was loud but calm. "Draw—"

For all Amris seemed to be affected, Darya was just another soldier; neither the soul who helped defend her, the hour or so they'd spent earlier, nor the tentative sentiments they'd exchanged had made any difference to him as far as she could tell.

Darya would have smiled about that too, but she had no time.

Chapter 34

"Shift change, sir," said the voice at his ear. "Here." A hand tugged the bow from Amris's hands and stuck a flask of water in its place. "Go down and sit."

He nodded. The twistedmen were digging in rather than charging, since the first attempt hadn't worked. Amris took his eyes off them, looked to the figure taking his place, and saw that it was Byrnart, the man who'd almost come to blows with him—the night before? Two nights ago? The sky was starting to lighten.

Byrnart took his place with no sign of embarrassment or word of apology, which was no surprise; there wasn't time, and there wasn't space in either of their minds for such a conversation. "Thank you," Amris croaked out, and stumbled toward the ladder.

Slowly his vision expanded to take in the space within the walls. At the end nearest the manor gates, four torches had been staked out to mark the square where the Mourner and his helpers tended to the wounded. So far, Amris noticed, there were only three or four men on the pallets, and only one covered shape off to the side: under the circumstances, a decent tally.

Far nearer the wall, unwounded soldiers sat against the walls of buildings, or on chairs and benches that they'd scavenged. Many drank or ate; many more slept.

We're to your right, said Gerant, and indeed, when

Amris focused his attention on the spell, he could feel Darya's presence by a small house. *If you do wish to join us, that is.*

"Thank you," he rasped.

Hallis was as likely as not to be nearby, so there was no conflict with his duty. Having thus rationalized, he made his way toward a small knot of people.

Darya sat a little to the side, slowly interspersing sips from her own water flask with bites of bread and cheese. When Amris cast himself down beside her, caring less about the bruising from his armor than no longer asking his legs to support him, she passed him a ration as well. "General."

Don't tax him too much, said Gerant.

"Wasn't going to," she said, and then, a little louder for the benefit of those around them, "The inside of his throat's probably in worse shape than those hides right now." She indicated the walls with a chunk of bread.

"No bloody wonder," said Isen. One side of the stablemaster's face was deep red and starting to blister, as though he'd spent too long in the sun. He was rubbing ointment on it as he spoke.

Darya herself appeared unwounded, which gave Amris what happiness he had energy for. Her face was drawn and paler than usual where it wasn't smoke-smudged, though, and her eyes were red-rimmed and none too focused. "How are—" he began, and then held up a hand to indicate.

"Same as they ever were," she said, while Amris sipped water. It had wine mixed in, which stung the inside of his scraped throat, but the pain felt purifying. "Only lasted a second."

I was able to mitigate the effects, Gerant said. *That's a vicious spell—and fortunate for us it only seems to work when the—*

"Blobby sons of bitches," said Darya.

—are the direct targets.

What of wide-ranged attacks, Amris wondered to himself. Would a stone from a catapult, or a firestorm if a mage could call one, get around that defense, or expand the return stroke to the entire army? He made a note to himself to speak with Tebengri about that, when he saw the mage and when he could talk.

Gerant continued, *Repeated attacks might wear down whatever the protection is, just as enough strain would break through my spells, but that's only a theory.*

"And no real way to find out," Darya added. "Counting the one I took, I think maybe half a dozen of us have had clear shots at the squirming-faces, and nobody's taken one since we passed the word."

Amris nodded his approval. If the spell, unshielded, was as bad as Gerant said, there was no point taking risks to find out.

"Katrine says she'll talk to the Mourner, when he's got a free minute. If this is Gizath's work, Letar's power might fuck it up," Darya added.

"Good thinking," Amris said. "Good work, everyone." Then he fell silent again. His throat was feeling better, but he had no desire to push his luck.

Eat, you fool, said Gerant.

He did. The bread and cheese tasted of blood, whether because of the smell in the air, the damage to his throat, or both. Darya, Isen, and the other soldiers spoke around him.

"No sign of Thyran, huh?" Isen asked.

Darya shook her head. "Biding his time, likely. We don't have a Blade, and even they probably aren't good enough assassins to get to him through a couple thousand of his creatures."

"Where'd they all *come* from?" asked a young man.

"This lot?" Isen shrugged. "North, or so I hear." He glanced at Darya and Amris, and when neither of them corrected him, went on. "Originally? Thyran made 'em out of the people who followed him. I don't know how."

There are creatures outside the world, Gerant said, and Darya repeated him, with a gesture to indicate the real speaker—though the choice of words would likely have given that away. *Parasites, like ticks on the body of a hound. Thyran, and his god, called them up. His most dedicated followers walked into their embrace and came out changed.*

A woman sitting nearby coughed on her water. "*All* of those went over willingly?"

"No," said Darya, still speaking for Gerant, though she started to use her own words. "The first lot, the strongest, could…split themselves after a certain point. Stick a tooth or a finger or whatever into a human corpse and five or six twistedmen come up the next day, all with the same grudges as their…sire?" She grimaced at the word. "It lessens the big ones to do it, and nobody knows if the parts that split off them grow back, but Thyran and his top creatures made them."

Amris nodded again. He'd seen such a parody of birth once. It was among the memories he most hoped death would blot out. He had to force himself to swallow his food, and washed it down quickly with the water and wine.

"Well, then," Isen said, thin-lipped and pale, "we don't let them get their hands on our dead, no matter what."

"Another thing to watch out for," said Darya.

We never knew if the transformation would work on the living, Gerant added, *nor what the results would be if it did. It remains, I fear, an unknown and a possibility.*

Darya didn't repeat that, only glanced down at her sword with a sigh. Amris didn't feel any need to state those facts either. There were plenty of obvious reasons not to let the living fall into the hands of Thyran's army, not least because the path from hands to mouths was likely to be a short one and might not involve death first.

Where bad ends were concerned, Thyran and his forces provided no shortage of choices.

———

"Sleep would be wisest, now," said Amris. "Until we're needed in our turn."

He was lowering himself to the ground as he spoke, though he didn't start to take off his armor—likely for the same reason none of them had gone into the buildings. When they had to go up on the walls again, every second would count. They had to stay easily found and ready to fight.

Darya understood that, and gods knew she'd slept rougher. It was the thought of sleeping with live enemies so close at hand that made her stare at Amris.

She didn't ask, though. The man looked ten years older than when he'd left her side and pulled his tunic back on, and he'd spoken through a throat of broken glass, from the sound. If he could manage rest, Darya wasn't going to bother him with questions.

The soldiers were following his example. A few had gotten there before and were already breathing steadily, either asleep or close to.

"Might as well try," Darya muttered, and lay back as well.

I'll wake you if matters grow dire, Gerant promised, *but he knows his business.*

"Never doubted it."

"Touched," said Amris, amused but sincere.

"Stop talking before you start spitting blood."

And she's not wrong about that.

"The judge has spoken," said Darya.

You're damned right.

Not caring who saw, she moved as close to Amris as his armor allowed. Plate mail, when she tried, proved too uncomfortable to be any sort of pillow. She could imagine how bad it was for him—could feel a trace of it, for that matter—but he was relaxing nonetheless, slipping closer to sleep with every moment.

He'd done this a few times before.

The idea smoothed out the knots in Darya's spirit. War, this large-scale fight, was new to her, comparatively new even to the soldiers, but familiar to the man at her side. Somebody she trusted knew what he was doing—and Gerant, as he'd always done for her, was keeping watch for danger.

She closed her eyes and felt both of them in her mind. "Wish this wasn't happening," she muttered, hearing her own words muddled with sleep, "but couldn't ask for better people to see it through with."

Chapter 35

"Climbing!"

And they were. Darya had no time to put a face or a voice to the warning. The twistedmen had reached the base of the walls, where arrows from above couldn't reach them, and were swarming upward. Their claws dug into the wood, giving them hand- and footholds that a human army would never have had.

The midday sun was bright. Every hideous feature showed as the monsters came closer, and while they'd cringed and hissed when they first started climbing, they faced the walls and pressed onward.

Darya shot the last of her arrows, taking another twistedman in the side as it made for the wall. Then she dropped her bow and picked up one of the spears close at hand. It was little more than a long stick, sharpened between bouts of training and stockpiling at the same time that she'd been poisoning arrows, and it too was coated with venom.

"Hold!" came Hallis's voice, steady through the noise, though it was as cracked and ragged as Amris's had been. "Wait—"

Darya gripped her spear one-handed, drew her sword, and peered downward, watching as the mass of skinless muscle and barbed black teeth grew closer, estimating range as best she could.

"Ready?" she asked Gerant.

Always.

"Now!" Hallis roared.

Soldiers along the walls braced themselves and tipped up huge pots of hot oil. Black and tarry, the stuff slid down along the walls, engulfing the twistedmen who were too far up to retreat. It flowed over the faces of the uppermost, suffocating as it burned, not giving them the breath to cry out. Others, lower down or to the side, shrieked plenty.

Joy, equally hot and dark, flowed up through Darya, and she felt her lips slide back in a grin. "That's right, you bastards."

But there was little time for celebration. The oil didn't cover every patch of the walls. Many of the twistedmen fell, dying, to join the others on the ground, but more followed, and some of the wounded only snarled and kept coming.

After heat came cold. Darya reached out to Gerant as she'd done a hundred times before, joining her focus with his power, and pointed her sword downward along the wall.

The spell wrapped her in an invisible blanket of ice for a heartbeat. Then it concentrated at her heart, ran down along her arm, and howled forth out of the tip of her sword. The twistedmen just below her stopped in place and writhed in pain as the water in their bodies froze. Amris was too far away to lend his strength, so neither died, but Darya saw the eye of one cave in with a spill of black ichor. Those around them flinched, and while they kept coming, they were slower.

Gerant's presence vanished from Darya's mind, and so, she knew, did the shield around her. Quickly she sheathed her sword again and grabbed the spear with both hands. It would come to blows very soon.

———————

Death made up all the world.

No orders remained to be given. The vats of oil had spilled over the attackers; while more was heating, it would take time. Archery did little good now, with the twistedmen at such short range. The mages, the priests, and the Sentinels knew their business and were carrying it out with no need of Amris.

Now there was only the weight and motion of the sword in his hands, the backward swing to gather momentum and then the thrust or the slice, the wet, yielding squelch of flesh and the jarring scrape of bone, the withdrawal and the next assault. Twistedmen came up like grim children's toys, met Amris's blade, and fell back screaming, when he left them a head to scream with. Claws raked along his armor, and the air was too full of noise for him to notice the shriek of sharp chitin on metal.

The man next to him fell back, his throat opening red down his chest. Amris turned and gutted the twistedman as it came up over the wall, then spun backward to shear half the skull off another. He knew the hole in the line next to him, and held it while that was needed, but saw no more of his replacement than a human figure with a spear; just so must the man in his turn have seen Amris earlier, when he'd come to relieve a wounded soldier.

Faces and names were no longer important. There were arms with weapons, and there were bodies that took blows so that the arms vanished and had to be replaced, flesh that fought and flesh that absorbed.

Ichor ran down the blade and over his gauntleted hands and arms. The stink of it was one with the smells of smoke and human blood, and the whole of it was familiar. Amris had been fighting the battle for a hundred years; he would be fighting it for a hundred more; there was nothing outside of the patch of wall he defended and the creatures swarming up to try and take it from him. Even his own body was remote in a fashion, the senses he needed focused on their targets and no others intruding into his awareness.

In such a state, he could have gone on shouting until the very cords of his throat snapped and not have felt the pain of it, any more than he felt the straining muscles in his arms and back, or the bruises and cuts where his armor had pressed through the padding and into his skin under some onslaught. He couldn't have thought of many words—maybe his own name—but he could have kept shouting.

But there was no longer anything to be said.

———

Darya yanked her blade up and out of her opponent. Avoiding the rib cage was always the trick—that, and not letting the creatures run up the blade and bite you, as a few tried. She let her weight fall backward, shook an oncoming cramp out of her arm, and then saw the man on her right.

He'd lowered his spear. That wasn't good. She didn't turn, because the next twistedman would get into range soon, but she called to him out of the corner of her mouth. "Guard up, there!" It might be time to get a replacement up, if they had any.

The man stepped forward. The spear dropped.

"Shit," said Darya.

A large clawed hand shot over the top of the wall and grabbed the soldier around his ankle. He didn't even scream when the twistedman started to drag him toward it.

Darya hurled her boot knife at the forehead of the twistedman climbing up toward her. Sword in one hand, she flung herself over across the blood-slick top of the wall in a barely controlled leap, bringing the blade down on the twistedman's arm as she landed. At the same time, she planted her free hand in the man's chest and shoved him backward.

He yelled *then*. So did the twistedman. It clawed its way up with its remaining hand, the stump of the other arm gushing ichor, and its head shot forward on its too-long, too-bendy neck, oversize jaws open and aiming for her face. Darya raised her blade to meet it.

One of the bird-things, clinging to the handholds the twistedmen had gouged in the wood, raised its own head and opened its beak. Rows of yellowed teeth looked like ivory spearheads. Between them a cloudy gray shape...

danced? Twisted? Pulsed? It *moved*, and the movement suggested that if you watched long enough, you might be able to figure out what it was, and what the shape was, and any number of other things. Stare long enough, and you'd learn anything you wanted to know.

A sudden chill shot up Darya's back and into her mind. She wrenched her head away and around, and the twistedman's jagged black fangs snapped together just short of her cheek.

Instantly, rage took over. A stab and a slice sent the son of a bitch's head falling to the wall, where she stamped a booted foot onto it just to be sure, reveling in the crunch. She wished it had still been alive and suffering—that thing that had almost hurt her, and all through its comrade's trickery.

Well, she could put an end to *that* too.

She grabbed the soldier's fallen spear. The recruits on the walls had been told not to bother throwing them— the chance of hitting anything was too slim—but Darya was a Sentinel, muscles and vision alike forged by the gods, and if she hadn't cut her teeth on a sword like rumors said, she'd had her hands on weapons since not long after she'd learned to walk.

Aiming without looking fully at the beaked horror was a new wrinkle, but she'd overcome worse, and fury fed her will. She lifted the spear, flexed, and threw.

The point took the beaked creature through the neck. Its teeth gnashed together, obscuring the bewitching pattern between them, and then opened too wide, as its grip loosened in death and the spear bore it backward and down to smear itself on the ground below.

Farther down the wall, another of its comrades burst into sudden, howling flame. Emeth had probably just used her blessing.

"Don't look at the bird ones!" the cry went up from one of the lieutenants. "They'll bewitch you! Shoot 'em if you can!"

"You don't say," said Darya.

Then there were more twistedmen coming up, pressing toward Darya's spot on the line. They saw one woman guarding a range that used to have two people. She'd been a good hand with a spear, but now she only had a sword, and they'd have her at shorter range. They saw, she knew, a weakness.

Darya brought her sword up and smiled, once, before going out to greet them.

Chapter 36

TOOTHED BEAKS GAPED WIDE, AND EVEN FORE-
warned, soldiers fell prey to the dancing patterns within.
When a chance look could entrap a person's mind, and
when the monsters had closed so that there was one
every few feet, warnings only did so much good.

Strong-willed Isen stepped to the edge of the wall.
Amris saw him and cried out a warning while he kicked
away the reaching claw of a twistedman and brought
his sword down to hack away at another attacker. The
woman at Isen's side called to him too and reached, but
a claw swiped at her face. By the time she'd fended it off,
the head groom was gone, dragged down the wall under
a mass of writhing claws and fangs.

To note that it had happened, and to save up the
mourning for later, was almost itself too much. That
was nothing new to Amris. He kept slicing through the
ranks in front of him, his mind leaden with a weariness
he couldn't let his body feel. Around him, the troops he'd
trained and joked with barely pulled one another back
from disaster, or went down bleeding and screaming, the
lucky ones back to their own side of the wall to heal or die
among humans.

He saw events elsewhere, background to the rictus
grins and claws in front of him. Branwyn's arms and face
shone pure metal, and the twistedmen struck at her in

vain, while behind her wounded soldiers crawled back
to safety and her sword spun deadly arcs in the air. On
his other side, Olvir leaned forward, looking with neither fear nor entrancement at a beaked monster, and
then took its head. Old Gleda paced her section of wall
behind the soldiers, hands moving in constant gestures,
and the troops near her shook themselves out of their
bewitchment.

They struck and struck again, aiming at the beaked
creatures when they could—with arrows from the side,
with spears, with fire and sword from those who could
manage it, moving through the sea of flesh that the twistedmen made on the wall. More hot oil came up, and
though the pots weren't as full as they had been, men too
wounded to hold a sword lugged them the more easily,
and poured them over the places where the mesmerizing
things were. Some got out of the way. Not all.

In time, the creatures faltered. There was a pause
between the one that fell to Amris's blade and the one
that came after. In it, he gazed out across the battlefield
and saw two of the squirming faces, as Darya had called
them, step forward, robes shining in the sunset. They
raised spatulate hands and, without a sound from them,
the monsters on the walls began to pull back.

It was no situation for quarter. A rain of arrows and
even rocks followed, as the wall's defenders struck with
anything they had, and more than one retreating twistedman found a blade in the top of its head as it started
the journey down.

They did go, nonetheless. Amris didn't lower his

blade until those on the wall were too far out of range to surge back up. Then he shot, though without Darya's expertise, until the retreating forces were out of arrow's range.

Only then did he let his vision expand, taking in the walls and the troops on them: bloody, exhausted, but still standing.

"Third guard!" Hallis yelled. "All others, food, water, and rest!"

Amris repeated the order, then made for the stairs with legs he'd almost forgotten still worked for walking.

Bodies burned with a thick, choking smoke and a smell like bad pork beneath the sweet spiciness of incense. There was no time for individual rites, no space for individual pyres—just a pile of twenty soldiers, laid out as well as the priests and their assistants could manage. Isen wasn't among them. Darya, who'd heard about his death—hopefully quick, probably not—thought of him as she watched the fire, and whispered a prayer, though she didn't expect it'd do much good. The Dark Lady was doing what she could. They all were.

Amris's hand was warm on the back of her shoulder, even through the armor. Neither of them spoke for a while, not until the flames had reduced the bodies to facelessness.

"How are we doing?" asked one of the people who stood near them. Darya recognized the girl who'd been helping Isen when they'd come to the fort. A bandage covered one of her eyes, and her lips were split. When she spoke, Darya saw the gap where a few of her front teeth had been.

"For where and when we are," Amris replied slowly, "well. That's not to say our losses don't exist, or that we don't feel them, but"—he spread his hands—"Thyran's forces have come against us twice, in large part, perhaps three times. Each time we've beaten them back. We hold, and we keep holding."

"Your mages and I are thinking of a way to guard against that trance," said Dale, the Mourner. His gray-streaked blond hair stood out in untidy spikes, and his hands were bloody to the elbow. "Likely it'll be unpleasant."

"What isn't?" Darya asked.

"Just so."

Gerant's emerald flickered, and she felt his presence in the back of her mind. He wasn't entirely back yet, not enough to talk, but clearly the conversation had caught his attention. "If there's time," she said to Dale quietly, "I'd want in on that discussion. Or he would," she added with a gesture to her sword.

"I'll find you," said the Mourner, unperturbed by the mention of Gerant as few outside the Sentinels and Letar's service were. Amris was another exception, Darya thought, and leaned her head against his chest for a second in silent gratitude.

"It's been two days," said Aldrich, who'd met them at the gate. His eyes were redder than the smoke could explain: maybe for Isen, maybe for another friend—or friends—in the pyre or elsewhere, maybe only for the situation. "And another two since we heard. Criwath is sending men, yes?"

"The men will be their answer," said Darya.

"But," added Amris, "they will. Hallis is certain of them—and if the map holds true, they'll be another day or two away, and with them will come mages and knights."

"Mourners too, perhaps even a Blade," said Dale, "and another two or three of your order, Sentinel, I shouldn't wonder."

Amris nodded respectfully, talking as if he had no idea that the grieving crowd had gathered around him, as if he were only conversing with friends. "We have only to stay standing, and with the walls more or less intact, until they arrive."

"And you think we can," said the former stable hand.

"We'd best," Aldrich replied, "or it'll all be for nothing."

"We can," said Amris in slow, measured tones. "And it won't."

The courtyard wasn't silent. Soldiers some distance out talked. Those in the square with the healers groaned, and some screamed. People carried supplies to the wall, and beyond the wall, the twistedmen growled and slavered and taunted the defenders. Closer at hand, the fire kept crackling. Bones popped from time to time.

But around Amris, a hush seemed to fall. When he spoke, the words weren't louder than normal, but bolder, heavier, written with thicker lines or set into metal rather than wood.

"How do you mean?" asked another soldier, not challenging but inviting: *Tell us more. Please.*

"We have allies fighting with us here already," Amris said, and gestured to either side of them. "The mountains and the forest that funnel Thyran's army into one spot. The walls that give us cover and height. All of these mean that we can do a great deal, even a hundred-odd against a few thousand—and all of this I've said before. But—"

Overhead, a cloud darkened the sky, throwing the light of burning bodies into greater contrast over all of them. Amris went on. "What I hadn't said, save to myself, is that those beyond us, those with perhaps more troops and more mages, yet lack the advantages we have now, and that the twistedmen are not infinite. You've seen it yourselves; when they die, they stay dead, and while they can reproduce themselves, they can't do so endlessly, or without wearying."

He paused and looked around at the crowd, at faces that were bruised or sunburned or pale with loss of blood. Darya saw him meet each of their eyes in turn. She knew that *he* knew he spoke to those who might die within a few hours or less, and who'd likely already lost friends under his command. The tension in the hand he'd returned to her back gave her some idea of what that cost him, but his voice stayed low and calm, and his face was serene.

We're right here with you, said Gerant. Darya didn't want to interrupt by speaking aloud, but she took Amris's free hand in hers. Fresh strength went through Amris at both. Darya knew that he could endure better because the two of them were there, drawing strength from them to lend the others, and the sense of it left her honored.

"I'll tell nobody what they should feel," Amris continued, "nor why they should fight. But what I tell myself is that even if we fall here, even if I lie unburned for the Twisted to find, I will have killed more of those corrupted things than they can make from my body. Each of them that dies before our walls is one that won't go on to prey on a village, or to face Criwath's troops on better ground. I will die knowing that my death means my enemy has less to work with, and that our friends without the advantages of this place have less to face. I speak for myself, and I speak as a general, and for me, no action is for naught if it leaves our foes weaker, even if that weakness comes with victory."

The faces around the fire lightened, and the shoulders beneath them straightened. Isen's stable hand smiled, and even Aldrich nodded, though grimly.

"And," Darya added, slipping back into a cooler, less immediate version of what she'd felt as the oil flowed down the wall and those below it screamed, "we're hurting the scum, and we're probably pissing off Thyran and his commanders pretty well."

"Oh, yes," said Amris. "He never was prone to being philosophical about failure."

Darya grinned, with the hot joy of a wild predator twisting inside her. "That right there is enough for *me*," she said. The Mourner, unarmed as he was, smiled back with the same hatred that sustained her as she went on: Letar was the lady of vengeance as well as healing, after all. "They're not getting through here without paying."

Two appealing arguments, Gerant said, still faint. *I'd be interested to see who picks which—though, of course, they're eminently compatible.*

Chapter 37

A HAND ON HER SHOULDER WOKE DARYA FROM A DOZE. She wasn't sure where she was at first, but there were fewer people screaming than there'd been in her dreams, and the face in front of her was whole and not in pain, though the brows were furrowed in concern. "Olvir?" she asked.

"Sentinel," he replied. "They've not yet picked up their attack, but there's action afoot. Your Emeth had it from a crow."

"Katrine's Emeth, if she'll admit to being anybody's." Darya unfolded herself from where she'd been sitting, back propped against a building. Her arms hurt. Her feet had gone numb. She shook life back into both. "Any specifics?"

"They've been killing their own wounded for the last hour," Olvir said. He offered her a hand and she took it. After three days of fighting and scarce rest, pride was long gone, and getting to her feet a fair-sized chore.

Darkness had fallen again while she slept, punctuated by the glow of fires in the courtyard and under the cauldrons on the wall. Soldiers moved through it like she did, vague shapes on vaguer errands. The wounded had been taken to one of the buildings once Dale and his assistants had treated the worst of their injuries, and their moaning had diminished either naturally or with painkillers.

For a siege, it was fairly quiet.

Darya took a few drinks of water from the flask

Olvir offered and tried to get her thoughts in line. The Twisted had been retrieving their wounded for a while, almost since the last attack had stopped. Darya had sort of assumed it was for the same reason most armies did— not that she suspected Thyran or his commanders wasted effort on tenderly nursing their monsters back to health, but a warm body was a warm body, or so she'd thought.

Olvir was leading her toward the wall. She followed, thinking of questions. "The worst wounded, or all of them? And why bother to get them back if you're just going to slit their throats—unless they're going in the stewpot, I guess."

"No," said Olvir, and sighed. "The crow couldn't give very much detail, Emeth said, or didn't notice very much, but she did say it was the healthiest—'the most moving'—and that some aspect of it disturbed her crow, but all he could say was that it was 'killing in a bad way.'"

Probably *not* just eating one another, then. There'd been plenty of that on the battlefield already. If the food had already been dead, she supposed it would have been a cold kind of practical, but usually it wasn't.

That sounds like magic, said Gerant, *though specifically for what and through what methods I couldn't say without a closer look, which I have no expectation of getting.*

"Shit," she muttered, and drew her thumb and forefinger across her eyes to the bridge of her nose, wiping away the last traces of sleep. "Magic."

"More or less," said Olvir, stepping aside so she could climb the ladder. "I hate to wake you with such news, but it seemed good to have as many of ours as we could get awake and on watch—particularly as many of us." He gestured between the two of them. "Casting no slight on the regular troops, you understand, but we're fewer in number, and each of us has information they may not."

"No, you're right. I don't like it, but you're right." She glanced down at Olvir, all big eyes and square jaw beneath the mop of auburn hair. Blood and other things kept the armor from shining, but he managed to look the part otherwise. "Has Tinival given you any hints?"

"No, Sentinel, but he wouldn't. Justice is very clear in this matter, and they"—he waved a hand beyond the wall, where the fires of Thyran's camp dotted the plain— "haven't bothered to lie to us. He strengthens my will and my arm; that's his part in these matters."

"A lightning bolt wouldn't hurt," Darya said, but didn't press the issue. The gods had their constraints, just as mortals did, and that was why she and Olvir were who, or what, they were. "Dale say anything?"

"No," Olvir said again, with a regretful shake of his head, "but he is dead to the world. After the last stint of healing, he lost consciousness. Amris and Hallis say to wake him only if the need is dire, and I agree. The Dark Lady's power is hardest of all the gods' on mortal flesh and bones."

"And there's only one of him, of course." Darya sighed. "Mages?"

"Awake, and analyzing as best they can. If Master Gerant wishes to confer with them—"

Master Gerant doubts he can add much to the discussion, but they're welcome to come over here. And tell the young man thank you for the consideration.

"You always seem your real age at this hour of the morning," said Darya, "and I never know why. It's not as though you need to sleep most of the time." She looked back to Olvir, who was politely waiting. "Glad to chat if they come over here, but doesn't have much to add right now."

Conveying messages was surprisingly annoying. Either her nerves were going to pieces or she'd gotten spoiled talking with Amris.

"How are the commanders holding up?" she asked, hoping to sound professional and impartial.

Olvir allowed her the luxury of thinking so, whether she managed it or not, answering gravely. "The strain is great, but they're strong men, and brave ones. They endure well enough. Better than I could, I think."

Neither of them talking about it, Darya not even thinking about it in advance and suspecting the same was true of Olvir, they each drifted to a Sentinel post on the wall, close enough to talk but spaced to cover a decent range if they need to. "You haven't led armies, then?"

"No," he said. "A squadron once or twice, at need, but that's five or six at most."

"More than me. I never really thought about what it took until now."

I didn't know the whole of it, by a long shot, said Gerant, *and I lived with Amris for years.*

"Must have been good for him," Darya said quietly, as Olvir tactfully didn't ask questions, "to have you. Even if you weren't always around, it seems like a person you love," the word came oddly to her lips, "could be a method of keeping you together in those situations."

Thank you, said Gerant. *It went both ways, of course. He listened to me when I was tearing my hair out about theory, and put me to bed a few times when I'd overstretched my abilities and collapsed. But I'm glad to think I helped.*

"I think you still do," said Darya. "I don't like thinking of how this would weigh on him if you weren't around."

You care about him too.

There was no accusation in what Gerant said. Darya was too exhausted to deny it. "Very much."

"The Golden Lady wove well when she sent the two of you to Klaishil," said Olvir. "Or it seems that way to me, from the outside."

"Fate's odd." That was part of theory that neither she nor Gerant had dwelled on. Sitha's most senior priests, or the spiders they bred, could tell vague bits of the future if conditions were right. Some people said the Golden Lady herself could see more, or that the Golden Web was not just civilization and craft but fate itself. "But it's a comforting thought. Thanks."

People nearby shifted their weight, murmured to their neighbors, sharpened weapons. Darya looked out again, from the walls to the forest beyond.

Among the fires of the twistedmen, there was motion—and a seething orange glow.

―――――――

Amris knew that light of old. Orange though it was, none could have mistaken it for fire. There was a sickly hue about it, as though the person who viewed it did so through a film of dust. No fire moved the way the light did, either, for it swarmed and squirmed as no flame ever had. To either side of him, soldiers turned greenish and swallowed, or looked away.

"What is it?" one of them choked out.

"Gizath's power," Amris replied. He squinted against the light, wanting badly to give the order to shoot, but knew it would be a waste of needed arrows. The one they needed to kill would be out of range even for the Sentinels. "Rouse the Mourner, please, and have Sitha's priest standing by as well—and all of our mages. Send them to Hallis. I know not what this will do, but it's likely we'll need them for it."

They took off down the ladders. Out on the plain, the light kept twisting, looping over and over on itself, and gradually the lower part of it began to darken. Huge legs formed, then a massive block of a trunk.

Amris heard prayers along the wall, quick, garbled, and desperate. He added his own, but silently—those in command had to stay in control. The hilt of his sword dug into his palm, cutting the skin.

Arms came next, each the size of three men. The figure bent, not picking up two human-sized forms from the ground but lowering a hand for them to step on, and then raised that hand to the flat top of its torso, onto which the two walked. A head, it seemed, was not necessary.

"Archers ready!" Hallis called, and Amris repeated it down the wall. He wasn't certain what good it would do—he suspected the humans on top of the figure had their own protections, or they'd not expose themselves as targets—but it was worth finding out. Perhaps the priests or the mages had been able to enchant some arrows, at that.

The figure started to lumber forward. As it came close enough to see, lit by the fires without and Gizath's decaying radiance within, the prayers along the wall turned to screams.

It was the dead.

The corpses hadn't risen as they'd done in Klaishil, as individuals. Twistedmen didn't seem to. Instead, Thyran and his mages had built the figure out of them, lashing corpses and body parts together into a blocky giant of rotting flesh and broken bones. They'd cared not about specifics, so the arms, each as thick as three men, were made of legs and ribs as well as hands, and splintered faces stared from the legs and the center of the torso. Power had merged them in parts, but it still flickered at the edges, and individual...bits...moved slightly out of sync with the others at times.

Yet they moved, and they moved forward, as one. The figure wasn't heavy enough to make the earth shake, but Amris nonetheless felt his footing tremble beneath him.

———

Darya shot and shot again, but the arrows skidded away when they got close to the figures on top of the corpse-thing, and when they stuck into it, they did as much good as sticking pins into a wall. At last she dropped the bow and drew her sword, waiting.

Emeth, elsewhere on the wall, sent forth flame. Bones

smoldered. Hair caught in places, flickering, and the fire spread feebly to flesh, but the amalgamation of corpses didn't pause or flinch. A few pieces fell away, none significant.

Cold may work better once the fire's died, said Gerant, without much hope.

"Worth a try," she said. All the delight she felt in a normal battle was missing. There was no dance, no pattern, just sick and slow progress.

Olvir didn't ask what she'd meant. He stood immobile, staring at the giant creature. Darya couldn't blame him. Amris might have found something helpful to say. He wasn't there, and Darya kept quiet.

Now, she could make out the riders themselves. One was a crawling-face, though it was larger than the others, and two extra arms sprouted from its sides. From the side, the other seemed human enough—ordinary, in fact. He was a man of middling height, round-chinned, with dirty blond hair receding back from his forehead. If not for the way he was dressed, Darya would have passed him on the street and not looked at him twice.

He wore jewels set in bone on all his fingers, and a crown of bone rested on his head, a great diamond at its center. His robes were gray silk, embroidered with gold.

"Thyran," she said, and it came out in a child's whisper.

His creation raised a colossal arm.

Darya lifted her sword and let the cold flow through her. It swirled around the construct. Maybe a bit of the flesh looked grayer. She couldn't really tell.

The fist hit the gates with a crack that Darya could

hear from her place on the wall. They didn't break then, but they shuddered, and splinters flew.

And Thyran turned his head toward her.

The priestess of Sitha was rushing toward the gates, calling on the goddess. The corpse-thing was raising its fist for another blow. Thyran stared in Darya's direction with rotten orange fire dancing across his eyes.

She didn't know if he saw her or was just looking at the section of wall that the latest attack had come from. She was too far away to be sure that he was sneering, triumphant, but she was sure of it anyway. Darya held tight to Gerant, missing the spirit now that he was resting, and waited for the next blow.

Thyran's gaze passed over her, moved on to Olvir at her side—and stopped.

Orange light flashed off the sorcerer's bone-set rings as he raised one hand to his brow. He froze in place, then actually staggered back a step. His companion on the corpse vehicle turned toward him in surprise and alarm.

Darya grabbed her bow again. If there was a time to shoot, it was now.

She fitted an arrow to the string, began to draw, and saw sunset-red light gathering on top of the gates.

Katrine, she thought. Of course. Letar and Tinival, the blessing that scourged all things turned against their own nature, whether they were undead or Twisted. The lady chose her time.

Thyran still had his hand pressed to his forehead. The crawling-face reached for him. He shook it off with an impatient gesture.

Katrine's light washed down from the gates, a wave larger than Darya had ever seen from her. It struck the corpse-monster just below the knees.

Vibrant red drowned out the orange-gray hellfire. Within its radiance, bunches of limbs and skulls began to fall away from either side of the construct, dropping like leaves in an autumn wind. It swayed drunkenly. Thyran dropped his hand—dropped both of them—and clung to the top. His companion, not so lucky or so quick to react, stumbled, then fell. Darya heard it screaming until it hit the ground.

She fired only to see the arrow crumple before it could hit Thyran, like a dozen others sent by people with the same idea. It was no surprise. It didn't make a dent in her mood, either: that was soaring as she watched the construct fall to one knee, then saw its other leg crumble. Within minutes, it was down to a torso and arms, with fists pounding ineffectually at the ground.

Thyran stalked off it then, his back stiff with rage. His army parted before him with the speed fear inspired. After a few steps, he turned and made a violent gesture to the union of corpses, which stopped hitting the ground and followed, dragging itself after its master on crumbling arms.

"Praise the gods and give me a damn drink!" Darya cheered, paying no attention to her raw throat. "What the hell did you do there, knight—ah, *shit*."

Olvir was slumped over the edge of the wall, only his breathing showing that he still lived.

Chapter 38

THE COURTYARD WAS FULL OF THE SOLDIERS HALLIS had called forth, knowing the twistedmen would be right behind any breach of the gates. He and Amris walked among them, sending the most exhausted to get some rest and the walking wounded back to what recovery they could manage, calming where they could and giving what answers they knew. Hallis put together a squad to help reinforce the gates because wood and stone would give Sitha's magic more to work with.

In the infirmary itself, Dale the Mourner still slept like the dead, and nobody had felt the need to rouse him. The recent attack had wounded nothing but the gates themselves—and Katrine, the Sentinel who sat in a dark corner with her eyes closed and her hands wrapped around a mug of strong-smelling tea. Emeth knelt behind her, rubbing her temples.

"Will you be well?" Amris asked quietly, stopping in front of them.

"With herbs and time," said Katrine. "I'm seeing two of everything just now."

"That was a blow most well struck out there," Amris said. "That we held is thanks to you, and to your sword-spirit. I hope," he added, clearing his throat and thinking of Gerant's sudden absence and the conversation he'd had with Darya, "they don't suffer from it in any lasting sense."

"No, thank you," Katrine replied. "I think they're well enough. The gem didn't crack."

"And neither did you," Emeth added, stroking the blond curls fondly, "though it was too damned near for my liking. That thing…" She looked up at Amris. "I've seen her take down a half-dozen undead and not suffer like this. And it's still out there."

He nodded. "It is. And Thyran is. Yet we're still here, and I'll take some comfort from that. The mages are working on defenses even now, and perhaps on spells that will hurt that creature if it should return." None of them had sounded very hopeful about it, but he didn't need to say so. Emeth's dark gaze held no trace of hope. "He seemed hurt for a moment, just before you struck, Sentinel. Do you believe he could sense the power as you called it forth?"

"I don't know. Nothing else has."

"And there's another root in this particular stew," said a voice from behind him.

Even though the spell had reassured Amris all through the fight, hearing Darya was still a spot of warmth in his chest. He turned and saw her, straggle-haired and tired and lovely, carrying a helmet and gorget that would have never fit her. Behind her came Olvir, white-faced and unsteady of gait.

"Are you injured?" Amris looked swiftly over the knight, seeing no immediate signs of fresh blood, nor any new bruises as far as he could make out. Mingled with a friend's concern and a commander's responsibility for those he commanded was an unpleasant sense of upheaval. He'd been certain there were no wounded.

"Not exactly," Olvir said, sitting with none of the grace Tinival's warriors usually showed. "I don't really know how to start."

It was Darya who started, summing the situation up from her perspective in three blunt sentences while Olvir tried to find words. Thyran had stared at Olvir. He hadn't seemed to like the results. At some point afterward—"though I hadn't exactly been paying attention; I'd say I'm sorry, but you wouldn't believe me and you wouldn't want me to be, if you had any damn sense"—in Darya's words, the knight had collapsed.

"She's right," said Olvir. "And that's as much as I can be certain of."

"Be uncertain, then," said Darya, "but be uncertain out loud, dammit."

Startled, Olvir laughed, and Amris with him, though he was less surprised. The other man began, "I remember Thyran looking at me, of course. It's not likely I could forget."

"He's very memorable," Amris agreed grimly.

"Yes. He..." Olvir lifted his hands, then dropped them back to his sides. "At the time, I thought it was a quality of his alone. There was a—I don't know quite how to put it—a sense... I wouldn't call it recognition. I didn't know him at all, save from tales. But when I looked at him, I felt as if, oh, as if I'd heard three lines of a song and would be humming it all day until I could bring the fourth to mind. It was far more overwhelming, though, and not in my mind. Not in words at all, and I don't think I could have put it into words at the time. None of you felt it?"

"Nothing like that," Darya said. "I'll admit he scared the hell out of me, but just the regular way."

"I was completely unflappable, of course," Emeth said. "And if I hadn't been, I'd have been like Darya here. Kat? Don't move your head, darlin.'"

"No," said Katrine. "I barely saw his face."

"I knew him," said Amris, "but because we'd met before. Otherwise, no. It was that which overcame you?"

"In a way," Olvir said. "My memory of the event isn't what I wish. I recall that feeling, and I had been starting, as much as the situation would let me, to try and work it out. I leaned forward to look at him more closely, and I called up Tinival's power to see truth. I saw blackness, and not only because I was falling unconscious—shattered, shining darkness. Then I *did* go under."

"Had I struck before you did?" Katrine asked. Waiting for an answer, she sipped her tea gingerly.

"I don't believe so, Sentinel, no."

"Then I suspect it wasn't my power Thyran sensed," she said, "and I suspect he wasn't fond of whatever you did. Could it all have been down to Tinival?"

"Perhaps," said Olvir slowly. "He was—is, I suppose— Gizath's brother. The familiarity would make sense. Tinival's presence has always felt very different to me. But Gizath's power is to turn things against themselves, and maybe that would have made a difference."

"It might have." Amris called up his memories of meetings in tents and on battlefields, as well as the occasional session of tactics that had managed to take place within four walls. "None of the knights I fought with mentioned any such thing, nor did their presence affect Thyran so. It may be that the years have caused him certain vulnerabilities or, given your order certain strengths, though I'll not count on either."

"Looks to me," Emeth said, "like we already know what we can count on. Us, and those things out there."

"Can he rebuild that walking abattoir?" Katrine asked.

They all exchanged glances. Amris was about to hazard a guess when Gerant spoke inside his head, faint and weary. *I have no certain way of knowing,* he said, *but if there's any left of it, yes. And if there isn't, I'm almost sure that he can make another.*

"That—" Katrine's voice caught. She cleared her throat and went on. "That stands to reason, I suppose. Gods know he has the raw material."

"He does that," Amris said. He'd paraphrased Gerant with a few words. Now he paced to the doorway of the infirmary and stood looking out, leaning one shoulder against the wooden upright.

Darya went to him. It was what she could do just then, and it wasn't much, particularly since his armor covered his back, but she reached up a little and rubbed the back of his neck gently. The muscles were taut cords under her fingers. His skin was still hot and damp. They all needed baths, not to mention about two days of sleep. It didn't seem like they were going to get any of that on the mortal side of a funeral pyre.

"I'm sorry for asking, Sentinel," Olvir said, "but how long until you can repeat what you did just now?"

"At least a quarter of a day."

"And that," Emeth said, "is if she wants to risk killing herself."

"It might not work even then," said Katrine, eyes shadowed and red. "That was more power than we've ever handled, and it only partially destroyed that thing, and then maybe only because Thyran was distracted. He'll be ready next time."

"Yes," said Amris. "Although it, or he, will likely be weaker against a ground assault than to archers or magic. Iron helps in these matters." But the words were laborious and he didn't sound certain. Darya knew why; on the ground, the numbers would still be very much against them, and that didn't include all of the twistedmen's special tricks.

Beyond him, Darya saw a shape approaching from the darkness. It came clearer and resolved into Tebengri, walking slowly and holding a large bowl in both hands. They paused in front of the doorway and nodded respectfully.

"I apologize for the interruption. We've put together a defense against the entrancement—and perhaps against the way the crawling-faces send pain back as well. I know it seems of little account just now."

"No," said Amris. "Just now we need every thread of hope that we can spin."

"Then I'm glad to help. There's enough here for half a dozen. Hallis sent me to find most of you, in fact, while the other mages take care of him and the soldiers at his location."

Nicely done, Gerant said. *Ask them, though, if it will impede the spell we have.*

"Good news, and thanks," said Darya, "but Amris and I have a spell on us already. Will that be a problem?"

"It shouldn't," Tebengri replied. "As Gizath's power is to turn parts of a whole against one another, this anchors you to who you are and what you want." A slightly devilish smile crossed their lips. "It shouldn't be obvious either. If you act well, you may be able to lure them in and catch them off-balance."

A light that Darya hadn't seen for too long reappeared in Amris's storm-gray eyes. He studied the mage for a second, nodding slowly. "So, indeed, we may."

Chapter 39

IT WAS FAR FROM A PERFECT PLAN, EVEN BY THE imperfect standards of any plan in a time of war. To begin with, the townsfolk of Oakford were going to be extremely unhappy about the results, even if their forces won the day. Knowing they'd probably be paid for the damages, that not all of them would return in any case—one hasty evacuation was one too many for some—and that a far worse fate awaited them all in any case, Amris still felt a pang, thinking of his father and sisters and what their reaction would have been.

That none of the Sentinels, nor Tebengri and Gerant, nor even Olvir, objected soothed him a little, but it also said that none of them had come from peasant stock. He wondered what Hallis would say, or the soldiers.

"Well," Emeth said, voicing a more tactical objection, "how do we know that even swords at close range will work? You said *likely*."

"We'll try all we've got," Darya responded before Amris could speak. "Swords, fire, magic... Hell, I'm willing to stand back and throw rocks at the damned thing if that's what's left. But we've got to figure the thing's not invulnerable, or we just lie down and let it squash us."

"But," said Olvir, "it might be wise to focus on the twistedmen at first, or when using weapons we know *don't* work. The one blessing of that creature is that it's slow, and it looks as though Thyran must be with it to control it. On the ground, clear of his soldiers, a few warriors could likely keep it on the run—so to speak—and survive."

"There's also Thyran's magic to consider," said Amris, as several unpleasant scenes crossed his memory. "He may not be able to use it and control the abattoir at the same time, but I wouldn't wager on that."

"Pardon," Tebengri said, stopping in front of him. Amris knelt in front of them and lifted his head.

The mixture in the bowl was cool and gritty, and smelled like ashes from a forge. As Tebengri traced a symbol with it on Amris's forehead, it seemed to sink into his skin, traveling through his skull and down his spine with a weight that was unnerving but comforting. He felt himself shaped around it, all the more solid for its presence.

"That," he said, when Tebengri took the brush away, "is quite a spell, all the more so for its haste."

"Thank you, General," they said. "This magic of Thyran's... What is it? Can it be defended against?"

"Yes, or dodged, but it's difficult in both cases. He can call forth fire from his hands, and when I say 'fire,' that's not quite accurate. It has the speed of flame, but it's more vicious, and it's...less wholesome."

It consumes from within, said Gerant. *It turns all that's strong and good about you against itself, and you eat yourself alive. Not literally, or not with your mouth at any rate, but in essence. It's Gizath's power in its purest form.*

"Great news," Darya said, and repeated the information. "But we can get out of the way?"

As you can dodge a bolt of lightning. Magic can protect

against it, and so can shields, for that matter, but those
defenses will fail more quickly than they would against
normal fire, say.

Amris translated, and added, "But he can only choose
one target at a time, or could in my day. That doesn't
mean he'll be completely vulnerable at such times, mind
you. He always had other protections established before
he ever rode into a battle."

"No disrespect intended," Olvir said, "but are you
sure he'll follow our lead?"

"Anger was ever his undoing, and we've thwarted
his purposes a few times now," said Amris. "He'll have
been vexed that we were prepared at all, and his wrath
tonight will be great. Few have ever thwarted him when
he brought that much might to bear."

"You have," said Katrine, "or so all the histories say."

"In different forms. I wouldn't take all the glory of it,
but I suppose—" He stopped. Gods knew how many of
the histories Thyran had heard, but Amris had been the
last face he'd seen before they'd been trapped, and Amris
the one to trigger the spell. Before that, Amris's army
had evacuated most of the targets Thyran had wanted in
Klaishil, had taken back other cities, and had held Thyran
and his forces off the longest of any general.

Whether Amris deserved the credit or not, Thyran
had likely given him the blame.

"I have faith in Thyran's anger overwhelming his
judgment," he said to his waiting companions. "But a
wise woman once told me that it's a shame to waste a big
shiny target."

"You've got to be joking," Darya said, almost immediately.

"Why?" Amris wasn't testing her, and he wasn't being smart. His face showed only worry that he'd missed a detail. There was nothing about him just then that showed they even knew each other, other than as two people on the same line in the battle.

That was the way it should be. Darya tried to respond in kind. "What if he kills you"—she thought she did a decent job of sounding neutral there, though she didn't look at either him or Emeth before she went on—"and you don't take him out? You're the only one who's fought him before."

"So I was. After this, any of you knows as much as I do of meeting him or his forces in battle—particularly now, when we've seen the twistedmen in their current forms. I've told Hallis and a few others all I remembered of the war, and though, yes, it's possible that I forgot to mention a detail, I don't believe there's enough risk there to balance what I might achieve by focusing Thyran's attention on me now."

None of the others spoke to support or challenge him. Tebengri carried on painting a sigil on Emeth's forehead. Olvir stood with his hands clasped behind him, waiting to hear more, and Katrine watched Darya with a sympathetic twist of her mouth.

"I know myself to be an excellent warrior and commander," Amris went on, "but not magically so, or blessed by the gods. Even if I were, none of us is irreplaceable, not now. Each of you would have told me that yourself, in my place."

He's right, said Gerant, sounding more tired than he had when he'd said Thyran would likely be able to bring the abattoir back. *I hate it, but I can't deny it.*

"Neither can I," said Darya. "All right."

Tebengri moved on to Katrine, and Emeth stood. "You don't survive this and we get our hands on Thyran, the bastard's dying by inches," she said. "But in all honesty, I'd want to see that regardless."

"I'd advise otherwise, Sentinel, tempting as it is. Better to make his death quick and certain." They faced each other in the dim room, two people who'd met only days before, two people of the four who understood love and valor best among all Darya knew. Amris heard the real sentiment behind Emeth's flippant, angry speech, and nobody could have doubted his sincerity when he added, "But I thank you."

None of the others spoke. The room was full of breathing: the snores of those wounded lightly enough to sleep normally, the shallow breaths of those hanging on by will and Letar's grace. Darya stared into the darkness, blinking hard.

Amris stepped in front of her and took both of her hands in his. "Darya. Sentinel."

For a second, Darya was conscious of the others around them, but then decided that if Amris didn't give a damn, neither did she. She looked up into his face, as she'd done before she'd said his name back in Klaishil, and tried to smile. "Not like any of us couldn't have died an hour ago," she said.

"Or at many other points in our lives," he replied quietly.

"I wish you hadn't woken up just to get thrown back into it, is all."

"The world is as it is." Amris's breath stirred her hair. "You told me that. I could wish to have more time in it—with both of you—even in war, but here and now is more than fate affords to many, in the end."

"Yeah," said Darya, and cleared her throat. "There's that."

I saw you again. That has to be worth something. We did the best we could in the time that we had, and I'm glad that it was the three of us, in the end.

"All three of us," said Darya, through the thickness in her throat.

On the cots some distance away, the wounded breathed steadily. A few stirred in their sleep, or moaned with nightmares, and the young woman on duty did what she could. Perspective, Darya told herself, was good.

I'll recast the spell on you both now, said Gerant, pulling himself together. *That should strengthen it, and combined with the sigils, it may keep the worst of Thyran's attacks from you. Your resignation does you credit, but there is, after all, a chance you might both survive.*

———

As before, Amris knelt before Darya, one hand in hers and one on the hilt of the sword where Gerant dwelled. Her hand had fit well within his even then, little as he'd known her, and it had been easy to look into her eyes. Now, as the world narrowed to her face and the slim fingers wrapped around his, he went eagerly into that temporary refuge—one familiar not just from lust but from stolen sleep between battles, from trust within them, from the comfort of her quick speech and quicker grasp of circumstances.

He'd known the weight of a sword forever, but the soul-blade felt better balanced, even upright and in one hand, than any weapon he'd wielded. The emerald was cool beneath his fingers, a balm to the abraded skin there.

The others gathered around them. It had started with Emeth going to stand by the doorway "because one of us needs to be ready with an explanation," she'd said. That had put her in the south, with Katrine sitting in the north. Olvir shifting east and Tebengri west had seemed only natural. None of them had spoken of it, but Amris, for years the lover of a mage, had smiled. They had a magic circle this time, one made of their friends. That was no promise of victory, but there was nobility in the moment, and that would suffice.

Magic grew in the air, humming faint and low. Amris breathed in slowly, watching Darya as she did the same: the depth and brightness of her eyes, the fine, stubborn lines of her face and the rainbow play of light across her scales. He felt the ache in her sword arm, like his own pains but different as her body was different. He caught a glimpse of vision through her reforged eyes, as shapes in the darkness became clearer and took on color.

Going deeper than before, he felt her anger and her grief, the desire for—and the revelation in—vengeance, far deeper than his own. Amris had learned battle and been glad of his skill, but Darya had been made to take joy in it. Feeling the shadow of that in his heart and gut, he embraced it. She was herself. No other, perhaps, would have been able to free him, nor to make a place for him in the world as it was.

Amris squeezed her hand gently and she returned the pressure. Tears sparkled on her eyelashes, mirroring the ones in his own eyes. It was a shame to die, as he thought they still likely would, and give this up, but they'd known it for a few minutes. That would have to be enough.

Beyond Darya, Katrine was watching them, her face solemn. Amris met her gaze—the spell expanded. It brushed her only lightly, far more so even than it had touched him and Darya the first time, but briefly he knew her flesh working over the last few years, changing her body into what she needed it to be beyond being the gods' weapon, and her lingering headache in that moment. From her it spread eastward to the keen young strength of Olvir, then south, as Emeth turned.

Her brow was furrowed and remained so for a second, and the quiet sound halted. Then she gave a very small nod, and the magic flowed over her and on to Tebengri, adding their quiet patience to the mixture. There it slowly faded, becoming an echo in Amris's ears and a faint perfume, or whatever form the others sensed.

It's complete, said Gerant. *Utterly unexpected, but complete.*

Nobody but him and Darya seemed to have heard, regardless of the spell. "Thank you," Amris said, not letting go of Darya's hands.

"I'm glad to have helped," said Emeth, "but what the hell did I just do?"

"We all agreed to be part of the spell," Tebengri said, "or at least I had the sensation that my will was necessary. But what that means for it, or us…" They shrugged.

I wish I had a more definite answer too. This didn't work when I tried it before—granted, the circumstances were different, but many of the participants were the same. Perhaps I need both of you as an anchor, or perhaps the sigil helped, or… I'll have to think about it. I perceived many things just then, and I'll need time to sort them all out.

"Gerant's got no idea either," Darya translated.

"I suppose we'll find out sooner or later." Leaning back, Katrine picked up her tea again. "If we all survive long enough for my head to feel normal, I'll be glad to answer questions. For now, though, I'd like to sleep. This scheme will go off better if I'm alert. Or if you are," she added, beckoning Emeth over with a free hand, "and I know you won't sleep for fussing."

"I don't fuss."

"And I had better find Hallis," Amris added. Slowly, he got to his feet, keeping hold of Darya's hands until the last second. She prolonged the contact by standing as well, easily mirroring his movements.

Now they were far more deeply linked. As a tactician, Amris hoped that it would be an advantage later on. For himself, he was simply glad.

Chapter 40

KATRINE AND OLVIR HAD BOUGHT THEM MOST OF SIX hours. Standing on top of the wall with her bow in hand, smelling the reek of a three-day-old battlefield in midafternoon, and watching Thyran's abattoir advance with the rest of his troops behind it, Darya could only hope they'd used it well.

"He's not taking any chances," she said to Gerant. The wizard had brought three of the crawling-faces with him, and two others marched on either side of the rebuilt juggernaut. "Wonder why he didn't have the whole pack along before."

Most likely, he was afraid one of them would use the opportunity to further its own ends. Gizath's nature has its downsides, and not only for us.

"Which means he's scared now." She nocked an arrow as the twistedmen grew closer and, along with the rest of the defenders, fired it on Hallis's command. None of them aimed at the abattoir this time. Twistedmen and beaked things made more satisfying targets, and they died by the score, while others shrieked with the pain of wounds. "I don't know if that's good for our plan or not."

Neither do I.

If Gerant had been able to breathe, Darya knew he'd have been holding his breath as the abattoir took position before the doors again. She sure as hell was. So was

Amris, making his way to the center of the wall, just above the doors themselves.

He stopped there, helmet under an arm, the wind blowing through his dark hair. They'd polished his armor to as close to a mirror sheen as it could get after days of battle, and the light caught it now, making him resemble a figure on a stained-glass window. Darya thought of Veryon, Letar's doomed lover, and wished she hadn't.

"Thyran of Heliodar!" he called, and drew his sword with his free hand. "We meet again. Accept my challenge, and let us end this with honor."

"Don't you dare fucking do it," Darya whispered.

She didn't have to worry long. Thyran looked up and his face grew white. His eyes widened and filled even more with the grayish fire of Gizath. "Var Faina? Who... How..." Then he flicked one ringed hand outward, and the face beneath the bone crown filled with contempt, leaving no room for curiosity. "What would you know of honor, you jumped-up farmer's brat? You, who feared me enough to turn your pet sorcerer's magic on me at the end? None of my blood would lower himself to cross swords with the likes of you."

"None of your blood are left, Thyran," Amris called back. The armies had fallen silent, preparing, waiting. Darya knew how badly the others on the wall wanted to keep firing—she did too—but arrows would be wasted on the abattoir and its riders, and killing the twistedmen would make too much noise. Thyran needed to hear every word. "You made certain of that long ago. Perhaps I had forgotten that the murder of sleeping households was your strength when you had a weapon, that you could never face a warrior without your god holding your hand."

Thyran screamed in rage then and raised one hand. The construct's fist fell hard on the doors, cracking them and shaking the walls themselves.

Arrows started flying again, but not as many. Most of the men on the walls were getting themselves down the ladders, dropping bows and pulling spears, swords, or axes in preparation for a fighting retreat on the ground. Darya reached for another arrow, felt the sigil on her forehead, and targeted one of the crawling-faces—not the riders, for they'd be protected, but one of those on the ground.

Her forehead and her hands both burned, but didn't hurt; it was like sitting a shade too close to a fire for comfort. The arrow stayed in one piece, flew straight, and took the monster right below its ear. It fell, shaking, and its companions turned in what Darya thought was shock.

"Not so safe now, are you?" she called down, laughing giddily as she strung another arrow.

The dozen others on the wall followed her lead. Some arrows still crumpled midair, or missed, and those aimed at the giant still bounced away, but more of the crawling-faces fell, dying or voicing high, burbling screams.

Thyran didn't turn his head. At his command, the construct hit the gate again, and the wood that had previously held shattered under its strength. One more blow and the doors buckled, then fell.

Darya didn't bother with the ladder. She dropped her

bow, grabbed the wall, and half slid, half climbed, using the footholds she'd carved earlier. As soon as she hit the ground, she drew her sword and ran toward her section of the town, a cluster of buildings where a tenth of the soldiers were trying to imitate a third.

"Hey." Emeth grinned at her from behind the ranks. "Let's have some fun before we die."

"It's always fun with you," Darya volleyed back.

Then the charge reached their position.

———————

All but the best of the archers had retreated already to the comparative safety and high ground of the manor walls before Thyran's second blow against the gates. The archers themselves had only waited a little longer before swarming down the ladders and joining their fellows, while slightly over a score rushed out to replace them, carrying pikes or swords and wearing the grim expression that said they had no expectation of coming back.

Amris took his place in front of the inner wall, sword drawn and helm back on. Thyran would recognize him now, even with his face hidden. Olvir took his right side, and Branwyn his left. Behind him, Hallis ordered the rest of the soldiers into formation, setting up a shield-wall bristling with weapons. It would hold, Amris hoped, as long as it needed to.

The mages were in the manor. The priests and the wounded were with them. The other Sentinels—Darya among them—were in their places, a good idea whose merit Amris could never have let his heart challenge. He commended his soul to the gods, set his feet, and watched the twistedmen pour through the outer gates and into the town.

Amris marked the charging hordes and saw, too, the movement to left and right. The soldiers in the town, he knew, were fighting a retreat before Thyran's forces, fleeing into empty buildings halfway between his position and the outer gates and throwing spears from that cover. He saw the twistedmen follow, a few of them falling but the rest pursuing undaunted.

Soldiers ran out the back of the building that Darya would, if all went to plan, have entered. There were fewer, Amris thought, than had gone in, but he couldn't be sure. He knew that Darya wasn't among them; he could feel that she was alive, and more or less unhurt. Knowing what came next, that was little comfort.

Slavering, the first ranks of the twistedmen began to close in. Amris braced himself.

The building Darya was in exploded into flame.

Violet fire flared into the sky, and Amris could smell the acrid smoke—only unpleasant for him and those with him, but deadly at close quarters. Gleda and the herbalists had mixed the powder, and Darya had just set it off. Her reforging would protect her, as it did against all poisons, and the twistedmen should die, but that was less certain. The spell told Amris that she was all right, but not whether she'd remain so.

As he brought his sword around to cut the legs out from under the first twistedman, Amris, for the first time in his life, rejoiced in the fight. Beyond satisfaction at his skill or the hope of victory, he felt, bone-deep, the relief at not thinking for a while, and the glee of avenging himself on those who'd made that comfort necessary.

———

Poison didn't bother Darya, but fire hurt like a bugger, even through Gerant's protection and her battle lust. She dove out a window and left the dozen twistedmen behind her to their fate, hit the ground, and rolled, both to stifle the flames and so she could come up swinging. She gutted a beaked thing and took the hand off the twistedman behind it as she found her feet. To be fair, they were a bit distracted.

From the alchemical explosion and Emeth's more normal fires, the buildings collapsed, roaring. Flaming debris hit roofs and walls nearby, not to mention the hay that the defenders had scattered around. As the mages had intended, walls and roofs caught fire far more readily than they normally would have, burned with more force, and sent more bits of themselves flying around.

Thyran's army screamed as it burned.

The ones on the other side of the fire ran. Many within the walls tried, and some made it out, scaling the walls or even dashing through the flames, probably hoping to lick their wounds on the other side. Those remaining quickly realized who was to blame.

Darya glanced behind her, saw a clear path to where Amris was fighting with the main force, and eyed the score or so of twistedmen advancing on her. "You bastards don't smell any better cooked," she told them, made an obscene gesture, and then turned to run.

They chased, as she knew they would. Darya darted sideways, dodging the swipe of a claw, feeling breath hot on her neck, and trusting Sitha's gift to let her find the safe places, as her memory wouldn't serve. She rushed across ground strewn with hay and dirt, leapt as the weight of her pursuers caused the false land to give way, and landed on the other side of what had suddenly become a pit. The noises from below said that the sharpened sticks, coated with poison, had found their marks.

She spotted a building ahead that hadn't caught fire yet, leapt to a windowsill and then to the roof. From there she saw Emeth, naked and wreathed in flame, laughing as she spun and sliced through her enemies, and Katrine on the other side of the town, glowing with blue light and always moving toward the ground that gave her the best advantage, even as she, like the other two Sentinels, moved generally backward to the rest of the army.

Darya saw the fight by the manor walls, claws scraping ineffectually off Branwyn's skin, swords shining beneath black blood, spears run through twistedmen and soldiers falling at their comrades' feet. She saw Amris, standing as a bulwark in the center, armor still shining.

And she saw Thyran, high on his construct, his face inhuman with fury.

Chapter 41

A BEAKED CREATURE DROPPED TO THE DIRT, STILL looking faintly surprised that Amris hadn't paid any attention to its attempt to entrance him. The ranks of monsters parted for a few seconds, as happened in war, and Amris shook the ichor from his blade and glanced around.

The traps had done their work well, as had the siege before them. Thyran's creatures now outnumbered Oakford's soldiers only by two to one, and many of those remaining were scattered, fearing the fire that belonged, by association, to their patron's deadliest foe. Any who came on them by accident, or was foolish in their purpose, would still meet a quick and messy end, but they had yet to mass and charge. In such disorganization, they were relatively easy prey for the three Sentinels who'd been in the town.

Emeth's corona of flame and Katrine's blue glow were hard to miss, but best of all was the sight of Darya atop a roof. Her clothing was in tatters, her armor singed, and her neat tail of braided hair was now short and uneven, blowing around her face in the wind from the fire. She was hurt, the spell revealed that much, but the Sentinels healed quickly.

From her perch, she smiled quickly at Amris, then looked past him to Hallis and waved her sword in a quick but emphatic gesture. The flash of green directed their attention beyond the immediate ranks of twistedmen, who were already moving to the side, and to the giant trundling toward them, its stink of corpses masked by the battlefield stench and the sharp lingering odor of the poison flames.

"*Now!*" Hallis shouted, and the soldiers scattered as well—but not blindly like the twistedmen before the flames. They broke into small groups, covering one another's backs as they sped off, leading Thyran's forces into terrain they knew to be treacherous. Hallis took charge of one group, Olvir and Branwyn each headed another, and Amris led a third.

His were the veterans, ten soldiers who'd been fighting on the border between Oakford and the twistedmen for years. Each had a sigil on their head, each a sword or ax in their hands. Following Amris's lead, they held their position as the abattoir lumbered nearer, until Amris could no longer see Thyran's face when he looked up, but only the clumps of bone and sinew forced together by Gizath's fell power.

Then he and his troops ran to the side, pretending that their nerve had broken at the last. Thyran laughed loud enough to hear over the battle as they took cover behind one of the buildings. The twistedmen closed in on them; the men peeled off to fight them.

Amris put on an extra turn of speed, rounded the other corner of the building, and charged.

———

The time was now. Her heartbeat, loud in her ears, provided the rhythm. And gods knew she had her choice of partners.

When Amris charged, so did Darya—but in a different direction, screaming, into the crowd of twistedmen. A blast of cold came from her sword before it struck, stronger for Amris being near—much stronger, this time. Five of the monsters facing her simply burst, as the toad-thing had done back in the forest. Another few literally froze in their tracks, though the looks on what passed for their faces said they'd felt the touch of Gerant's magic beforehand and hadn't liked it at all.

The others, surprised and slow and scared, became so many targets in the field. If they stayed and fought, Darya cut them down, sensing dimly that their blood was splashing her face and their bones breaking on her sword's edge. She let them run if they wanted to. That didn't bother her.

She couldn't spare a moment to search for Amris. Their bond told her he was alive and relatively well. That was all she knew, until she ran her sword through the chest of another twistedman and had a space to breathe, to wipe the blood away from her brow, to look toward the abattoir for the figure she knew would be there.

He was. For a man in armor, Amris was dodging well—slashing and pivoting, stabbing and running, using the abattoir's size and slowness against it as well as Thyran's rage. "No fire," Darya panted. "Not yet."

I think, said Gerant faintly, startling her with his presence, *he must be using all his power to control that thing.*

"That's something," said Darya.

Then she was fighting again, ducking under claws and whipping the arms they belonged to off at the shoulder, kicking backward as one of the twistedmen had a half-bright idea and using the force to cleave up through the rib cage of another. Pain raked down her back, there and then gone in the heat of battle. If she lived, she'd hurt later.

Thud on the ground not far in the distance as the abattoir's fist struck. Darya ran one of the toad-things through, yanked her sword back, and spun to meet the next attack. Beyond the grisly shoulder of her foe, she spotted Amris, still alive and now moving in, as two figures rushed the abattoir from behind: Katrine and Olvir.

They struck first, each taking a leg at the knee, as far up as they could reach. Divine might backed both of their steel, and the construct felt it. The legs didn't collapse, but they wavered, wobbled, and gave Amris the opening he needed.

Darya saw him take it before he leapt: knowledge of him and of war took the place of fortune-telling. It was their best chance, and he sank all his strength into it, rising off the ground farther than one mortal man in armor should have been able to do and driving his sword into the exact center of the abattoir.

━━━━━━

In his landing, Amris felt more than one bone break: a rib, he thought from the immediate, intense pain, maybe more, and his sword arm between the elbow and the wrist. He'd left his sword itself in the abattoir, losing his grip on the hilt almost as soon as he'd sunk the blade full-length into the walking pile of corpses.

Through the eye-watering pain, he saw it frozen above him. It, Thyran, and the remaining faceless creatures seemed caught out of time again, and for a heartbeat that and the pain confused him. Had he truly awoken? Had he truly slept? Was Gerant still living, and the notion of a hundred years of stasis a fancy?

No—he felt Darya and Gerant present in the spell, and regretted that she must be sharing some echo of his pain. As Amris had the thought, the abattoir crumbled.

It was sudden and complete, and only the lack of force when the corpses fell apart made it a landslide rather than an explosion. The creature's riders fell with it, and tumbled through the smoky air above Amris, the mages with their arms flung wide as though they could fly and Thyran still transfixed in disbelief. This was not how events were supposed to unfold.

Hands gripped Amris's shoulders, and so great was the pain that he started to fight before he realized they were human, and that the face peering into his was Olvir's. "Thank the gods, you're alive," he said. "Can you stand?"

"With help."

Help he had in Olvir's strong back and arms, and in Katrine's tall armored figure standing between them and the twistedmen, who stared at the glowing woman and showed no inclination to approach. They learned, if slowly, and they'd learned fear of humans that day— particularly fear of Sentinels.

"We'd best get you to Dale," said Olvir. "I don't like the way you're breathing."

"As it is breathing, I like it very much," Amris replied, but rather spoiled his point by wincing when he talked.

"If you can make jokes, then—Ah, Silver Wind, *no*."

Wreathed in sickly fire, Thyran rose into the air from behind the pile of corpses that had been his creation. He glanced at Olvir as he hovered there and grimaced, but a jewel in his crown flared and he seemed to take no more hurt from that moment of contact. "You," he said, with a wave of his hand, "are a problem for later. But you, var Faina—"

He turned his attention to Amris. "Mongrel filth." Thyran's lips drew back too far, exposing dark-gray teeth as long and pointed as those of his creatures. "I hope you think your insolence was worth its price."

He lifted both flaming hands.

———

Darya was too far away.

The twistedmen had started retreating. Her path to Amris was clear, and she was pretty sure no son of a bitch would stand in her way, not just then. Simple distance was the problem—there was too much for even her reforged body to cover.

Given that, it was damned mean of chance to give her a clear view of Amris, leaning helpless against Olvir, who was wavering on his feet and had blood pouring from his eyes, and Thyran rising up in front of them with awful power crackling around him. Olvir feebly raised his sword, a well-crafted sharp bit of metal with no magic about it at all, and Thyran's hideous smile twitched. Katrine had turned from the twistedmen, but, like Darya, she was too far from Thyran.

Darya ran toward them, knowing she'd be too late, eating up the ground in half-leaping strides that left her thighs burning and a sharp pain down her side. As she passed over the blood-slick dirt, she had time enough to find reasons. The first blow might not kill them both; maybe she could stab Thyran while he was distracted. He might run amok with Amris and Olvir down, instead of retreating like a reasonable person, and somebody needed to try and stop that.

None of them were the real reason. If she'd had breath to scream, she would have been shrieking denial at the top of her lungs.

Gray-orange flame flowed like water from both of Thyran's outstretched hands, right toward Amris and Olvir.

A summer cloudburst of magic washed through Darya and outward. It took her strength with it, and she stumbled over the uneven ground on suddenly liquid-feeling bones, but she saw green radiance flicker around the two men and was glad and sorry at the same time— sorry, because she saw how faint it was, and knew it would make very little difference.

Then, as Gizath's power met Gerant's shield and began to tear through it as though it were wet paper, strands of violet-blue wove themselves into the green radiance. Lighter blue joined that in the blink of an eye, and Darya's skin tingled with the heat of a smith's forge, then the red of hearts' blood and the smooth feel of worked wood, and finally a pale silver and a cool spring breeze. Each wove itself into the rest, bolstering the places where Thyran's twisted flame had done damage.

When all were there, Darya felt the combined power rise. It surrounded the corrupting force coming from Thyran—even at a distance, and not a mage, she felt the hunger and the hate within the flame, squirming like maggots in a corpse—and, as a child might have done with a ball, threw it back at its source.

———

Surprise that he wasn't yet dead, and wonder at the magic he dimly sensed around him, quickly took lower priority for Amris. When Thyran's spell rebounded upon him, deserving as he was, nobody could have viewed the results with anything but horror.

The former Lord of Heliodar had flung up a ringed hand to guard himself, and he managed to shield one side of his face, but the hand itself rippled and changed. Fingers melded, grew, and blended with his bone rings, so he ended with a spatulate mass, raw flesh grown around three concentric circles of bone and blackened gems.

On the side he didn't shield, the bone crown likewise became part of his face, melting and growing so it covered the eye entirely. The cheek below that eye sunk in, forming a ragged hole through which all of his teeth and a large part of his jawbone could be seen, and his lips sheared away, leaving everything below his nose a spiked maw.

He screamed, and went on screaming, but he didn't die.

Above the screams, Amris heard, from outside Oakford's walls, the sound of horns and horses: the army of Criwath, come at last.

"*Take* him," he croaked at Olvir. "Now. Leave me—"

With a pained look, Olvir obeyed. Amris slumped to the ground, and Olvir rushed across the short distance, sword raised. Katrine came from the other side, glowing even more brightly.

Around Amris's pain, dulling the worst of it, he felt love wash over his consciousness. Darya, nowhere close enough to reach Thyran, fell to her knees beside him instead. She reached out with infinite gentleness to lift Amris's head into her lap—bloody and burnt, but hers— and together the two of them watched the others charge forward.

Thyran's single eye narrowed and his malformed mouth shaped a single, unpronounceable word. As the last syllable hit the air, a pillar of rancid smoke rose up. Olvir and Katrine drew back, coughing—and Thyran had vanished.

Chapter 42

NINNIAN, ARCANIST-GENERAL OF CRIWATH, WAS ONE of the rare people significantly taller than Darya. She was still sore after two days of rest, and the difference was beginning to matter.

"Etiquette be damned, sir," she said, pointing to the other chair in Hallis's study. "If I have to look up at you for another minute, my head's going to fall off. Don't even think about it," she added to Amris and Olvir. "You're both in worse shape than I am, and neither of you heal like a Sentinel. Sit or I'll put you through a wall."

Sleep and victory improve *some people's temper*, said Gerant.

"Nothing wrong with my temper. Now hush and let the nice man do mage things at you."

She passed over her sword, and Ninnian took it with ceremonial care. Darya leaned against the desk while he made mystic gestures over the hilt, peered at it, whispered a few words, took another look, poured a fine blue powder over Gerant's gem, studied it again, and finally shook his shaved head.

"I have no notion how you managed any of that. This blade, like those of the other Sentinels, seems as it was. I can sense—I *have* sensed—the spell on all of you, and it's an unexpected creation for certain, but it shouldn't have had the capacity for such a feat, not by any mechanism I can think of."

The open window let in the smell of summer rain. Two days of it, not to mention active cleaning with the aid of Criwath's forces—including two Blades, a Mourner, and a mage who'd specialized in fire spells— had cleared the stench of the battlefield. Darya suspected a weather mage might have pulled some strings, but she'd been either asleep or too busy to ask.

My supposition, Gerant said, *is that it had to do with Olvir.*

"Olvir," said Amris, not sounding too surprised. To be fair, he wasn't sounding too much of anything just then. The Mourners had done what they could, but they'd had their hands full with the more severely wounded, and fixing the hole in his chest had taken a fair amount of magical effort. The broken ribs that had caused it were still strapped, and his arm was in a cast and a sling.

"Me?" Olvir blinked, but he didn't sound surprised either. His damage wasn't as straightforward as Amris's, but he'd passed out again shortly after Thyran disappeared, and the whites of his eyes were still entirely red. He moved more gingerly, and seemed not to be quite aware where objects or people—even the ground, half the time—truly were. The Mourners, he'd told Darya, had said that would heal.

You've heard of his reactions to Thyran's presence, Gerant said. *I was...not at my best when I shielded him and Amris, and there's plenty I likely missed, but I did feel my spell anchor to him and grow stronger from it, and I believe it*

*called to the others in the same manner. After that, I was…
overtaken.*

"I don't remember much either," said Olvir, when he'd been filled in. "The sigil, and being prepared for it, helped me go on when Thyran was close, so long as his attention was elsewhere. Maybe they saved me from a worse fate later, but once he started to focus on us…it felt like being torn apart."

"Shame Thyran didn't feel it," Darya said.

"I suspect either the ornaments he wore—likely magical, after all, given their construction—or his followers helped him shunt off the worst of it." Ninnian smoothed a hand over his scalp. "It *could* be Tinival, I suppose. In a metaphysical sense, Gizath's power is to turn bonds against themselves, or their holders, and Tinival's domain is largely the upholding and maintenance of those bonds freely entered into."

"He stands as firmly against the Traitor God as his sister does," Olvir agreed, "but with less hatred, or… less personal hatred. Loathing what Gizath became, not what he did. But none of my training ever spoke of"—he waved his hands—"any of this."

"Nor has any theory I've ever read."

Nor have I seen it, Gerant put in, *and I've read a great deal. The Mourners or the Blades, or the Adeptas, might be able to shed more light on the matter.*

"Many might hold the knowledge, or parts of it," said Amris, "and we'd best begin to search. I know not what Thyran will do next, but if he hated us before this, what he feels now is likely beyond imagining."

"Well," said Darya, coming up behind Amris as he stood by the outer wall, sheltering from the rain under one of the walkways where they'd stood for so many hours of desperate battle. "Looks like we're bound for Affiran."

Amris turned from watching the first efforts at rebuilding, and smiled at her. "Oh?"

"Gerant and I, definitely. Probably Olvir. The Order has a chapter house there, and they've got plenty of mages to study us, not to mention being the closest army." Darya shrugged diffidently. "I told them I couldn't speak for you and I didn't know if you were taking orders these days. Ninnian said I should let you know, if I encountered you."

"Taking orders is no hardship," Amris said, "and I'd be glad to go, but I thank you for the choice." He reached out his good arm. Darya blinked, but came to his side with every evidence of gladness, though she kept most of her weight to herself, not leaning against him the way she'd done when they'd rested during the siege. Briefly, Amris wondered if peace, or the prospect of going with him to a civilized land, had given her second thoughts. Then she looked up at him with her brows furrowed and said, "Are you sure your ribs will hold up? I don't know how this works for normal people."

Gerant snickered, and Darya muttered an obscenity.

"My ribs," said Amris, drawing her more firmly against his side, "will endure—though sadly, likely not for anything more energetic than this for a few days yet. And," he added, glancing down at the gem that held Gerant, "any comments about my normality or lack thereof can go unsaid, thank you."

They certainly can...

"Oh, you save a few lives and suddenly you're not worried about being made into saucepans," said Darya.

You know I don't live in the blade.

"All right, I'll make you into a pendant and give you to some court lady in Criwath. One fond of sentimental poetry and badly trained dogs."

I do, Gerant said thoughtfully, *occasionally miss being able to stick out my tongue. Or to make other gestures.*

"The feeling comes across, I assure you," said Amris. Darya was warm and strong against him, her hair smelling of the rain, her scales shining with it. Gerant was laughing in his mind, cheerfully content. He deeply regretted his ribs.

Moving with care, she slid one of her own arms around his waist, and then laughed softly. "This is so much easier without armor."

"I'd nearly forgotten how it feels not to wear it."

The town was full of people once more, though not yet those who'd fled. Amris wasn't certain how many would come back. Criwath's troops were starting the rebuilding, with the priests of Sitha to help, and already wooden frames had gone up on most of the blackened squares where houses or shops had once stood.

But Thyran was likely rebuilding, too, or would soon start. Knowing that, Amris thought, and having fled from one attack already, a farmer or a shopkeeper would likely

hesitate before returning—and certainly before bringing
their family back.

"Are the others staying here?" he asked. "The Sentinels?"

"Emeth and Katrine are."

Much to Ninnian's disappointment.

"Really?" Amris asked.

"He's been doing experiments with Katrine and
Olvir, since her main blessing comes from Tinival. But
they haven't come to much, and given how effective she
is against Gizath's creatures, the Order couldn't justify
sending her to Affiran. Emeth's animals can give good
warning if Thyran or his people move in this direction
again, and those two work well together."

Not unlike some other people, said Gerant.

In a phenomenon almost as rare as that which had felled
Thyran, Darya actually blushed. "Last I heard," she went on
quickly, "Branwyn's going to Heliodar. Criwath can send
word to the other kingdoms and they'll listen, but there's
too much bad blood with the Heliodar Council—and
more, maybe, things that a Sentinel might need to check
into. Bran's the best of us at passing for a regular human."

"Gods go with her," said Amris. He remembered
Heliodar only vaguely firsthand. It had joined the war
eventually, but after a great deal of division.

I always thought, Gerant added, *that we should have
turned over more rocks there and found either what loyalties
Thyran might have left or how he found his way to Gizath
so quickly.*

"Yes," said Amris, "but there were ten things to fill
every hour by then—and more after, I'd imagine."

Precisely.

"And that's Bran's mission, thank the gods. Court intrigue—ugh." Darya made a face. "Even if it is in pretty surroundings. Criwath's got nearly as much real art, in its own style, and not nearly as many political mazes."

"It was a pleasant country, as I remember it," Amris agreed, "though I'd imagine it, too, has changed."

"Probably." Darya looked up at him with a small, rueful smile. "I'll do what I can, but I'm not much of a guide, especially once we get off the borders. Best you can do with me is being outsiders together, you know."

Amris didn't have to bend far to kiss her. It was an awkward process with his sling, but it was soft, slow, and gentle. The rain fell quietly beyond their shelter, soldiers called cheerfully to one another while they piled stones, and Darya's mouth was warm and seeking against his. Gerant surrounded them both, a gentle presence in their minds, a faint haze of green, and a soothing hum, not intruding on the kiss itself but a happy witness and one whose joy added to their own.

Eventually Amris drew a little way back, but he didn't let her go. "Beloved," he said, "if you gave me another hundred years to consider it, I could think of no fate I'd prefer."

*The story is far from over. Keep reading for a sneak peek of **THE NIGHTBORN**, coming Spring 2021.*

Chapter 1

SHE WAS GOING TO DIE.

Yathana would have reminded her that everyone was going to die. But Yathana was leagues away, where the spirits that charged the magic of each Sentinel's sword-soul went to rest after exhausting themselves channeling the gods' gifts. That burst of magic had left Branwyn with temporary metal skin and an absence at the back of her mind—which was normal—facing a horde of mal-formed, malicious creatures.

That had become normal, too, over the last few days.

Now the twistedmen came on, pouring through the shattered gate of Oakford. They swarmed past the colossus of warped bodies that shambled across the yard, a moving charnel construction that held their leader, Thyran.

Branwyn knew the name, a shadow from the past given horrible life. She'd glimpsed the man himself, but her more immediate concern was his army.

Together, they formed a writhing mass of oversized claws and skinless-seeming red flesh. Some looked as though their faces were melting. Others had the beaks of birds, full of teeth and traps for the unwary who viewed them too closely.

She threw herself at them. Talons screeched as they ran along her arms. Black blood hissed in the air. The enemy never became individual bodies, simply one entity with lines of vulnerability: a leg here, a neck there. Branwyn carved a path through the shifting wall of flesh, Yathana slicing away what obstructed her.

Hallis's voice rose above the shrieking of Thyran's troops, yelling the signal that Branwyn had been waiting for.

One of the beaked creatures had caught her by the wrist when the word reached her. It yanked her forward, opening its mouth too wide. The shifting grey presence within had entranced more than one of Branwyn's companions to their death—but now the sigil on her forehead let her mind turn the charm as easily as her metal skin turned claws. She spun into the monster's grip, let Yathana's edge take its head from its shoulders, and then, when she'd made a half-circle, started running.

She wasn't alone. A dozen others, soldiers stationed at Oakford and half-trained peasants who'd stayed to face the siege, kept pace, leading Thyran's troops on. They raced for the middle of the shattered town, where archers hid behind piles of rubble and the ground concealed a dozen sinkholes.

The twistedmen followed. Arrows did take some, and others stumbled, becoming easy marks for the archers' second volley or simply having to slow down, letting Branwyn and her companions gain a few precious feet of space.

More to the point, they had followed, away from the

rest of the troops, away from the walking abattoir that carried Thyran. Branwyn saw the construct off to the side as she turned to fight. It lurched onward, crushing the wounded beneath its rotting feet, and Amris var Faina, Thyran's foe from a hundred years before, charged forward to meet it.

One of Thyran's wizards raised its boneless hands and sent a bolt of icy power screaming toward Branwyn. She threw herself sideways to avoid it, crashed against a pile of rubble, and staggered backwards, slashing out at a twistedman that was grabbing for her.

She regained her footing in time to see Katrine, her fellow Sentinel, and Sir Olvir, an earnest draft horse of a man who served the god of justice, rush Thyran's mount from behind. It staggered as two swords sunk into the backs of its knees; in that instant, Amris leapt with all his strength. His blade hit the center of the colossus.

Then three of the twistedmen were on Branwyn—an arrow had taken out the wizard, thank the gods—and she turned her full attention to them.

Yathana pierced the ribcage of the first with her usual ease, the metal of a soulsword divinely sharp even when the inhabiting spirit wasn't present. One of the soldiers jabbed the second in the side with a spear—not a fatal wound but enough of a distraction that Branwyn had time to yank her sword free and plunge it into a more vital organ.

She simply slammed her head into that of the third. Its gaping maw sought purchase on her face for a futile second before Branwyn's full weight hit it, knocking it backwards and into a hatchet that had only cut firewood a few days before.

For a few heartbeats, the world was clear around her. The construct had collapsed into a pile of corpses. The air was heavy with blood and smoke, much of it acrid: Darya, who was immune to poison, had led a squad of the twistedmen into a building and then set fire to a nasty packet of herbs.

Branwyn inhaled deeply anyhow.

There were still too many of the twistedmen, she realized. Only eight of the people she'd led still remained. She knew that she had only a few more minutes until she became flesh again, with the enhanced strength and skill of any Sentinel but no more.

And Thyran rose from the mountain of dead meat glowing with sickly fire. Olvir and Katrine stood below him: they'd been helping Amris to his feet, but now all three were still. Branwyn saw Darya start running toward them, and knew that she herself was too far away to possibly intervene.

She was going to die.

Everyone was going to die.

There was nothing to say to the soldiers around her. There was nothing to do but face her death as bravely as she could. More twistedmen were running toward them already. Branwyn braced herself, lifted Yathana—

—and saw the twistedmen freeze in place, staring at the same multicolored radiance that Branwyn glimpsed from the corner of her own eye, as it surrounded Katrine, Olvir, and Amris. Thyran's flame froze too, when it struck the shimmer, and then went hurtling back at its creator.

They had a moment. Branwyn didn't know why, but she knew they'd better use it.

She broke into a run, crossing the distance toward the nearest still-distracted twistedman, saving her breath but shouting a battle cry in her mind.

From beyond Oakford's walls, she heard the clear, sonorous sound of a war-horn.

Reinforcements had arrived.

About the Author

Isabel Cooper lives outside of Boston, where she spends her days editing technology research and her nights doing things best not discussed here. (Actually, she plays a lot of video games.) She likes road trips, but camping is best left to fiction.

You can find her sporadically updated blog at isabelcooper.wordpress.com.